Praise for Kate Johnson's *I, Spy?*

"Kate Johnson has created a wonderful set of characters. Sophie Green is adorable. She's quirky, full of smart comebacks, mom to Tammy, and ready for a "to die for" career....this book has everything!"

Jan Crow, ParaNormalRomance Reviews

"Kate Johnson tells an outrageously funny story about a ticket agent/wannabe spy who has no clue which end of a gun shoots the bullet and drives a totally conspicuous car called Ted! It is good to see that a ditsy blonde can save the day and when Luke and Sophie finally hook up readers will just not believe where! I, Spy? is one hot read and too funny for words."

Alisha, Two Lips Reviews

"If you like the Stephanie Plum series, I believe you will like I, Spy? as it has a similar feel to it. This book is modern, quirky, ironic and sassy. It hooked me in from the start...I can easily see how this will spin out into an excellent series."

Janet, Once Upon a Romance

I, Spy?

Kate Johnson

A Samhain Publishing, Ltd. publication.

Samhain Publishing, Ltd.
512 Forest Lake Drive
Warner Robins, GA 31093
www.samhainpublishing.com

I, Spy?

978-1-59998-635-7

Editing by Jessica Bimberg
Cover by Scott Carpenter

First Samhain Publishing, Ltd. electronic publication: March 2007
First Samhain Publishing, Ltd. print publication: September 2007

Dedication

To Alysia, without whom Sophie would never have been written, and Amy, without whom she'd never have been published.

Chapter One

Okay, I can do this. This is not a problem. This is what I'm trained for. I can stay calm in a crisis.

Only, the crisis was I switched my alarm off and now I had twenty minutes in which to get out of bed, washed, dressed, up to uniform "neat and tidy appearance" standards, gulp down some coffee, find my keys and get to work.

It takes me twenty minutes to find a frigging parking space.

I hit the first hurdle when I couldn't find my uniform shirt. Not by my bed. Not under my bed. Not in the laundry basket. Not in the washing machine. Christ, I only took it off yesterday, where the hell could it have gone? I found myself looking in the most insane places—under the sofa, in the shoe cupboard, the oven—*everywhere*—before I finally found it in the first place I'd checked. Stale and creased in the laundry basket.

I sprayed some Febreze on it, shook out the creases—I couldn't even remember where my iron's *supposed* to be, let alone where it might actually have ended up—and slung it on. I nearly strangled myself with my scarf before I got it right. Making some heroically quick instant coffee with half cold water, I nevertheless scalded my tongue and the roof of my mouth gulping it down.

Tammy, my little tabby cat, watched with a total lack of interest as I hopped around, swearing and moaning at the pain.

"Keys," I slurred, and she blinked at me. There was no logical place for my keys; why would there be? I was nearly crying by the time I found them on the kitchen counter. A quick check of my watch told me it was ten to five—even if I raced up to the airport and left my car on the front concourse, I'd still be late.

"So why am I rushing?" I asked Tammy.

Tammy didn't know.

Finally, finally finding my shoes, gulping down some mouthwash as an alternative to toothpaste (and nearly choking myself in the process), I ricocheted out of the house. Seven minutes to. This was not going to be possible.

At least the roads would be quiet—but no, against all reasonable laws, I got stuck behind some ancient grandpa doing two miles an hour in his Rover. Finally leaving him behind as I took the back road to the staff car park, I skidded up to the car park barrier—and realised I'd left my security pass at home.

Shit, fuck and bugger. With a side order of bollocks.

Slamming the car into reverse with no thought for who may be behind me—thankfully no one—I zoomed back home, startled Tammy by grabbing said pass from the back of my bedroom door—well, where would you keep yours?—and left again.

I parked up at quarter past five. T plus fifteen minutes. By the time I made it up to the terminal, breathless, red and wheezing, it had gone twenty past and the queues at check-in were hitting the desks opposite.

I slunk up to the office, ready with an excuse about my car breaking down—hoping no one would remember it's physically indestructible—and found it deserted.

Ha. I grabbed my time sheet and signed in on time. Hell, they weren't going to check.

Probably I should stop being this late every day, though.

You know, when you think of airline staff you think of cute uniforms and bright lipstick and glamour. You don't think about getting up at an invisible hour of the morning, wearing a bright turquoise shirt and polyester scarf, covered in cat hairs and so tired you could fall over mid-stride. The reality isn't checking in celebrities on first class flights to New York. It's surly businessmen and drunk girls on hen weekends to Prague.

Within five minutes of me sitting down at a desk, one of several things will have happened: the computer will have broken down, the bag tag reel will have run out, the boarding card reel will have run out, the flight will have been delayed, the passenger in front of me will refuse to pay their excess baggage, the passenger behind them won't have the right visa. The Norwegian guy I fancy will have got chatted up by a woman with condoms on her veil. Or all of the above.

Within thirty minutes, I'll feel like curling up into a ball under the desk, sobbing hysterically.

So, why did I do this job? Why demean myself daily, prostrate my exhausted body in front of the baying masses clamouring for my blood because their lives have been disrupted by five small minutes? Why work longer hours than the sun for worse pay than a supermarket shelf filler?

Well...

I did look good in the uniform.

And the Norwegian guy was really quite cute.

And because when people asked me what I did, I had an answer for them that wasn't "student", "shopgirl" or "office junior", which was what had happened to everyone I went to school with. Apart from Jason Miles, who's a pothead and went to prison three months ago for ramraiding the post office.

And that's about it. I suppose you could say there was the illusion of glamour. My job really wasn't very glamorous, but people thought it was and I liked them to think I was too.

My name is Sophie Green, and I live a very small life.

My alarm clock went off and I knew I had to get a new job.

The thing was, I'd been in this job two years and I'd been saying the same thing every day for the last... seven hundred and twenty-nine days.

I checked my roster sheet. Sven was in today, Luca too. Excellent.

Sven was the Norwegian. He was twenty-nine, from Stavanger on the west coast. He had hair that was like sunshine and eyes the colour of the Caribbean, and when he smiled, interesting things happened in the pit of my stomach, not to mention other places I'm not going to tell you about until I know you better.

Luca was new. Ish. I mean, he sort of crept into the schedule, like maybe he had his hours changed. I don't remember him getting trained up with all the other newbies. He's sort of Mediterranean-looking, dark hair and eyes, and he always looked like he knew what I was thinking and found it very amusing. And he had a very sexy rolling Italian accent. And fantastic cheekbones.

It was weird, because I don't really go for Latin types. Ever since I went to Majorca with the girls and practically got stalked. I mean, don't they have blondes over there? Generally I like men who are like me—blond, blue-eyed, tall and, erm, built.

Therefore Sven fit the bill. He was very sweet, too. He smiled at me and asked in that lovely accent which always sounds so serious, "Are you all right?" The first time I wondered what the hell was wrong with me that he was asking so seriously. Then I realised this was his version of "Hi, how are you?"

An honest answer would be, "Very warm now that you're smiling at me," or, "Slightly flustered because you're leaning over to get to my bagtag machine." But being a Brit chick, I always answered with a cool, "Yeah, I'm fine. How are you?"

Who am I kidding? I looked like a beetroot whenever he talked to me.

So when Paola, the little sweetheart, put me on a desk next to him I didn't mind so much that I was checking in the biggest flight that day. Or even that it was full of skimpily dressed wannabes flying off to Ibiza. And DJs with their record bags that they always wanted to take as cabin baggage, but were always too heavy.

Every single girl flirted with Sven. And Sven flirted right back.

But then he would, right? If I was as brain-breakingly gorgeous as him, I'd flirt, too.

"Hey," came a voice, shattering through my reverie (me and Sven on a beach in Ibiza. He was practically naked and I was a lot thinner). "Do you have an end-bag?"

I blinked up at Luca. "A what?"

"End-bag." He stretched over the desk to look. "It's the little bag we put a special tag on so the guys downstairs know there are no more to come," he explained helpfully, because how would I know that? I'd only been there two years.

Ha ha. He was funny.

"I don't see one," Luca added.

"No one travels light to Ibiza. The guys all have record bags and the girls take twenty kilos of make-up. You want me to put my back out grabbing a huge end-bag?"

He gave me a look I'm sure would have worked on a more susceptible woman. "Come on," he was almost pouting, "you can find me a little end-bag. Just, maybe, fifteen kilos?"

Ha ha. Fifteen kilos was a medium wheelie case. One of the hard shell ones. An end-bag had to be small, or there was no room for it behind the desk, and also it was easier to lob on the top of a dolly to drag out to the plane. Not to mention the heavy ones were hell on your back, and we weren't insured to lift heavy things.

"Okay," I said, "but I'm not promising anything. But just because I like you," I reached under the desk and pulled out a bag smaller than something I'd take clubbing, "I got you this, for Venice."

Luca gave me a look of adoration. "They always over-pack for Venice," he said, taking the little thing with its huge end-bag tag. "You get me bags for Munich and Malpensa too, I take you to dinner."

He sauntered off, and I allowed myself the luxury of checking out his fine arse. Hey, a girl can look.

The woman who was next to check in looked mildly stunned and very jealous, and it wasn't until I saw her watching Luca that I realized why.

"He was joking," I said. *I hope.*

"If he offers you dinner, you take it," she said, and I smiled.

"Do you have any bags?"

I checked her in and noticed she spent the whole time looking over at Luca. And his arse. The next passenger was Italian. I could tell as soon as he swaggered up, looking cool, still wearing his shades even though he was inside, in England, in April. He looked over his shades at me.

"Where are you flying to?"

"Roma," he rolled the R. "Is Rome in Eenglish."

I snorted, then realized he hadn't been joking. "Right," I said. "Can I have your passport, please?"

He spent the whole time looking at my chest, especially when I stretched over to tag his bag. But, hey, it is a rather impressive chest. I can't really complain.

"You are ver' pretty," he told me as I handed him his boarding card.

"Thank you."

"A Eenglish rose, *sì?*"

"*Sì.* Thanks. Here's your boarding card."

Now naff off, you're creeping me out.

Halfway through my shift, I was pulled off the desk. "Can you board the Edi for me, love?" Paola asked, looking up at me, very tiny and adorable. Paola was seven months pregnant, and I swear, the baby was bigger than her. Apparently she was thirty, but I felt like calling a children's charity on her, because she only looked about twelve. And then there was me, almost a decade younger and looking like her nanny.

I took a fresh gate report out of the drawer and headed off. So I was heading away from Sven the Sublime, but I was also getting away from check-in. Any respite was welcome.

I liked working at the gate because you got time to yourself. There was maybe ten minutes of frantic action when the flight boarded, but you had to be there an hour before departure. For quite a while, there wasn't a lot to do but mess around changing the status of the information screens and making announcements that people rarely listened to.

The domestic departures satellite was quiet. There was a Ryanair flight boarding as I went past, but my end of the lounge was empty. The Edinburgh flight wasn't very full and I didn't need anyone else to help.

I messed around getting everything to my liking, seeing how many people had checked in, looking for funny names, changing the flight status to "open" and listening to the radio burbling away behind the coffee stand.

"Hey, sexy," called Dino, the coffee guy. "You look hot."

"You too, Dino," I called back, rolling my eyes. See what I mean? They saw blonde hair and big boobs and some instinct kicked in. Must hassle female. Must make innuendoes. Must make her blush.

Okay, well, I stopped blushing when he did it in front of a flight full of people. Now I played along. He shut up faster that way.

I checked the status screen again. The plane callsign wasn't quite right and I called up Ops to check.

"No, darling, it's a Titan plane we're using for Edi," Kelly from Ops told me. "Got three off tech today. Just do them a little announcement so they don't wander all over the tarmac, will you?"

Another Titan plane? I seemed to board more of them than Ace planes. Stupid piece-of-crap cheap planes.

I put down the phone and picked up the microphone. Learning announcements was a jump-in-and-swim experience, and most of us made them up. You put on the sing-song voice and repeat yourself over and over, hoping they're listening and won't start bleating in panic when they see the wrong logo on the wings.

"Ladies and gentlemen, this is a passenger announcement for all passengers traveling on the Ace Airlines AC109 flight to Edinburgh. We would like to inform you that, due to a technical problem, the service today will be operated by a Titan Airways aircraft. Please board as normal through gate eighty-seven and follow the Ace Airlines staff to the steps of the aircraft when you are called forward for boarding. We estimate this to be within the next twenty minutes," I said, glancing at my watch.

It didn't matter how long I thought it was going to take to start boarding, I always said twenty minutes. It was just long enough for people to forget how long ago you said it. "On behalf of Ace Airlines, we would like to thank you for choosing this service and wish you a very pleasant flight."

I estimated that about five people heard me, and that two of them were actually listening.

More of them turned up after a while, and I did all the procedures on auto-pilot. I repeated the aircraft change announcement twice more, but by the time we came to boarding, I still had people asking me in panic where their plane was.

I mean, really. I'm sure these were very bright, sane, reasonable people. It was just that the second they stepped into the terminal they lost all their brains, not to mention manners, and started acting like angry five-year-olds.

"For the Edinburgh flight?" came a dark velvet voice from the other side of the flow of passengers. "Please form two queues, please..."

I looked up in surprise. Sometimes the dispatcher might help to pull cards if the flight is really full and we're understaffed, but I wasn't sure why Luca had come over to help. Still, it got things done quicker.

The last of them trickled through, and I started tapping the security numbers of the boarded passengers into the computer. We were two down, and the system had them as Lavery, Anne, and Brown, John.

Luca counted up the cards. "Forty-eight?"

"Yep. Two down." I reached for the microphone. "This is a further boarding call for the Ace Airlines flight AC109 to Edinburgh. Would passengers Lavery and Brown please make their way to gate eighty-seven where this flight is now closing."

Anne Lavery turned up straight away, flying through, racing out to the plane. Truth be told, there were several minutes before pushback, but it paid to get people boarded on time. The dispatchers could get pretty stroppy if there was any delay and they weren't all above putting it down to gate staff on their reports.

I checked the system again. John Brown had one piece of baggage checked in, and I radioed down to the dispatcher that she might want to start looking for it. It was highly illegal for a piece of luggage to travel without its owner. After Lockerbie strict rules were put in place to make sure every piece is scanned and accounted for. If a passenger didn't travel, then the bag had to be pulled off the plane. It was a bugger, especially since the ramp boys had to search through every bag to find the one they wanted.

I made another call for John Brown and got Ops to put out a call over the terminal PA. Luca was tapping a pile of cards on the desk.

"He still not here?"

I looked around with heavy sarcasm. "Not unless he's invisible."

Luca gave a faint smile. He looked pretty damn tense.

"You okay?"

He shrugged. "I'm tired. This is my third early, and I been doing overtime too. Looking forward to my day off, you know?"

I nodded. I was looking forward to it, too. Hours and hours of unadulterated sleep. Bliss.

Luca grabbed the microphone and made another impatient call for Brown. "Failure to report to the gate within the next five minutes will result in your bags being offloaded and the plane will depart without you."

That usually got them. You could tell them they had fair warning, repeat until you were blue in the face that the boarding time was printed and highlighted on their boarding card (and it always allowed oodles of time for boarding, too), but ultimately, to a passenger, if they missed the plane then it was your fault.

Passengers were stupid. I hated them all.

The dispatcher radioed up. "Any sight of him?"

"Not a squint," I replied.

"Right, that's it. I'm getting his bag off. If he turns up send him back to check-in. He ain't traveling."

Luca glanced up at me. "I'll go and get his bag," he said. "If he comes, keep him here."

I nodded, watching him go. I got all the sucky jobs. I liked to act the bitch but really, I hated telling people they couldn't travel. They got so mean. Sometimes they cried and I felt miserable. Sometimes they yelled at me and I got all angry, and when I was done being angry, I went away and cried, because they made me feel little and stupid and worthless.

I let them get to me—that was my problem.

Not long after Luca disappeared, a fat, balding man in a shiny suit came rushing up to the gate.

"Mr. Brown?"

He nodded breathlessly. "Am I too late?"

"I'm afraid so," I said. "The plane's about to push back."

He looked distraught. "I can still make it," he said, glancing out of the window where the plane was, indeed, angling out of its bay with the help of a tug.

The folly of passengers. They see the plane going down the runway and still, somehow, believe they can catch a wing and get to their seat. Like this is Charlie's Angels or something. You know that bit in the film where they open the plane door and freefall? At that height, everyone in the plane would have got sucked out with them and they'd have all died.

"I'm sorry," I said, not meaning it at all, because he looked like a loser. "It's really not possible. Your bag is on its way up. You can catch the next flight. I'll have to take you back to check-in—"

"No, you don't understand—"

At that moment the door from the jetbridge opened and Luca came out, a holdall slung over his shoulder. "Mr. Brown? A word with you, please?"

I frowned, and I'd just opened my mouth to say something when Mr. Brown turned and followed Luca like a puppy. The door swung shut behind them and I stood, frowning some more.

Then I went back to the desk and called through to check-in that a passenger had missed the plane, so could they remove him from the system and close the flight? I tallied up the boarding cards and scribbled a bit more on the report. I watched the Titan Airways plane trundle towards the runway and out of sight around the corner of the departures satellite.

I doodled a pretty design on the report. I shook out my hair and pinned it back up again. I sang the Ace theme tune through twice before I remembered how damn annoying it was. I latticed the boarding cards into a pretty pattern and shuffled them like a deck.

Then I leaned against the desk some more and waited for Luca to come back. What the hell was he doing? Reading Brown a personal riot act for not turning up on time? I know it was annoying, but it happened all the time. It wasn't really a big deal.

Then I heard a thud from the jetbridge and suddenly felt hot.

There was no one else in the satellite. No passengers or staff, even Dino had vanished somewhere.

I looked around in panic. Could just be Luca dropping the bag on the floor. Those floors were noisy sometimes. Hollow-sounding.

I edged over so I could see through the little window into the jetbridge. Luca had Brown by the collar, shoved against the wall.

Horror flooded me, and I fumbled for my pass to open the door. "Luca, what the hell are you doing?"

There was a sticky second of silence as both men glared at me. "Go away," Luca said, and his voice sounded different. I squinted at his face and thought I saw a bruise around his left eye. "Sophie, just go away."

"You can't beat him up! I know you're having a bad day, but Luca—"

Luca glared at me, and I suddenly realized what was different about his voice. His accent was totally gone. He sounded as English as me or Brown.

All sorts of awful thoughts ran through my brain. Since 9/11 they went through incredible security checks on anyone applying for an airside pass, but if Luca got his pass before that then they might not have been so thorough. That was how sleeper agents got in. They got their jobs years in advance, when they were still respectable citizens.

He could be anyone. He could be a terrorist or a lunatic or a criminal.

Oh, God, I'm in bad trouble.

"Sophie," Luca said, and his voice sounded like he was using a lot of control to sound calm, "will you please pick up Mr. Brown's bag and take it back to check-in? I'll escort him back in a minute."

The next thing that happened was really weird.

Usually I'm a total wimp, like I've said. I'm pretty good at fooling people into thinking I'm really mean, but inside, I'm as soft as a mouldy banana.

"No," I said, and even I must have looked surprised to hear it. Luca looked astounded. "Put him down, or I'll call the police."

There was a very, very long moment when I was pretty sure one or the other of them was going to pull a gun on me.

Then Luca, still gripping Brown by the collar, gave an exasperated little laugh.

"Sophie," he said, "I am the damn police."

I stared, frozen, as he pulled off the fire training pocket that hung from his security chain and tossed it over to me. "Inside," he said, and I opened it to find a warrant card and a second security pass, this one red instead of green like mine—an all-access pass, with an older picture of Luca on it.

Only it had him listed as Luke Sharpe, and his position was Special Agent.

Oh.

Holy.

Bollocks.

For quite a long while I stared at the pass, my head totally empty. I really couldn't think of a single thing to say or do.

Eventually Luke put out his hand. "I'll need that back," he said with a faint smile, releasing his hold on Brown.

I handed over the plastic pocket and watched him clip it back into place. Then he reached for something inside his jacket and pulled out a pair of handcuffs. He fastened Brown's wrist to his own and picked up the holdall.

"Sophie," he said, "I'm going to take him down to the station, and then I'm going to meet you in Ponti's, okay? Go straight there."

I stared at him.

"Sophie? Go straight there. I'll explain this when I get there. Don't go anywhere else or say anything about this to anyone, okay?"

Do not pass Go, do not collect £200.

I nodded dumbly and stumbled through the doors, swiping my card three times before I got it right, nearly dropping it twice, having to go back for my bag when I realized there was nothing heavy over my shoulder.

But I didn't go to the coffee shop. I walked back to the terminal, as fast as I always did, keeping my eyes away from everyone else. BAA had cameras all over the place: surely they'd seen what went on? Surely they'd know and they'd do something about it?

I walked up the steps to the office behind the check-in desks, put my gate report in the tray and turned to Tem, the assistant supervisor, another huge flirt.

"Hey, baby," he said. "You okay?"

I blinked. "Why wouldn't I be?"

"You look really white."

I shrugged, relaxing. I have pale skin and the Mediterranean staff are always asking if I'm okay.

"I always look really white, Tem. Where'd you want me?"

He grinned. "Anywhere, baby." He peered over the wall above the desks. "Just open up another desk, will you? It's pretty quiet."

So I opened up another desk, sitting there feeling almost normal, and even checked someone in without freaking out too much. But I'm pretty sure I hardly checked the passport and barely looked at the seat map as I did it. I don't know what weight I put in the system for the bag. I read out a totally inaccurate boarding time and sent the passenger away with a dazed smile.

Then the phone rang.

I almost didn't answer it. I was sweating all over. I was icy cold and nearly crying with terror.

"Soph, can you close down and come up?"

It was Tem. I stammered a reply and lifted my bag, which suddenly felt like the heaviest thing in the world. Fifty kilos at least.

When I got to the top of the steps Luca—no, fuckit, Luke—was waiting there, looking pissed off, his eye turning a shade of damson that clashed with his shirt. A uniformed policeman stood next to him.

"Hey," I squeaked.

"Hey," Luke replied, glaring at me.

Tem smirked. "You are in big trouble, baby," he said. "Look." He showed me the supervisor's log, which had *Sophie is wanted by the police* in big letters. Red ones.

"Cheers," I muttered, my teeth chattering.

"If you could just come with me," the copper said.

"Am I in trouble?"

He shook his head. "Just come with me, please."

Shaking, I tripped after him, looking down at the baggage belt as I crossed the catwalk over it, wondering if I could chuck myself on it and escape.

Luke nodded to the policeman as we left the Ace desks and the copper walked away, leaving me with Luke, feeling rather vulnerable.

He walked me over to Ponti's and asked me what I wanted to drink.

I stared at him. Was this like a last meal? Better make it good, then.

"Coffee," I whispered. "Black."

He got one for me and another for himself and we went to sit down at the table behind the serving station, where we were hidden from public view.

God, he could kill me, and no one would see. No one. I wished the uniform was still with us.

"Look, Sophie," Luke said, "this isn't really easy to explain."

"Am I really in trouble?" I whispered, visions of courtroom trials and prison sentences flashing through my head. What would I wear in court? I didn't have anything respectable enough.

Oh, though. That suit I had for Nannan's funeral. That was quite sober. And my pink blouse—no, the white one. Or would I need more than one? Those things went on for days. It could be really expensive. I wonder if the court would give me a clothing allowance?

"No," Luke sighed. "But you do know more than you should. We've been after a group of counterfeiters for a while now. Brown was one of them. Now we have him, we might start getting somewhere. I was going to board that flight myself, but whoever did the rosters obviously didn't know that. I thought we might have missed him."

He exhaled and stirred his coffee. One hand strayed up to gently touch his discolored eye, and he winced.

"I'm sorry you had to see that in the jetbridge. I was going to take him back like a regular decontrolled passenger. His bag was full of counterfeit notes."

My eyes widened. "Really? That holdall? Were they good forgeries?"

He gave a faint smile. "Not bad. You'd need a specialist to tell they were fake."

I sat back against my seat. "So now you've caught him, is that it? Are you leaving Ace?"

He cocked his head, looking more like sexy Italian Luca. "Would you miss me?"

"Only if my aim is off."

He laughed. "Funny. No, look, I have to stay on a while longer. I need you to keep it a secret who I am. The duty managers know, but no one else. You have to keep it a big secret. Understood?"

I shrugged, then nodded. "Seeing as I don't really know who you are, it shouldn't be too hard."

That brought a smile. "Good girl." He looked down at my drink. "Are you going to finish that?"

I hadn't even started it. I picked it up and gulped a load, scalding my mouth, managing a weak smile. "I need the caffeine," I said, and he nodded understandingly.

"I hear you. Are you on tomorrow?"

"Yeah. Early again."

"Okay." He looked at his watch. "Look, why don't you go home early? I'll square it with Paola."

I must have looked as doubtful as I felt, because Luke laughed.

"If you get into trouble, I'll cover for you. I'll even pay you the difference." He stood. "Finish your coffee, then go."

I nodded.

"And, Sophie?"

I looked up.

"If you tell anyone about this, I may have to kill you."

I stared. Luke grinned, then walked away.

Chapter Two

When I started this job, they told me the social life would be great. No one parties like airport people, they said. And there's such a mix—people from all over the world, different ages and backgrounds and languages and races—it's amazing. Your social life will go through the roof.

Really?

Last time I went out clubbing with the guys from work I went home, changed my clothes and went straight off to work again at four-thirty. And then I fell asleep at the desk and nearly got fired.

My usual social life consisted of watching *Buffy* videos, with or without my best friend Angel, and occasionally going to the pub. With my parents. God, I needed a life. I wonder if you can get them on Amazon?

I let myself in with a big sigh of relief. Tammy, my fluffy little baby, was mewling around her bowl, looking all tiny and helpless.

"Aw, poor baby," I scooped her up and felt her purr against me. "Did you run out of squirrels to kill?"

Tammy gave me a dirty look and squirmed to get down. She killed anything that moved: mice, birds, squirrels, even small dogs if she got the chance, and yet she was so small I could hold her in the crook of one arm, like a baby.

A baby with teeth, and really sharp claws.

I found her some biscuits, remembering guiltily that she hadn't been fed since lunchtime yesterday, and forked out a huge can of food.

It must have been twice her body weight, but she ate it. God, I wished I was a cat. You got to eat and eat and eat and never get fat, you had gorgeous glossy hair and fantastic cheekbones, and people were always telling you how beautiful you were. Well, they were always telling Tammy, anyway. Right now I didn't feel very beautiful. I felt haggard.

I moaned as I remembered I had a third early tomorrow. That was the last time I swapped shifts with anyone.

The way my shifts worked was that I did two late shifts, then two earlies, then I got two days off. If you were totally insane, like Angel, you could apply to work twelve-hour shifts, four days in a row or four nights in a row, then four days off. There were all sorts of overlaps, and the part-timers sometimes worked on a three-on, three-off pattern that would drive me mad. This was how it was hard to remember who was going to be on when, because we all only got the roster sheet for the people who were on the same shift as us.

But this month they stuck Luca's roster on the end of my sheet. Or should I say Luke?

The whole thing was insane. An undercover… what? Policeman? Government agent? Spy?

Ooh, a spy. That was quite sexy, actually.

I wondered if he'd have any other stuff to spy on? I wondered if he'd been spying on me?

Pervert.

Four in the morning and I was on my way to work again. When the alarm went off, I muttered my usual "I have *got* to get a new job," but like I said, that was my morning mantra. I never did squat about it. I mean, everyone I trained with had moved on to supervisor level, or to dispatch, or down to the ramp. The really smart ones left. It was really only just me who was still on check-in.

Chalker, my brother, said I had a lack of direction. Well, it was fine for him. He knew when he was five what he wanted to do. "I wanna be a rock star," he said when he saw *Back to the Future* and how cool Marty looked with his guitar.

I saw *Back to the Future* and wanted to be an inventor. Or a mechanic at the future car garage. Or a gunslinger in the Old West.

By the time I was ten, I had run through every possible career, from pearl diver to Tom Cruise's personal assistant (that one was crushed when Chalker pointed out I was already taller than my hero). When it came time for my unutterably boring careers interview at school, I was told to play to my strengths and apply to university to study whatever I was interested in.

And thus we have the great academic drive to utterly belittle a university degree by making sure even the illiterate have one. I actually know someone who's half qualified to be a teacher, and she can't read words longer than five letters. They're so desperate to send you off to university that even when Chalker stood up and said he'd no interest in taking A levels, they still tried to persuade him that studying Schubert for another two years would be really worthwhile to a future rock star.

And me? I'm so directionless that I applied to six universities on the sole premise that they were the same ones my boyfriend wanted to go to.

His great plan was to become an accountant. I should have seen it coming from that. His name was Pete, he worked in a supermarket, he was okay in a boring sort of way, and the only thing I remember actually liking about him was that he fancied me. When I was eighteen, I was so fed up of being single I just took the first guy who came along who was a) taller than me and b) not into hard drugs. Now, of course, I know better. There are so many arseholes out there—it's sooo much better being single. I don't have to shave my legs or anything.

Okay, forget I said that. That's gross.

Two months into an English Lit course (what everyone studies when they don't know what to study, right?) I walked into his room to find him boning the tart from down the hall.

I was really insulted. If he was going to cheat on me, it could at least have been with someone really hot.

So I packed up and left. I think I intended to go to some other college at that time, but it was Chalker who made me realize that wasn't what I wanted to do at all. He was doing what he wanted, and it made him happy, and my parents hadn't kicked him out yet. That and my gran died, so I moved into her flat temporarily, and just never moved out.

Truth was, I didn't know what I did want to do. That was really why I was still doing my job at the airport. I didn't seriously hate it, despite how much I complain. I didn't really like it, either, but I figured a lot of people actively hated their jobs, so I was a step ahead.

According to my roster, Luca was supposed to be on shift today, but I didn't see him as I trudged up to the office and signed in. Angel was there, looking tired but excited at the prospect of going home in an hour. The unexpected bonus of working nights.

Cow.

"I've got you on a desk next to Sven," she winked. "You're checking in the Stavanger so you'll be able to ask his advice a lot."

I smiled gratefully. Angel understood my desperate need to be close to the beautiful people. There really weren't a lot of hot men around here, so I had to take what I could get.

Angel, of course, could get anyone, or really anything, she liked. Her mother was a famous actress and model, her father a songwriter. Between them they generated enough royalties to keep Angel living in a very nice style. Plus she had inherited her mother's tiny blondness, with big blue eyes and glossy curls. If I didn't adore her so much I'd really hate her.

Sven greeted me and told me I looked tired. Chalker reckons that's an insult but to me it's observation. And concern. It was sweet of him to care.

I touched up my lipgloss when he wasn't looking.

I settled into the sleepwalking routine of checking people in, wondering if any of them were counterfeiters, if Luke was secretly watching any of them. Occasionally Special Branch contacted us when we were running a Belfast or Derry flight, because they wanted to do surveillance. It never freaked me before, but then before this all I ever saw of it was people filling out embarkation cards.

Everything went normally—that is to say, chaotically—for the first couple of hours. I took a coffee break and sat stirring my drink until the plastic spoon splintered. Part of me wanted to see Luke again. We shared a secret now. I was *In On It.* But part of me was scared. Maybe I'd blow it. Maybe I'd call him Luke instead of Luca. Maybe something else would happen and I'd miss it.

Maybe that Brown guy would come back, or send one of his mates round, maybe they'd recognize me (I'm pretty easy to describe and I sound good on paper) and gun me down.

Maybe I was caffeine deprived and needed to get out more.

I trudged back to check-in and slobbed back down to the desk. Stavanger had closed, Sven had moved on, and I was checking in Roma. *Is Rome in Eenglish.* I couldn't help comparing the Italians' accents with the way Luca spoke. Thing was, he sounded authentic, and I'd heard him speaking Italian to Italians, and they hadn't looked suspicious.

I guess you believe what you're presented with until someone tells you otherwise.

We had maybe a dozen more passengers to check in when the floorwalker's clipboard slapped down on my desk and a familiar voice purred, "Do you have an end-bag for me?"

Luca. Of course.

I looked up, and there was no hint in his face that he was anyone else. But I knew he wasn't called Luca, wasn't Italian, wasn't at all who he presented himself to be.

"Sure," I said, handing him a little case. "No offer of dinner this time?"

"But you only got me one bag," he replied. "It's three bags for dinner."

Another passenger strolled up, wearing expensive sunglasses, immaculately turned out. Italian. She handed over her passport and I looked up at Luke with my most charming expression.

"Would you like to ask her the security questions?"

Without missing a beat, he rolled them off and the woman answered with a smile, obviously appreciating Luke's dark liquid eyes and casually attractive biceps.

He gave me a smug smile and leaned against the desk next to me. I glared at him and ripped the boarding card out of the machine.

"*Ecco la porta*," I ringed the gate number, "*e l'ora d'imbarco. Grazie*."

Don't get all impressed. That's pretty much all I can say in Italian. That and I can ask for directions to the post office, but if someone answered I'd never understand.

Luke raised his eyebrows. "You look tired," he observed as the passenger sashayed away.

"Will people stop saying that? It's seven-thirty and I've been awake for four hours. Of course I'm bloody tired."

"Did you have sex last night?"

I stared, cheeks flushing. "Excuse me?"

"You look like you had sex last night. Tired and..." He waved his hand. "Happy."

I was pretty sure I didn't look happy. He was just trying to rile me. And I hadn't had sex in... Well, I stopped counting when the months got into double figures.

"Don't you have anything better to do than stand here and harass me?"

He shrugged. "I'm going to the gate in ten minutes. Not really anything better to do."

"Can't you go early?" I muttered peevishly.

Luke grinned. "You want to get rid of me?" He swung my monitor round to face him and tapped a few things on the keyboard. "Only two people checked in on my flight."

"Milan?"

"*Si*."

"And drop the bloody accent," I hissed.

Luke regarded me with his head on one side. "You want to get rid of me?" he repeated.

Now I felt rotten. He was only behaving the way he always had, flirting outrageously with me. I used to find it flattering. Now it unnerved me.

"Keep an eye on things for me," he muttered, accent gone, and chucked me under the chin.

Then he was gone, taking his dark eyes, his rolling accent and his fine arse with him.

Get a grip, Sophie. Don't start lusting after a man with a fake ID.

It happened when I got up to change the LED display to read *flight closing.* I happened to glance down the line of desks, checking out Sven's profile, and then I gazed out over the queue of passengers in front of him.

Then I did a marvellous double take.

John Brown was standing about twenty feet away.

I swear I nearly rubbed my eyes in disbelief. The same man Luke had grabbed yesterday was standing in the check-in queue for Alicante.

I moved fast. Luke was boarding the Milan flight, so I opened that up in the system and got the gate number. They hadn't started boarding the passengers in the system, but that wasn't to say they were all already on the plane and the gate agent just hadn't put the information in the system yet.

I got out my little black book of useful airport information (sadly, not Sven's number), grabbed the phone and dialled the number for the Milan gate.

It rang out.

Shit.

I glanced up at Brown again. He had a laptop case and was gripping a holdall tightly against him, and I just knew it was all full of counterfeit money.

Palms sweaty, I rang the airport police. This had never freaked me before, because usually I called them with an enquiry or to get them to check firearms documents. Never because I thought there was a criminal standing very close.

He shifted his grip on the holdall and all the hairs on my arms stood up, because if he wasn't carrying a gun under his jacket then he had a thing for replicas. They were illegal on flights—understandably, they scared the hell out of people—so whatever he was doing, he was in trouble.

And so was I.

The dial tone droned on against my ear and my foot tapped in impatience. *Come on, answer it, you're the damn police*! Maybe I should have called the emergency services. Maybe I'd still be there next year waiting for someone to answer.

Eventually a woman came on.

"I need to get hold of Luke," I babbled. "Luke Sharpe."

That had to be a made-up name.

"Excuse me, who is this?" the WPC asked.

"Sophie Green, from Ace. He's working undercover for Ace and I need to get hold of him because there's—I think there's a situation he needs to deal with here."

There was a long pause, and it occurred to me that maybe even the police didn't know about Luke. Maybe Luke had lied to me. Maybe none of it was true.

Then, "I'll give him the message," she said, and my heart started beating again. "What number are you on?"

Seconds later the phone rang and without any preamble, Luke said, "What's going on? Sophie, you can't just call—"

"Brown," I interrupted, and Luke shut up. "John Brown, from yesterday? He's standing right in front of me. Three desks down. He's about to check in for Alicante."

"Brown?" Luke said. "That's impossible, he's—"

"I swear it's him," I said. "I'm really good with faces." If I was wrong, I would never live it down.

Sven's passenger moved on and the line shuffled forward. Depending on whether the group in front of him were all together or not, Brown could be next to check in.

"Shit," Luke said. "I know what this could be. Okay, I'm coming back."

"There's not enough time! He's nearly at the desk!"

"Then you'll have to keep an eye on him for me. If he checks in, excuse yourself and follow him. Try to delay him but don't alarm him."

"But—"

"I'll be right there."

Liar, I thought as the phone went dead. It took at least fifteen minutes to get back from Sat 1. Unless Luke could fly, which I was pretty sure he couldn't.

Although really, I wouldn't be surprised.

Sweating all over now, I watched Sven check in the group in front of Brown. Then they left. Then he checked Brown in.

I looked at the passenger list. There were no Browns listed, but of course he wouldn't be that dumb.

The holdall was tagged and sent down the belt. Sven weighed the laptop case and waved it away as hand luggage. He gave Brown his boarding card and sent him away.

Double shit!

I got to my feet, my legs shaking, and switched the belt off as I climbed over it. A woman came rushing up to the desk.

"*Scusi, scusi,*" she bleated, waving a flight itinerary at me. I tried to ignore her but she pointed at the *flight closing* display and babbled desperately in Italian.

I threw a frantic look at Angel, who was the next one down, two desks away, next to Sven. "I have to go," I said. "I really have to run. Can you…?"

She frowned, but nodded and beckoned to the woman, who was giving me a filthy look.

I ignored her and bolted. Brown was nearly at the bookshop on the corner now, and he didn't look as if he was going straight to Security. He was heading away, around the other corner, and I speeded up, grateful I wasn't wearing huge heels.

"Excuse me," I called, not knowing what I was going to say to him, "sir…"

I'd make up that he'd left something behind or there was a problem with his ticket. Yes! The payment hadn't been processed. That always takes forever to sort out. I'd be safe.

But he saw me, blanched and darted away.

Triple shit.

He was running back towards check-in. What was going on? Had I got it wrong? Where was he going?

He rushed up to one of the empty desks up at the end and leapt over the little gate on the baggage belt. For a second I halted, staring, disbelieving. Surely he wasn't going to do what it looked like he was going to do?

He ducked and threw himself onto the main belt.

He must be insane! Apart from the fact that it was unbelievably illegal to even lean out over the belt (not that it stopped us, heh heh), it was really dangerous to walk on it.

Or so they always tell us.

But I couldn't just let him go. If he really had a gun, he could pull it on the ramp guys. I had to stop him. Nobody who acts like that is innocent.

"Crap." I stamped my foot and ran after him, tripping over the little belt and throwing myself onto the main conveyor.

Really it was just like one of those moving walkways that go on for miles and miles. Except that this one had more twists and bends, flaps and poles to make things lie flat, scanners to make sure no one was packing anything they shouldn't. I heard a siren go off up ahead, presumably as Brown went through, and steeled myself.

I scrambled along the belt, knowing my quarry was doing the same thing ahead, and barely noticed as I passed under the scanner.

It made no noise. Apparently I was legal for airline transportation.

I could see him up ahead, climbing over the edge and dropping down into the undercroft. People were staring, some of them were running, but no one was trying to stop him. To give them the benefit of the doubt, I think they were shocked. I don't want to think they were all such cowards.

"For fuck's sake, stop him," I yelled, peering over the edge then closing my eyes as I threw myself over.

I landed with a thump on my side and dragged myself to my feet. People were rushing over to the plastic flaps that led outside, and I followed them just in time to see one of the airside cars speeding away.

Fuck.

I glanced around wildly for something to follow it in, but all I could see was a baggage dolly. Not helpful.

"Bloody stop him," I hollered, breathless, and a couple of guys started running after the car. Good boys. But it was going too fast and they would never catch it.

Brown rammed the car over the grass verge and the wheels started spinning. Thank God they never shelled out for a decent car. I spied a wheel chock on the ground, picked it up and hurled it as hard as I could at the car.

It smashed the rear windscreen good and proper.

"Yes!" I aimed a fist at the sky and ran off after the car. The wheels were still spinning, spattering mud all over me and the three guys in their hi-vis jackets who were trying to get into the car. Brown had locked the doors and was looking at the back window as if it might be a good way to get out. But the glass was shattered all over, it'd be instant death.

He and I stared at each other through the driver's window for a long second. Then I grabbed the chock and swung it at the window, wincing as the glass shattered. I reached in, snatched the keys out of the ignition, smashed them across his face before he'd had time to react and grabbed his gun.

I'd like to state here and now that I've never fired a gun before and I hardly know which end is which. But apparently I looked convincing, because Brown raised his hands in surrender.

Someone in an Ace uniform reached in and opened the door, grabbed Brown and held his arms behind his back. "The coppers are coming," he said, looking at me. "What the hell's going on?"

I shrugged, the gun still aimed at Brown's head. "I'm just following instructions," I said.

"Me too," said the Ace guy. "Yours."

A cop car came whistling up and out catapulted a couple of uniforms, followed by Luke.

"Sophie?" he said incredulously. "Put the bloody gun down."

My hands were shaking. "Are you going to take him away?"

"Yes. He's going into custody. And so are you unless you give me that gun."

Not taking my eyes off Brown, I handed the pistol over and felt my body slump. Luke put his arm around my shoulders, holding me up. It was probably an inappropriate time to notice that his body was very warm and hard, but I noticed it anyway.

"This yours?" Luke asked Brown, passing the gun, wrapped in a handkerchief, to one of the uniforms.

Brown nodded.

"You are in so much trouble," Luke said as the Ace guy handed Brown over to the coppers.

I wasn't entirely sure who he was talking to.

Chapter Three

When I got home it was dark.

I'd been at the airport police station for hours, tired and hungry, shocked and dirty. My uniform was probably beyond repair, torn and splattered with mud, but I didn't really care. Probably they'd fine me for it. Fuck them. I'd had an unbelievable day. No one was going to fine me for anything.

Was I in trouble? I kept asking the policemen but they never really answered. They took full statements on every part of the incident and I signed billions of things without really looking at them. Probably I should have looked. I didn't really care.

Tammy was scratching around the gate as I unfastened the latch and tripped down into the yard. Really it was supposed to be a little courtyard, but my nannan used to live here, you see, and where she came from it was a *yard*. It had one sad-looking conifer in a tub and a washing line and a metal dustbin, and that was it. Not what you'd call pretty.

The security light came on as I pushed the gate open and I didn't see Agent Sharpe at first, sitting with his back against my door, elbows resting on his knees, changed out of his Ace uniform into jeans and a fleece.

He looked up at me. "You're late."

I shrugged. "Got held up."

"Did you come straight back?"

I nodded. I'd wanted to go to Tesco's for some ice cream but I couldn't face walking around in the state I was in. I'd planned to get changed, walk up to Total and get five of everything that was bad for me. Then I was going to get in a hot bath and stay there until tomorrow.

"Were you waiting for me?" I asked, rather unnecessarily, but I was feeling brain-dead.

Luke nodded and got to his feet. "You okay?"

"I will be." I pushed past him to unlock the door, and when the key stuck I felt like crying.

Luke shoved at the door and it came open easily.

"Thanks."

"Can I come in?"

I shrugged, and he followed me in. My flat is rather small, just one room with an open-plan kitchen, then a bedroom and postage-stamp bathroom, but it was all mine.

Well, actually, it was my mother's, because she inherited it from my nannan, but it was mostly mine. I paid rent and everything.

I dropped my bag on the floor and went through to the bedroom, picking up comfort clothes as I went and changing in the bathroom. I wasn't sure I entirely trusted Luke not to walk in on me, so I locked the door.

"I've been waiting about an hour," he said from the kitchen. I could hear the kettle being boiled. "It's bloody freezing out there."

Poor baby. I threw my uniform in a pile on the floor and kicked it.

"I didn't think they'd keep you so long."

"Yeah," I called back, opening the airing cupboard and switching the heating on to max, "well, they did."

"It wasn't all necessary."

Now he tells me.

I stomped through to the kitchen with my muddy clothes, pushed past Luke and dumped them straight in the washing machine. So the colors might run. Did I look as if I gave a crap?

"Hey," he caught my shoulder as I turned to the kettle, "are you sure you're all right?"

I shrugged. "Yeah. Nothing a hot bath won't cure."

"You look like hell."

"Thanks." I picked up the coffee jar, then thought better of it and got the hot chocolate out instead. Then I ran some hot water in the sink, got out my first aid kit and rolled up my sleeve.

"Shit," Luke grabbed my arm, and I winced. "What happened?"

"Nothing. Just a bit of glass. Nothing."

He narrowed his eyes at me. "Those two broken windows..."

"Had to stop him somehow."

"Did you really smash them with a wheel chock?"

I gave him a sullen look and reached for the cotton wool to wipe away some of the crusted blood. It was just a few cuts on my elbow and lower arm, but they'd been stinging all day. I kept thinking longingly about that hot bath and wished Luke would go away so I could get some sleep.

"You're a menace," Luke said, pouring out water for my chocolate and his coffee. I didn't remember him asking if he could drink my coffee.

It was good coffee, too.

Even Tammy, the little traitor, was happily weaving around his ankles as if he was a great friend. So much for cats being good judges of character.

"Just doing my job," I said tiredly, dabbing Dettol on the cuts and trying not to let him see my eyes watering.

"No, you were doing my job. Why didn't you wait?"

I stared at him. "You said to follow him! He had a gun. I wasn't about to let him try to board with it."

"They'd have picked that up at Security."

"Not if he didn't go through Security."

Luke shook his head. "Even the staff Validation Points have scanners. Nothing gets through. It's tight. I've checked them all."

I sighed. Probably this wasn't the best time to bring this up but...

"There is a way," I said.

He stared at me. Great, now he thought I was a terrorist. It was just an idle thought I'd had once, in between ranting about bloody cyclists taking their bikes with them on holidays. So they don't have bikes in France? Yeah, right.

"When someone wants to travel with a bike, what do we do?"

"Tag it and send it to Outsize," Luke said promptly, like a proper newbie.

"What if it's unpackaged?"

"We escort it to the undercroft. It gets scanned there."

"Yes, but only after it's been down in the lift. With an agent. All alone."

He gave me a hard look. "What are you getting at?"

I peeled the backing off a huge plaster. "Okay. You're a terrorist or a counterfeiter or whatever, and you want to take a gun through undetected. All you need is an airline uniform, a pass and a bike. Everyone knows the picture on your pass looks nothing like you. It's like a passport photo. Did you search Brown?"

Luke looked mulish. "He had a pass. Forged. Ryanair."

"Right," I said. "And he was wearing a white shirt, yes? Lots of people don't have full uniform. Security aren't going to pull you up on that. All he had to do was get a bike, put his gun in a saddlebag or something and go through VP9 with it. He gets scanned, he's clean. The bike goes through the gate to be scanned later. While he's in the lift, he takes out the gun, puts it in his pocket, leaves the bike in the undercroft and wanders off airside."

I stirred my hot chocolate and looked up at Luke. He looked dumbstruck.

Ha.

"Jesus," he said eventually.

"I know."

"How do you know all this?"

I shrugged. "Figured it out one day. I was bored, okay? It was even easier when we did the foot-and-mouth spraying. Even packaged bikes had to be taken down there. You could hide shedloads in one of those bike bags, then stash it under your coat, in the lift. Those Ace coats are bloody huge." They were fat parkas, and I looked like the Michelin man in mine.

Luke was still staring at me. "Shit," he said. "So anyone could have taken anything through?"

"If they were smart enough. If they knew how to work the system."

Luke shook his head. "Does anyone else know about this? Why didn't you tell anyone?"

I raised my palms. "Didn't think anyone'd ever try it. You've got to be clever to work it out and pretty dumb to try it."

"A common criminal combination," Luke said. He pinched the bridge of his nose and rubbed his fingers into the corners of his eyes. "Can I use your bathroom?"

"Sure."

Off he went, and I flumped down on the sofa. Tammy leapt up and settled on my lap. Apart from the grazes on my arm, I had bruises all over from being bashed about on the baggage belt. BAA had been really mad at me for that, but I pointed out that I'd been doing what no one else had done. I caught the criminal.

I figured there'd be hearings and fines. I figured I might lose my job. I didn't really care. I think I was in shock.

Luke came back out, jiggling a small case in his hand. A contact lens case.

I looked up at him. "You wear contacts?"

He grinned. "Only for show." He fluttered his eyelashes, and I realized in shock that his liquid brown eyes were now pale blue. And rather lovely.

"Jesus," I said.

"I figured Luca would have dark eyes. You don't see many blond, blue-eyed Italians."

It was on the tip of my tongue to tell him he wasn't a blond, but then I realized it was probably dyed. He seemed to take this undercover thing very seriously.

"Why Italian?"

"I can speak it. I've lived there. Girls like Italians."

I'm afraid my lip curled. "Look," I said, "not to be rude or anything, but why are you here? Am I under arrest or something?"

Luke sighed heavily and took a seat beside me on the sofa. I shuffled away from him. There was a very slight possibility he was mad. Hot as hell, but mad.

"I'm going to tell you something," he said, "and you have to keep it a secret. I mean this, if you tell anyone—your mum, your best friend, your brother, even your bloody cat—" Tammy looked offended at that, and rightly so, "then I'm not joking, I will have to kill you." He lifted his pullover fleece and showed me the pistol holstered at his side.

"What happened to Brown's gun?"

Luke gave me a look. "You know that wasn't his real name, right?"

"Duh." It hadn't occurred to me, but I wasn't about to tell him that.

"It wasn't even the same guy."

I stared, horrified.

Luke laughed. "It's okay. The guy we caught yesterday has a twin brother. What we didn't know, when he used up his one phone call, was that he was giving out some kind of code. The brother was following instructions. If you hadn't spotted him, he might have got through."

"To Alicante?"

"No. Actually he was booked on the Geneva flight, but that's by the by. What gets me is that he was stupid enough to use the same airport and the same fucking airline."

"Very bright and yet so very thick."

"They all are." Luke held out his hand to Tammy, who sniffed at it, then licked his fingers.

Bloody cat. Took me weeks to earn enough trust to pick her up.

"Was that the classified information?"

"What?" He looked up. "No. Not really. We've been after the brothers for a while. What I have to tell you is who 'we' are."

I braced myself.

"Twenty years ago the government set up a special branch of military intelligence, based at Stansted, to deal with illegal airport traffic. Everything from drugs to terrorism. They called it SO17—Special Operations Seventeen. To begin with everything was excellent, the agents did everything they should and caught dozens of bad guys. At the time it was thought Stansted was going to grow into a huge airport, bigger than Heathrow."

"Not if I can help it," I said with feeling. Airport expansion was something I was pretty much against, mostly because it would involve building over my house.

"But of course the airport didn't get that huge, and we shot ourselves in the foot."

"Feet."

"Whatever. The problem was that we worked too well. There were no more bad guys to catch. Word had got around. So they downsized us, didn't want to spend all this money on an operation that wasn't doing anything. Agents retired and they weren't replaced. SO17 got pretty much forgotten by the government."

I can't say I had any sympathy. As far as I was concerned he was talking bollocks. I didn't believe for a second that there was a special governmental intelligence agency at the airport. We had Special Branch and that was it, right?

Right?

"Right now SO17 consists of four people. I'm one of them. We have license to do pretty much whatever we want, hire new people, et cetera, but we don't have the funding. When I was hired they were skimming the cream of the military. I was in the RAF, then the SAS, before they picked me for this."

So now he was boasting to me? Ooh, look at my military record. Does that make you horny, baby?

Well, quite frankly, no.

"But now we can't afford to do that. Our director has given us orders to each find and train new agents. My old partner is currently searching for a suitable recruit. I've been looking around for a while."

He looked right at me. Tammy clambered from me to him, and I focused my attention on the cat, because I wasn't sure what Luke was saying.

"That's nice," I said uncertainly, quite aware that I sounded like a complete idiot.

"I was impressed with you today," he went on. "Yesterday, too. You're not very good at following orders, but I get that, because a good agent understands artistic license."

"Bond never followed his orders strictly," I said helpfully.

"Of course not. In *Licence to Kill*, he was a rogue agent. He still saved the day and got the girl."

I ignored that. I wasn't really interested in getting any girls. "So you want someone who's disobedient?"

"No, I want someone with a brain. A lot of squaddies, they're in it because they're good at following orders. And they're good at following orders because they're crap at thinking for themselves. And that's great, because the army always needs squaddies. But we need intelligence. We need stubbornness. We need someone who'll see the mission right through."

I took Tammy off him. I needed a diversion. My head was whirling.

"I was impressed with you today," Luke said again, reaching out and touching my hair. "I've been watching you since I started at Ace. You're bright and confident and you can think on your feet."

This was true. When you had a hundred and fifty passengers demanding to know what compensation they were going to get for a two hour delay (none) and threatening you with legal action, you learned to spout comforting drivel.

"Plus," Luke added with a smile, "you're like a bulldog with a rag. Tell me, if the twin had driven away in that car, what would you have done?"

I shrugged. "Got in one of the tugs and gone after him."

"You think a tug can keep up with a Corolla?"

"I think Tammy could keep up with a Corolla."

He smiled properly. "And what would you have done when you caught him?"

I blinked. "What I did today."

"Did you plan that?"

"No. How could I?"

"You thought on your feet. You didn't consider the consequences for yourself, you just went after him. Sophie, do you want to come and work for SO17?"

Chapter Four

It was weird, but after he'd gone I didn't feel as surreal as I'd thought. I fed Tammy and ran a bath and read my book and went to bed, but I couldn't sleep. I ended up switching on the video and watching Buffy the Vampire Slayer throw herself into that abyss for the millionth time.

You see, it was like when she found out about the Initiative and became one of their sort of agents. Only Buffy could do all this cool Slayer stuff, all her athletics and stamina and accelerated healing and super senses and stuff, whereas I...I could touch my toes. If I warmed up, I could kick Chalker in the head. But only if I wasn't wearing jeans. Which I usually am.

Oh, bollocks. It was nothing like *Buffy* at all.

Hey, I wonder if Luke has all those cool gadgets like Riley had? Or like Bond? If I was a secret agent would I get to run around in sexy leather outfits and outrageous wigs like Sydney Bristow?

Note to self, try and watch an entire episode of *Alias* without going off into fantasies about Michael Vartan.

Luke gave me a mobile number to call him on with my decision. But how the hell did I make a decision like that?

When it came down to it, was there really a single reason why I should become a spy?

It was sexy, yeah, but it was dangerous, really dangerous. There was a scar on Luke's upper arm that I saw once when I thought he was Luca. He said he got it in a motorbike accident in Rome, but even at the time I thought that was made up. The scar was nasty, too. Looked like it was made with a blade.

I didn't like blades.

He carried a gun. The guy I caught today—I still didn't know his name, call him Brown 2—he had a gun too. Would I have to carry one? I didn't know anything about guns. I could tell I don't like them, and that was about it.

God, this was hard. He even told me the pay wouldn't be that great. But still a boost to my Ace pay, which in turn would go down because I'd be working there part time for appearance's sake...

He told me that if I take this up then it would have to be a total secret. I couldn't even tell anyone about the existence of SO17, let alone that I was working for them.

Because I was going to end up working for them. If I didn't, I'd spend the rest of my life checking baggage for a low-cost airline. And that was a thought so wretched it made me feel physically ill.

The name's Green. Sophie Green.

You know what? I need a new name.

I made the call not long after the sun came up. On a normal day, I might be on my way to work right now. But I had a feeling there weren't going to be many more normal days for me.

"Okay," I said when Luke answered. "I'm in."

I could hear the pause as he grinned. "Knew you would be," he said. "Okay. I need you to come into the office and sign a few things."

"I signed millions of things yesterday!"

"Yes, but these are important things. Do you remember where you did your Ace training?"

I was confused. My training was so long ago that it was a distant memory (and a laughable one—did I really think people would pay their excess baggage charges without a fight?), but I remembered where it was, because that was where a lot of the airlines had their back-up and support. Ace had an office in supersmart Enterprise House, by the car park, but they still had a few rooms they used for training round where the old terminal was.

I pulled up outside the building. Luke was waiting, a look of disbelief on his face.

"What?" I said, opening the door for him.

"*This* is your car?"

"What are you implying?"

"Why the hell are you driving a Land Rover Defender?"

I made a face as he got in. "I like it. It's reliable. Lara Croft has one."

Luke stared. I think I was doing okay until I mentioned Lara. "You know she's fictional, right?"

"I'm not stupid." Probably this wouldn't be the best time to tell him the car had a name. It was called Ted, after the character in *The Fast Show*... Okay, never mind.

He shook his head. "Go up here and turn right."

I did as I was told. I'm not sure what I was expecting: a bunker, maybe, something highly secret. But he told me to stop outside a totally ordinary, rather shabby looking prefab hut. The peeling sign outside said it belonged to Flight Services Inc.

"Has anyone ever come in asking about flight services?" I asked as I locked Ted up. He didn't have central locking, and Luke shook his head in amazement when I asked him to lock his door, as if he was wondering why anyone would ever try to steal the car.

I liked my car, all right? It was solid and dependable and a design classic, and the army had them. And if someone was parked in a stupid place then I could just trample all over them and not worry about the damage to my car. Ted looked happier with a dent or two in him.

Luke, after a moment's pause, glanced at the sign by the door and said no, no one had ever asked about flight services. Most airport people were very focused. It was sometimes hard to remember there was anything outside your own flight report.

Christ, I was glad I was getting out of that.

Inside was an ordinary, dated office where a pretty blonde woman sat behind a desk, glancing at something on a computer.

She looked up and smiled. "You must be Sophie! Luke's told me all about you."

I glanced at Luke. He flicked his eyebrows at me but said nothing, and wandered over to check a chart on the wall.

"I'm Alexa." The blonde offered her hand over the desk, and I took it. "Call me Lex. Everyone does."

Lex. As in Luthor?

I gave her a smile. She seemed very normal. She wasn't Moneypenny glamorous or GI Jane hard. She looked like a normal receptionist. She even had an aspidistra next to her desk.

It was all sort of disappointing.

"So," she leaned over the desk earnestly, "are you excited?"

I shrugged nonchalantly. I was so nervous I could barely stand up. It had actually taken me most of the night to decide on what to wear. Now the sun was up and Alexa was smiling at me in her New Look shirt, I felt a bit stupid for having agonised about whether to wear a skirt or trousers (in the end having plumped for trousers and top with high Lycra contents, just in case they wanted me to start doing any training, and a smart leather jacket).

Alexa turned to Luke. "I know we said you'd go straight in, but Maria just called. She's bringing up her catch from London. Should be here any minute."

I glanced at Luke for an explanation, but he didn't look at me.

"Did she say anything about him? Or is it a her?"

Alexa shrugged. "No idea. Just that she's very pleased with herself."

"Christ."

It was warm in the little office, thanks to the noisy air heater by Alexa's desk, and I took off my jacket.

"God," Alexa cried, "what happened to you?"

She was staring at my arm. So there were a few scratches on it, and the bruises were just beginning to come up. I shrugged. "I had a run-in with a baggage belt."

"I didn't know they fought back."

"Viciously," I said, and we shared a smile.

A car pulled up outside, and I glanced through the blinds to see a woman in a shiny PVC coat getting out of an aged Peugeot 205. From the passenger seat emerged a giant of a man, the sort of super-scary black man they post outside clubs to frighten off teenagers.

And they were coming inside.

"Hey," the woman greeted Luke and Alexa, then switched her attention to me. "Oh, Luke," she said.

That's all she said.

I looked her over nervously. She was beautiful in a way I'd never be—perfectly straight, glossy dark hair, no little frizzy bits like I get because I brush it too meanly and blow-dry it when I shouldn't. She had huge, mesmerising dark eyes, perfectly but sparsely made up, and gorgeous clear skin. Her figure was svelte, tightly wrapped in neat jeans and a little black T-shirt.

Ugh.

"I'm Maria," she said.

Of course she was.

"And what the hell have you brought us, Maria?" Alexa laughed, coming out from behind the desk. To my surprise, she was wheeling herself. Luke's highly secret government agency had a disabled agent?

Very equal-opportunity of them, but also kinda limiting. I was beginning to see how desperate they were.

Everyone was looking over the huge black man. He didn't look amused.

"What am I, cattle?" he said, and his voice rumbled.

"Sorry, sweetie." Maria placed a casual hand on his arm, and I saw Luke's eyebrows rise. "Everyone, this is Macbeth."

I stared. Alexa, safe in her wheelchair, started to laugh. "I'm sorry," she said. "Great name."

"He can quote it, too," Maria said, unfazed. "I found him nicking car stereos in Brixton."

"I figure, anyone who leaves a car unattended in Brixton deserves to have their car stereo nicked," Macbeth said.

Good point.

"He also single-handedly broke up a six-man brawl outside a nightclub before I'd even got my gun out," Maria said. She gave Luke a so-there look, then glanced back at me. "So, what did you bring?"

Luke nodded at me. “This is Sophie.”

I gave little smile.

Macbeth was looking at me like I was meat. Maria was looking at me like I was a Barbie doll. “What can she do?”

I blinked at her. “Well, if you wind my arm back my hair grows,” I said, and she burst out laughing.

“Okay, I see. She’s the airport girl?”

Luke nodded.

“Very nice. So, Lex, where’s One?”

“Gone up the road for breakfast. He said to go through, he won’t be long.”

Luke opened the door behind Alexa’s desk and Maria, Macbeth and I followed him through. This was another ordinary-looking room, with a desk and a table and several chairs. There were filing cabinets and potted plants and a decrepit projector in the corner.

“Don’t look very secret to me,” Macbeth said.

“It’s not supposed to,” Maria said. “If anyone asks, we’re the administrative force for an in-flight service company. Take a seat.”

“So, this One,” I tried to make conversation, “he’s in charge here?”

Luke nodded. “Time was, we all had numbers according to our seniority. Now, I guess Maria’s Two, I’m Three and Lexy’s Four. We just call him One out of habit. His real name is Albert.”

I considered it. One sounded much more Bond than Albert.

“So we’d be Five and Six?” Macbeth gestured to me.

“No, you’d be Sophie and Macbeth.” Luke drummed his fingers on the table. “I need to sort out those contracts with Lexy.” He stood up, and then so did Maria.

“I’ll come with you. Let the newbies get to know each other.”

I managed a very faint smile. Being shut in a room with a human riot shield was not my idea of fun.

“So,” Macbeth said. “What’d you do?”

"Do? Well, I sort of work at the airport, I do check-in..." I trailed off, because he was shaking his head.

"No, I mean, what did you do to get snagged for this?"

"I followed a guy down the baggage belt and damaged company property."

He grinned, a flash of white. "Nice one." He paused. "So, you reckon this thing's for real?"

I shrugged. I'd been wondering the same thing. "God knows. Luke has a warrant card, but then it could be a fake. I don't know."

"She," he jerked his head at the closed door, "has the sort of hardware you can't buy in shops, you know what I mean? That's black market stuff."

"You mean guns and stuff?" I thought about bluffing it out but ended up confessing, "I don't really know anything about guns."

Macbeth shook his head. "So why'd they hire you?"

I shrugged again. "I have no idea."

"You sleeping with him?"

"No!"

"Just checking."

We waited in silence for a few more minutes. I tried to think of something to say to Macbeth but my mind drew a whole load of blanks. Truth was, I was terrified of him.

Eventually, voices sounded in the outer office, and then the door opened and a middle-aged man in a suit came in. He had that sort of distinguished look about him, handkerchief in his breast pocket, old school tie, air of supreme self-confidence. The kind of guy you'd hate to have as a neighbour—until someone tried to build over your street and he called in his old chums at the Home Office. Luke and Maria followed him, looking like rebel children.

"This is the biggest team briefing I've had in a while," the distinguished chap said, taking a seat behind the desk and switching his computer on. "I'm One. You are... Sophie and... Macbeth?"

Macbeth nodded.

"Interesting. What's your real name?"

Macbeth looked impassive, but he took something out of his pocket and handed it over to One. A passport. An old black one. They were pretty damn rare now. It was hard to get them extended.

One read it, raised his eyebrows, then handed it back. “Miss Green?”

I stared at him for a bit.

“ID?” Luke prompted and I, blushing, fumbled for my wallet. I’d brought my passport too, but I hated the picture. I handed over my driving licence, figuring that if I could fly to Ireland with it, I could use it for government ID.

One looked me over, smiling. “Luke,” he said.

“Sir?”

“The British spy is elegant, suave and sophisticated. The British spy is not blonde, built and...and confused.”

I didn’t know where to look. I know I went red. Maria and Macbeth looked like they were having a hard time not smiling.

Luke had no such reservations. Grinning broadly, he said, “She’s smarter than she looks, sir.”

“Well, she’d have to be. All right,” One gave my driving licence back. “They’ll need new pictures for their cards,” he said to Luke and Maria, who nodded. To me and Macbeth he said, “They’ve told you the rules? Don’t discuss any business with anyone outside this room—apart from Lex. Not even a policeman. Hardly anyone knows we exist.”

I wanted to ask about the police cooperation yesterday, but kept silent.

“Don’t tell anyone you work for us. Don’t tell anyone we exist. If we find out you’ve been telling secrets, we will have you killed. Is that clear?”

I nodded. Macbeth nodded too.

“Lex has the contracts for you to sign.” He looked up at Maria and Luke again. “They’re in your hands now. Good luck.”

With that he turned back to his computer, and Luke came forward to me. We went back to Alexa’s desk, I signed a million confidentiality things and then we were outside and it was hardly breakfast time.

“We’re going to take a look round the terminal,” Maria said. “You want to come with?”

I shrugged, looking at Luke. He grinned. “I think we’ve seen enough of it for now,” he said. “I rigged it with Paola that you’re off when we need you,” he went on, as Maria and Macbeth got into the 205 and disappeared. “Now it’s time for some training.”

I swallowed nervously. Precisely what kind of training did he have in mind?

He told me to drive back to the village, but to take a different route. I’d lived there most of my life, and I thought I knew every part of every road, but when we turned off on what I’d thought was a dirt track and pulled up at a big converted barn with a sign outside reading “Smith’s Guns”, I was surprised.

“How long has there been a gun shop in my village?”

Luke shrugged. “Years. Why?”

“I—I just never knew about it.”

“Mostly they sell shotguns to game shooters,” Luke said, unfastening his seat belt, “but they do a few decent extras.”

“Such as…?”

“You’ll see.”

“Do I get a gun?” I asked hopefully. Okay, so they scare me, but I’d look pretty cool with one.

“Do you have a gun licence?”

“No—”

“Then you don’t get a gun.” He flashed me a smile.

“Well, how do I get a gun?”

“Be very nice to your local constabulary. Join a gun club. Of course, to join most gun clubs you have to have a licence…”

“That’s just stupid.”

“No, that’s very clever. That’s why we don’t have a gun control problem.” He held the door open, and I went in.

The walls were covered with every kind of shotgun, and there were rifles too. All of them were locked down with alarms and things. But there were no small guns. I looked at Luke, puzzled, and he smiled and went straight over to the counter.

"Mr. Sharpe," the man there greeted him. "Haven't seen you in a while. How're you getting on with your SIG?"

Luke grinned. "Perfect partners," he said. "Got any more bullets for me?"

The man reached under the counter for a key and unlocked a door behind him. "It was the .40 Smith & Wesson rounds, right?"

"Right," Luke nodded. "And, Joe? Need to have a look in your special cabinet."

Joe flicked his eyes at me as he dumped a box on the counter. "This is all on the level?"

"Totally above board. She's with me."

Joe gave a doubtful nod. "Right, then," he said, and disappeared into the back room. Luke beckoned for me to follow, and I walked through cautiously, right into Wonderland.

Well, maybe Macbeth's idea of Wonderland. The room was filled with guns of every size and calibre, ammunition, knives, defence sprays, bullet-proof vests.

"Jesus Christ," I muttered. "Is all of this legal?"

"Depends on who you are," Luke said thoughtfully. "Everything's legal for me."

"What do I get?"

He took something that looked like an electric hair tong off the rack and handed it to me. "Stun gun."

"You are kidding me."

"Defence spray."

"Seriously?"

"Kevlar."

I stared at the vest. "A bullet-proof vest? What for?"

Luke and Joe both looked at me as if I'd just landed. "Erm, to stop the bullets?" Luke said.

"What bullets?" My voice was rising, I was panicking a little. "You never said there'd be bullets."

Luke stared. "Joe," he said, "can you give us a minute?"

Joe left, closing the door behind him, and Luke gave me a serious look.

"I told you there'd be bullets," he said.

"No, you did not." Did he?

"I said it'd be dangerous! Did you think people would be coming after you with sucker-dart guns?"

Chalker has one of those. He used to fire it at Tammy. And then I used to hit him.

"Well, no," I said, feeling foolish, "but..."

"But?"

"But if they get guns, why don't I?"

"You need to prove to me you're not going to shoot yourself in the foot," Luke said dryly. "Start off with the basics. You probably won't need them."

I trudged out of the room with him. Only probably?

Luke paid Joe by credit card, and I took my stash out to the car. He'd added handcuffs and a couple of Velcro braces for all my stuff, but there still wasn't any gun.

I made a face.

"What?" Luke said patiently.

"Stephanie Plum gets a gun."

"Who?"

I shook my head. Philistine. "What now?"

Luke glanced at my feet. I was wearing my cool trainers—the pretty ones, not my muddy, dog-walking trainers that my mother keeps trying to wash.

"How fit are you?" he said, leaning over and pinching my waist.

"Hey!" I recoiled in shock. Next he'd be asking how much I weighed.

"I'll race you home," Luke said, getting out of the car.

"No way." It was at least a mile, and pretty much all uphill. Whoever said Essex is flat must have been in a goddamn tank.

"Yeah, come on. It's good for you."

I frowned reluctantly as I got out of the car and locked it.

"I'll even give you a head start," Luke offered.

Git.

"I'm fine," I smiled sweetly. "I'll see you there. Don't get lost."

He started running. I got back in the car and tried to run him over, but the bastard was too fast for me.

"Cheat!" he yelled, banging on the window, but I drove past, smiling serenely. Okay, I was cracking up, but let's pretend I was serene, okay?

I arrived home, let myself in, put the kettle on and greeted Tammy, who was making a nest out of my laundry. "Hey baby," I said, and she opened one eye at me. For a cat, that was a lot of effort. "Shall we lock nasty Luke out?"

But nasty Luke found my bedroom window open and climbed in.

"Cheat," I said, and he shook his head.

"Seriously," he said, "an open ground-floor window on an unsecured courtyard?"

"Oh, and I suppose you have CCTV on all your windows, and infrared alarms too?"

Luke shrugged. He probably did. He probably lived in a bunker or something, with lots of monitor screens and tripwires.

Freak.

The toaster popped and I took my bread out, spreading honey on it and then slicing a banana on top.

"What the hell are you eating?"

I looked down at my food, then up at Luke. "Lasagne," I said. "Want some?"

He glared at me. "Don't get smart. Is that supposed to be your breakfast?"

I looked at the clock. It was nine-thirty.

"Lunch," I said. "I've been up for hours."

Luke shook his head. "Shouldn't lunch be... savoury? Like, a burger or something?"

"I'm a vegetarian."

"Vege-burger."

"Do you know how many additives there are in those things?"

Luke stared at me like I'd just grown another head. I was getting used to it.

"I suppose you don't eat ready meals either?"

Of course I do. Everyone does. But he'd just run a mile uphill, I needed to beat him on something.

"Ice cream?"

I gave him a look. "I am still human."

Luke made himself a sandwich and found some crisps and ate it all without asking. I got some gratification from Tammy, who tried to nick everything out of his hand.

"Your cat is just like you," Luke commented after a while.

What, gorgeous, sinuous, almond-eyed, stealthy and deadly? I batted my eyelashes at him.

"Like a dog with a bloody bone. It's my food, you little bugger."

Offended, I picked Tammy up and nicked a handful of crisps for her. "I am not like a dog with a bone."

"You were yesterday."

"Are you even going to tell me their real names?"

"What, the Brownie twins? We're still not sure. They have a lot of aliases."

I mumbled something under my breath about the state of his military intelligence, but when Luke asked me to repeat it, asked brightly, "So what do we do now?"

"Go into town. Get you a phone."

"I have a phone." I gestured to the handset by the sofa.

"A mobile."

"Got one of those, too," I pulled out my little Siemens from my handbag.

"A company phone. A good one."

"This is a good phone!"

"Can it take hi-res pictures? Video clips? Is it Bluetooth enabled? Triband? Does it have my number, Maria's, One's, Lexy's and the office programmed into it?"

"It could have," I said sulkily.

"You're getting a new phone. Give the number out to *no one.*"

"Or what, you'll have to kill me?"

Luke didn't answer, but got up and put his plate in the sink. "Come on."

Whatever he drove, it was still up at the "office", so we got back into Ted and rumbled off into town.

"This is incredible," Luke said, looking around the car's sparse interior.

"Yeah," I said fondly.

"There isn't even a tape deck."

I frowned. "There's a ghetto blaster under your seat," I said. "But the batteries are flat."

Luke shook his head. "You're a weird girl."

"...thank you."

He didn't say anything about my parking, but I could feel him wincing as I pulled into a rather small space. And if government agents have any kind of dispensation for free parking, then Luke didn't share it with me.

I was half expecting another hidden Smith's Guns type place, and was mildly surprised when we walked into The Link and Luke picked out an expensive Nokia package. I wanted to wail that I didn't know how to use a Nokia. They confused me, all the punctuation was in the wrong place when you wanted to send a text—but he didn't listen, carded it and handed me the bag.

"Do you belong to a gym?"

I shook my head in faint horror.

"Join one."

"Sir, yes, sir!"

Luke gave me a sideways glance. "Are you on the Pill?"

I stared. "Excuse me?"

He handed me a slip of green prescription paper. "Present for you from Lexy. She's a qualified doctor. This is a no-period Pill. Maria takes it. Carry them in your bag, take them religiously, and even if you're captured and tortured, explain that they keep your heart beating or something."

He looked slightly flushed. Men never grow up, do they?

"Okay." I took the prescription. "So we're going to Boots?"

"Yeah. I need toothpaste anyway."

Just to embarrass him a little more, I made him come with me to Marks and Spencers and help me pick out a sports bra. If I was going to be tumbling down any more baggage belts, I'd need proper support, right?

We took all my new stuff home, Luke playing with my new phone and setting some numbers into it. He called Maria. "Does Macbeth have a phone yet?"

"Half a dozen," I heard her say in despair, "none of them his."

I smiled at that. I think I was beginning to like Macbeth.

My answering machine was flashing when we got in, and I listened to a message from Chalker. "Don't you ever answer your bloody mobile?"

I took it out. *Network Search.* Crap. I hoped the Nokia had a better network.

The second was from my mother. "Are you coming home for tea? We're having lasagne. Charlie's bringing someone to eat with us," she added with faint despair.

My mother is the only person in the world who calls my brother Charlie (no one in the entire universe has ever called him Charles). He's been Chalker ever since we were at school and he used to have to chalk out lines all over the blackboard every lunchtime for some new misdemeanour.

Luke's mobile rang as I was listening to my mother's message, and he went into the bedroom to answer it. I called my brother back.

"Vegetable lasagne?" I asked. "Or vegemince?"

"Vegemince," he said. "And garlic bread."

"The nice kind?"

"We have dough balls..."

"I'm there."

Luke came back in and abruptly took the phone from my hand and put it down.

"Hey! I was talking to my brother—"

"Don't care." He handed me my bag, his face stony. "Something's come up. Get your pass."

I picked up my airport pass and followed him, confused. We drove in silence up to the airport, Luke tense and still in the passenger seat. We dropped the car outside the terminal, and when one of the traffic wardens started yelling, Luke showed him his warrant card and pulled me after him.

"What is going on?" I asked as I was tugged into the terminal.

"You'll see," Luke said, dragging me past the Ace desks as I tried to cover my face. Wasn't I supposed to be off sick today?

He pulled me up to VP9, one of the Validation Points where staff go through to airside, and I went towards the scanner, dumping my bag on the belt in a reflex action.

Luke picked it back up again, showed his red pass to the BAA woman and pulled me through the gate without getting me scanned.

I remembered the handcuffs in my pocket and was pretty glad he had.

As we approached the lifts an announcement rang out, "We would like to apologise for the delay in baggage handling services. This is due to a technical problem. Thank you for your patience."

Was that why we were going down there? A baggage belt failure? Oh, crap. *Don't tell me it's* my *fault.*

Usually whenever the main belt stops, it's because something's got stuck—a bag that was too big or something with too many trailing straps. We were supposed to spot things like this and sort them out before we sent the bags on their way, but sometimes there just wasn't enough time to tie up every single strap on every single rucksack. I really hated rucksacks. So I sometimes, er, sent them down as they were. And they sometimes got stuck.

Sometimes quite often, actually.

So you can see why, if a rucksack would stop the belt, a person might sort of break it. Ahem.

We went down to the undercroft in the noisiest lift on earth. I swear there was a small rodent in the mechanism getting the crap tortured out of it. It screeched and moaned and shuddered, and by the time we got to the bottom, I was traumatised. I never used that lift if I could help it. It sounded like it was dying.

The undercroft was eerily silent, like it is late at night or early on a Sunday. We rounded the corner, past a still, silent baggage chute, and my skin burned as I remembered leaping out over it yesterday.

"Is this about yesterday?" I asked Luke meekly.

"I think so," he replied, and I frowned. What was that supposed to mean?

I found out when we came to the Ace chutes. Police tape cut off the whole area, and Luke and I ducked under it into a crowd of people in uniforms, a lot of them talking madly into their phones. I spied Maria and Macbeth talking to a guy in plain clothes. "She's with me," Luke said to the nearest copper, and the guy took one look at his badge and let us through.

I glanced at the chute in front of me. It looked pretty normal, apart from the huge smears of blood and the mangled corpse lying on the still conveyor.

I stared at it for quite a while. Blood doesn't scare me, if you had a cat like Tammy you'd understand that. Many mornings I have woken up into a scene from the Godfather with a squirrel head beside me on the pillow. Hardly a day went by when I didn't see the dismembered corpse of a rabbit, deer or fox on the side of the twisty little roads in and out of the village.

But I've never seen a human body before. Not a real, battered cadaver. Bodies on TV aren't the same. I'd never seen anything as...*raw* as this.

"Went right through the mechanism," the policeman was saying to Luke. "Take forever to clean it all out."

"You definitely have an ID?"

The policeman nodded and went over to the body. It was still dressed in a ripped Ace uniform, complete with hi-vis, and in a pocket on the sleeve was his pass. All the ramp and baggage guys kept their passes on their sleeves so they didn't get in the way.

"Christopher Mansfield," the copper read, smudging away some blood with a gloved finger. "Ramp operative."

I blinked. The name was familiar.

"Chris Mansfield?" I tried to bring up a face and got him almost instantly. He was the guy who'd had Brown in a lock yesterday.

All of a sudden I felt sick.

"Oh, Christ." I reached out for Luke, and he held me upright. "That was him, he helped me yesterday when I—when we—Jesus."

Luke pulled me over to a section of the belt where I could sit down and told me to put my head between my knees.

"This your first body?"

I nodded. "It's not that, it's... God, Luke, it's..."

"I know." He stroked my hair. "I know."

Chapter Five

He wouldn't let me drive and, after a huge hot chocolate from Starbucks, eventually shepherded me down to my car and drove me back to the office, glaring at the harsh gearbox.

"I heard." Alexa was halfway around the desk when we walked in. "Jesus, sounded brutal."

"Yep," Luke said. "Did you hear the extra dimension?"

She shook her head, glancing at me. "Are you okay? You look really white."

I shrugged. "I'm fine. I always look white."

"She's in shock," Luke said. "The victim helped her apprehend Brown yesterday."

Alexa covered her mouth. "Oh, God, you think that's why he was killed?"

Luke shrugged. "Wouldn't rule it out. In fact, I'd say that's pretty much got to be it. The Browns have an ally on the outside. A very vicious ally. One who has access to at least the undercroft. That's a green pass at least, right?"

I nodded. "Yeah. Green is most areas."

"Could even be red," Alexa said. "Maria and Macbeth are going through the computer looking up everyone who's gone through since last night. They reckon it must have happened this morning before the belts were started up, and he just worked through the system. Probably someone left him in the mechanism."

I shuddered, and Luke looked over at me.

"Maybe it might be a good idea if you stayed at your parents' tonight," he said.

I shook my head out of pride, although right now home seemed like a very good option. Lasagne and ice cream and football on the telly. Yeah. Home was good.

I nodded, meekly.

"Luke," Alexa said, beckoning him over. She spoke in hushed tones, but I still heard. "Maybe you should rethink this thing. Look at the state of her."

Luke gave her a level look. "Lexy, the first time you saw a fresh body, you threw up."

She made a face. "I'm just saying. It could be that someone's after her. From the reports I'm getting in, she was sort of high-profile yesterday."

Luke glanced at me. "You're saying we should keep an eye on her?"

Alexa nodded, and Luke sighed, like I was some big burden to him. Well, fine, but he got me into this.

"Okay." he looked at his watch, then at me. "Lunch?"

I shook my head. "I'm not hungry. Besides, I've been up so long it's really teatime tomorrow. Speaking of which, I said I'd go to my parents'."

He shrugged. "Okay. Do you think you can drive?"

I was so shaky I had to hide my hands behind my back, but I nodded and we went outside. I got into Ted, and Luke said he'd follow in his car. He'd need to know where my parents lived, for quite a few reasons, he said, but mostly I suspect he wanted to check they weren't ex-KGB or anything.

I drove back home with my usual abandon, and it wasn't until we were nearly at my house that I realised we'd gone the wrong way. Never mind. I parked up and went into the flat to get a few things.

Most of the stuff I needed was at my parents' house anyway, but I wasn't about to let Luke see I'd gone the wrong way. I picked up my post and checked the answer phone. It was flashing one call, and with a sinking feeling I remembered getting cut off from Chalker that morning.

I dug out my Siemens. Texts, missed calls, voice mails, the lot. I'd been concentrating so hard on learning about my new Nokia I'd forgotten all about my old phone.

"Crap." I took it out and read the messages. Chalker was pissed off with me for cutting the call, he'd heard Luke in the background and told me to stop shagging and get my arse over to Mum's for tea.

This was so stupid I started laughing. Luke read the message over my shoulder, and his face twitched with amusement.

"Your brother is, er, colourful," he said.

"You have no idea."

"At least your parents are expecting you."

I nodded and listened to the voice mail. It was more of the same. "They're expecting me to be bringing my new bloke," I said with a grimace. "Chalker told them about you."

Luke bit his lip. "Is there any way of getting out of this?"

I laughed. He looked so panicked. "Of course there is! Come on, Luke, they don't really expect me to be bringing someone home. I think they'd probably faint if I did."

This was completely and very sadly true. I couldn't even remember the last time I went on a date. Some time before Pete-the-philanderer, the one who was porking the tart at college. Actually, no, I think it *was* Pete-the-philanderer. There'd really been no one else. And to be honest, I still wasn't entirely sure why there was him. He was a bit of a loser. I think I was just so overjoyed that someone wanted me and I wasn't going to end up on the shelf at the tender age of nineteen that I said yes almost before he'd finished asking me out.

God, now I sounded really sad. I mean, I met men. I liked men. I flirted with them all the time at work. But since Pete I'd had very high standards. Losers need not apply.

Which did sort of rule out pretty much every bloke I met, apart from the fantabulous ones who only looked at you if you were rich, size six and so glossy they could see their own reflections.

A bit like Angel, really, but she was a sweetheart and honestly hardly noticed men falling at her feet most of the time, plus she lent me her vintage jewellery so I couldn't really fault her.

Luke was still looking at me.

"You keep your family and your love-life separate?"

I cleared my throat. "Yeah, that's it. The family is more important. Really important."

"So if you turn up alone and they ask where I am...?"

"I'll say you were the plumber or something." I managed a little shrug and just for a second allowed myself the fantasy of letting Luke into my parents' house. My mother would have a heart attack. Luke was all cheekbones and penetrating eyes and tight muscle. He was sort of lean-bodied, with long legs and a great arse.

Not that I spent a lot of time looking, you understand. Just every second he was turned away from me.

I threw some clean underwear in a bag and added my new secret agent extras...cuffs, defence spray, Kevlar, rape alarm... just overnight things, really. In case the psycho who mangled Chris happened to follow us.

I walked past Tammy's food bowl and was struck by a horrible thought.

"What?" Luke said, looking impatient.

"Tammy. Have you seen her?"

"Who?"

"The cat! Have you seen her since we got back?"

My heart was beating in double time. Little Tammy! What if someone took her and hurt her? My poor little abused baby!

"She'll be out on the prowl somewhere," Luke said. "You have a cat flap."

I nodded, trying to believe him. She was a rescue cat and people had done horrible things to her when she was a kitten. Even now she was terrified of strangers.

"Actually, that's sort of a security risk," Luke began, but I gave him a death look. I ran to the door, box of Go-Cat in hand, shaking the biscuits and yelling Tammy's name. What if she'd got run over? I knew I shouldn't have brought her with me when I was moving so close to the main road. What if she was hurt?

What if someone had taken her and was torturing her?

Oh God, what if...?

And then I heard the most marvellous sound, a fabulous, magical sound. I heard the gentle tinkle of the bell on Tammy's collar that was supposed to warn squirrels that she was coming, but of course never did.

"Tammy! Hello, baby." I dropped the Go-Cat and made a grab for her but Tammy, the wriggly little thing, escaped and started capturing stray biscuits.

I straightened up and turned to see Luke standing in the middle of the sitting room, shaking his head at me.

"Somehow I don't think your cat is going to be an easy target," he said.

"How do you know?"

"She just ran away from you."

I scowled and opened the hall cupboard for Tammy's travelling basket. She absolutely hated the thing, and I didn't blame her, because I probably wouldn't like to be locked into a wire cage only three inches bigger than me (and Tammy was a really tiny tabby). I lined it with an old towel and went back outside to pick her up.

I just said she was a wriggly little bugger. She was also a sharp-clawed little bugger. I doubt I could have inflicted more damage on myself if I'd gone down the baggage belt naked with someone throwing razorblades at me. By the time I'd got the lid locked shut with Tammy inside, I was hot, sweaty, messy and bleeding, and Tammy was regarding me like she'd have called the RSPCA if only we had a phone designed for cats.

Throughout all this Luke stood and watched me with his usual expression of faint disbelief.

"Can I just interrupt your swearing to ask why you're doing this to her?" he asked.

"Fuck off."

"Fair enough." He jangled his car keys. "Are you nearly ready?"

I flicked back my hair as coolly as I could and picked up my bag. "Sure. Let's go."

Ted was waiting for me, still unlocked (honestly, no one'd ever steal him), and I put Tammy on the passenger seat. She glared at me malevolently and gave an abused-baby mew.

"Not working," I told her. "I'm saving your life here."

For a second or two, I wondered if someone was really out to get me. If they really were going to break into my house and try to kill me.

Maybe they'd try to blow it up like in Stephanie Plum.

Maybe I was overreacting. I put the car in gear and reversed out of my space.

Luke followed me, sticking very close all the way. He was driving a three-year-old Vauxhall Vectra, and part of me (the very tiny part that wasn't stressed and frightened and tired) made a note to make fun of him later. I mean, a Vectra? How secret agent is that? Bond never drove a Vectra. Bond probably doesn't even know what a Vectra is.

My parents used to live in a very ordinary Sixties house in the middle of the village that was so normal and boring I often drove right by it without realising. But after I moved out, they paid off the mortgage and seemed to decide they missed being in debt, because they bought a new, more expensive house.

It was very pretty, with roses round the door and a stream and a big garden that my dad could potter around in. You knew your dad was getting old when he started pottering. It was up a longish drive from a narrow road, and my city-born parents thought it was marvellous.

When it rained, you could hardly get up the drive.

This meant that in every month, apart from sometimes July and August, I got distress calls from my parents begging me to come and tow their car out of the mud. My dad had a Saab, which was very cool but not so hot in the deep mud. In fact it'd been known to sink. My mum had a cute little Corsa, which ran away from all the mud. Really, it was car torture.

Then there was Ted, who can climb every mountain, ford every stream (even the one at the bottom of the driveway that was so cute when they bought the house, and which my dad threatens daily with a bridge he would never, ever build). Chalker laughed at me when I bought Ted, he said I was like those sad soccer moms who drive massive Discoveries five hundred yards down the road to pick their kids up from ballet lessons. But he'd shut up a bit now on my choice of car. Now he generally picked on my driving skills instead.

Luke, rather predictably, balked at the sight of the mud and when I was a couple of yards up the driveway, my new phone started ringing.

"What?" I said, trying not to sound too smug.

"You shouldn't be answering that while you're driving," Luke said, so I ended the call and chucked the phone back in my bag. Super-citizen, that was me.

The phone rang again, and I ignored it. If I stopped now I might get stuck. I ploughed on to the sound of the phone chirruping (I hadn't set voice mail yet) and Tammy warbling along in distress.

When I was parked safely on the paving outside the house, I picked up the phone.

"Now who's laughing at my car?"

Luke sounded very pissed off. "If I go up there, will I get stuck?"

"There's that possibility."

"Why didn't you tell me that?"

"Why didn't you get a decent car? Really, the kindest thing you could do to that thing is let it sink without trace."

"What's wrong with my car?"

Uh-oh. Did I just break the cardinal rule? Did I just insult a man's car? I mean, it wasn't that bad a car. It was just boring. Luke should be in an Aston or something. Not a Vectra. Not something so...ordinary.

Maybe I should refrain from saying so, though. I mean, we hardly knew each other, and he was sort of my boss.

Then I remembered him sneering at Ted and said firmly, "It's pants."

"How do you know?"

"My dad had one once as a loaner when his got mud in the carburettor. He hated it."

"Did you ever drive it?" Luke asked pointedly.

I made a face at the phone. I wasn't old enough at the time. "Look, you know where my parents live. There's a footpath just up the road a bit if you want to walk up, but really, I'll be fine. Do you need me for anything else?"

"I don't think so."

"So I'll see you tomorrow?"

"I'll call you."

"No!" If he called, Chalker would be merciless. "Text me. I'll tell them it's Angel or someone."

"Ten-Four." And he was gone.

I couldn't help grinning at Tammy as I lifted her cage out of the car. In real life, people always said goodbye at the end of a phone call. Or at least thanks, or see you later, or something. They didn't just cut the call. They only do that in *X-Files* land.

Wow. How cool was I? I was just like Scully. Except I had blonde hair. And Luke was cuter than Mulder.

Well, he was. Speaking purely objectively.

I kicked open the door and lugged Tammy inside. Strange for such a tiny cat to weigh so bloody much. She was making herself as heavy as possible, I knew, just to spite me. And I'd never be able to get her back in the box to take her home.

"Oh, hello. Why have you got Tammy?" my mother asked as she came out of the kitchen, tying her apron.

"There's a leak," I improvised. "In the kitchen. Because of the builders. You know, across the car park. I called a plumber but they can't get the part for it. So Tam and I are coming back here."

My mother shrugged. "Okay." She glanced at the spitting ball of menace that was my baby kitten. "She looks pissed off."

You sort of have to get used to my mother. She can be a bit full throttle. Don't get me wrong, I adore her and everything, but she's not what you might call normal.

Guess it runs in the family.

I poured out some Go-Cat for Tammy, then got some milk at the ready in case she hadn't forgiven me. But the biscuits seemed to work. She hissed at Norma Jean, my brother's loopy blonde dog, and made herself at home in seconds flat. Cats are easy to please.

"Charlie said you had someone over when he called this morning," my mother said, giving me the sort of "tell me *everything*" look I usually get from Angel. "Someone male?"

I'm afraid I blushed. "No, that was just the plumber," I said. "Sorry."

My mother did indeed look disappointed. "Thought you might have invited him over," she said.

"What, the plumber? I don't think so."

"It really wasn't anyone interesting?"

"Nope," I lied. "Sorry. So who's Chalker bringing home?"

My mother did a palms-up. "I have no idea. Lucy? Laura? Lulu? The one with the blonde ringletty things."

"Jessica?"

"Maybe. One of those skinny hipless things."

I smiled at that. My mother and I are united in our fight against turning into my grandmother (I have a good few years yet, and still have to look forward to turning into my mother first, but I still dread the day I wake up and think hair lacquer would be a good idea), who sort of melted outwards as she got older. Neither of us was built to be a hipless wonder, as my mother calls them, and we both know that neither of us would ever be able to run without wearing about three sports bras. We hated skinny girls.

Chalker's new bird turned out to be minuscule and hardly out of primary school. Her name was Jeni (had she not even learnt to spell yet?) and she ate about a square inch of lasagne before declaring she was full.

I should probably explain that while I am nearly a proper vegetarian (just chip shop fish, I swear), my family just cut out red meat. It was some thing my mother started years before we were born as a health fad, just like she started yoga and taking so many vitamins she rattled. The rest of us sort of went along with it.

I used to eat all kinds of meat until I was six, when I saw my first adorable baby lamb and asked my mother what it was.

"Lunch," she answered, and I've not eaten meat since.

Chalker was explaining this to Jeni, with rather more emphasis on me being really weird, and telling her that he ate chickens "because they're stupid".

I gave him a look. "Then you might as well eat Norma," I said, and from under the table, the dog gave a sigh. No one knew what breed she really was. She was just pretty and blonde and really stupid, and she'd roll on her back to have her tummy tickled by just about anybody.

Really, she was Chalker's ideal woman.

After tea, Chalker got a text from Tom, the singer in his band. Then Tom turned up, apparently to pick up a CD but really to check out Jeni. Chalker had by this point got his guitar out to impress Jeni, and then he handed it over to Tom and started on the piano to really rub it in. Before I really realised how late it was, it was midnight and we were still singing Beatles songs.

"Oh my God," Jeni squeaked, "I have to go to college tomorrow."

I blinked at her, feeling cruel. "Which college is that, Jeni?"

She gave me a defiant stare. "Cambridge."

Hardly. At dinner she'd said she adored *The Importance of Being Ernest*, and when my mother asked if she was an Oscar Wilde fan, Jeni had looked blank and said, "Was he the butler?"

"Really? What are you reading?"

Her pretty brow creased. *Dear me*, I thought, *better stop that or you'll get wrinkles. In, say, twenty years' time.*

"Well, my main text book is *Modern Business*. It's sooo heavy. It really makes my back ache!"

Since a glossy magazine would probably double her body weight, I wasn't surprised.

"Are you doing a business degree, then?" I asked, poisonously. I'd seen that book at school—at *school*—and it most definitely was not a degree-level tome. In fact, Norma Jean could have critiqued it.

I caught Tom's eye. He was trying hard not to laugh.

"Well," Jeni said, "maybe, once I've got my GNVQ."

I bit my lip and couldn't trust myself to say anything.

"A GNVQ is equivalent to two A levels," Chalker said.

"How would you know?" I asked pleasantly. "You never got any."

Chalker scowled, and I got up for more wine. My family was great, so long as you have been healthily immunised with alcohol.

Tom followed me into the kitchen. “What is she, sixteen?” I asked.

“Seventeen,” he replied, “she says.”

“She’s such a child!”

Tom grinned. “You want to know the best bit?”

I nodded eagerly.

“It’s not even advanced GVNQ. It’s intermediate. She failed all her GCSEs.”

I put my hands to my mouth. That was fabulous.

When we were at school, we called a GNVQ Generally Not Very Qualified. If you did A levels then you had to do three subjects and fill your timetable up, but the GNVQ lot rolled up for about three hours a day, including study periods. Plus, it was generally acknowledged that any qualification in business meant nothing. It was like on *The Secret of My Success* when Brantley finds out his college qualifications will only get him a job in the mail room.

Jeni left soon after to get her beauty sleep before going off to chew her pencil at Cambridge Regional (not quite the same as King’s) in the morning. Tom crashed out on the floor in Chalker’s room. I went upstairs and found Tammy asleep on my pillow, looking all lost and helpless.

“It’s okay, baby.” I scooped her up and she wriggled against me, all warm and sleepy and adorable. “The nasty scary people won’t get you here.”

She curled up in the crook of my arm and went back to sleep instantly. I lay awake, somewhat harder to convince.

Chapter Six

I was woken by Tammy licking my nose at half past six. My dad gets up early to go to work and usually feeds Norma Jean before he goes. I guess Tammy remembered the early breakfast from when we both lived here.

I pushed her on the floor and tried to get back to sleep.

Tammy burrowed under the covers and settled on my back, kneading and purring. It would have been a great free massage except that she has really sharp claws. I extracted her from the duvet and pulled it right up to my chin.

Tammy sat on my chest and started patting my nose.

I was about to give up when I heard Dad get up and go downstairs. Tammy bolted after him and I sank blissfully back into sleep. Ah, wonderful sleep. I love to sleep. It's one of the things I'm really good at.

Dad let Norma Jean out and she started barking at the rabbits on the other side of the stream.

I gave up on sleep and went downstairs, thinking, *I'll be productive. I'll work on the Nokia.*

I managed to set ring tones and voice mail and, by the time I'd finished, was so sleepy I dropped the phone on the floor and went back to sleep. Tammy joined me and we curled up together on the sofa, both of us exhausted by yesterday's very long day.

Then my new phone rang.

It was flashing Luke's name. "What?" I mumbled sleepily.

"Wake up."

"I am awake."

"I've got a job for you."

"Oh, goody."

"Lexy's gone through the computer and come up with a couple of names who could be behind yesterday's grisly murder."

I shuddered.

"And you want me to...?"

"Check them out. I'm doing it too. Give me five minutes to get my contacts in and I'll be back as Luca. Come up to the office in half an hour, I'll give you the details then."

He clicked off and I sat staring at the phone. Half an hour? I had to wash my hair and everything!

Tom was waiting as I came out of the bathroom, dripping, wrapped in a towel. He ran his eyes over me.

"Oh Sophie," he said longingly, "why don't you dress like that more often?"

"Because I'm part of a huge campaign to halt bathroom perversion."

He winked at me and slipped into the bathroom.

I threw on yesterday's clothes, stopped and swore and went charging around the house for my Ace uniform.

"I thought you were working a late today," my mother said.

"Change of plan. Overtime," I explained, grabbing a shirt from the laundry basket and trying to remember where my scarf was.

Crap. It was at home, along with my pass.

I made it to the office only ten minutes late and scrambled inside. Luke was reading through some paperwork, looking serene and sexy in his un-crumpled uniform, eyes brown, in full Luca mode. Alexa was immaculate and smiling. I was hot, sweaty and irritated.

"You're late," Luke said.

I glared at him and he shrank away. "Next time, give me more time."

"Half an hour is plenty long enough to get ready and come into work."

I flashed a look of despair at Alexa, who rolled her eyes. "Coffee?"

"Yes. Please."

She rolled over to the kettle and switched it on and, when she came back, handed me a large manila envelope. "This is all for you."

I looked inside. Oh God. Warrant card, red go-anywhere BAA pass, remote keys to the office, complete with passcodes, list of phone numbers for me to program into the Nokia.

It was like Christmas.

"Don't save any of those numbers under their real names," Luke said. "Put them all as Mum or Aunt Alice or make up a lot of names. But for Christ's sake remember who they are."

I looked down at the list. A lot of them were police chiefs and army contacts. "Let me guess, I have to eat this when I'm done?"

Luke and Alexa shared a look. "You could," Alexa said, "or you could just burn it."

Better plan. I was liking Alexa a lot.

"Don't let anyone see your red pass," Luke said, "you're not supposed to have one. Ace still thinks you're a Passenger Service Agent."

"What about the duty managers?"

"They know about me—at least, they think I'm with Special Branch. They know you're helping me. They don't know you're actually with us."

I nodded as if I understood.

We went up to the terminal in the Vectra. "Seriously," I asked Luke, "*this* is your car?"

"Ha ha."

"Why do you have it?"

"Why do you think?"

I raised my palms. "Lost a bet?"

He gave me a look. "Would you look twice at a Vectra driver?"

"I wouldn't look once."

"Exactly."

"...Oh." When he put it like that, it was rather sensible. Wasn't that why the police drove them as unmarked cars?

We parked up and made our way up through the undercroft to the terminal, Luke briefing me as we went.

Hark at me, a briefing. Look out, world, I was a real secret agent now.

"I need you to keep an eye on this guy." He handed me a grainy photo of someone with a shaved head. "Has a record. We're just checking him out as a precaution. Lexy hacked into the allocations, he's on the gate today. Checking in a flight to Frankfurt. Get your arse over there and flirt the information out of him."

"Precisely what kind of information are we looking for?" I asked, wondering how far I'd have to take the flirting.

Luke grinned. "Just where he was when Mansfield was killed. Lexy has it down to somewhere between two and four yesterday morning."

Eurgh. So while I was deciding whether to get out of the airport business, Chris was having it decided for him.

"Any questions?"

"Just one. Why was Chris in the undercroft in the middle of the night anyway? If he was on the morning before then he wouldn't be working that night."

Luke tapped me on the head. "Smart cookie. We don't know why he was there. He was supposed to be working middles, nine-to-five."

I made a face. We never did middle shifts. "All right for some."

"Don't be bitter. You don't have to do shifts any more at all, remember? Only when we need you there. Okay, kid," we'd reached the stairs now, and Luke seemed to be expecting me to go up them, "race you."

"Naff off." I walked past and pressed the button to the lift.

"Can't you even run up a flight of stairs?"

"That's about three storeys!"

"You need to be in good shape."

"I'm in plenty good shape," I said, offended.

Luke ran his gaze over me and I felt a little hotter.

"Prove it."

I sighed. "I am not racing you up those stairs."

"Why not?"

"You'll win."

"Defeatist."

"Yeah, and?"

"At least walk up them."

Eventually I consented to that, although Luke jogged up and taunted me from the top. I glared at him and stalked past.

"So where are you going?" I asked.

"Cameras caught one of the girls from Information going down there on the night in question. A Miss Ana Rodriguez."

I frowned. "I know her. We went to get our passes together." I frowned deeper. She was very pretty in a Penelope Cruz sort of way. "Luke, how come you get the tiny little Spanish girl and I get the big scary thug?"

"He's not a thug. His file says he's only six foot."

"Oh, tiny."

Luke grinned. "He's shorter than me."

"Show off."

He laughed. "Got your phone?"

"Yes. Both of them." I hefted my Ace bag. "And my other pass. And my warrant card—which, by the way, I have no idea what to do with. And I have my cuffs and defence spray and everything."

"Running shoes? Sports bra?"

"That's a very personal question."

"Don't flirt too hard. There's nothing unsexier than a big boulder-holder sports bra."

I stuck my tongue out at him and made my way over to the gate.

On the way over to the satellite the Ace jingle played at full volume. The Ryanair girls in their natty little blue suits looked over at me and tittered, and every single passenger zoomed in on my Ace logo.

I tried to make myself smaller. It was hard when you're five foot ten and wearing a giant black parka with the word ACE stamped across the back in massive letters.

I skipped into the ladies on my way to the gate. Luke had told me to invent a cover story, so I figured I'd make something up about a last-minute gate change that left me in the satellite with nothing to do for a while. I checked out my reflection, got out my make-up and added extra mascara and lip gloss, and wished desperately that the Ace uniform gave more leeway for sexiness. Probably people would notice if I unbuttoned my shirt halfway down. Besides, as Luke pointed out, my sports bra really wasn't too attractive.

It's not fair. Flat-chested girls can run whenever they want. And they can wear pretty little camisole strappy things. I have to have substantial shoulder straps. It sucks.

But then, I never have to pay parking fines…

I hefted my bag back over my shoulder and stomped out of the ladies, stopping halfway and remembering myself. I plastered on a big fake smile and sashayed on over to Gate 36, where the thug, known as Gavin, was playing with his computer.

I gave him a smile. "Hi."

He looked surprised. "Hi. Do you have a flight from here?"

No, I'm in love with you. "Yeah," I said. "Prague."

He nodded and went back to his computer.

Damn. I flicked through the flight systems. There was a Prague flight, but it wasn't for four hours and it was in another satellite. I toyed moodily with the machine for a while, then had the bright idea of pulling out the keyboard cable while he wasn't looking.

"Oh," I said aloud. "Damn. The keyboard's not working." I made a show of checking the wires. "Is it always like this?"

He shrugged. "Some of them are. D'you want to use mine?"

Bingo. I leaned across him and wriggled slightly, and checked a few random things on the computer, knowing full well he wasn't looking at the monitor.

"They're all in," I said, looking up at him on the "in".

"What?" He'd been looking at my arse. Men are so damn easy.

"The passengers. They're all checked in." I straightened up and leaned back against the desk. "So what's yours?"

He licked his lips. I actually saw it.

"My what?"

"Your flight!" I gave the silliest laugh I could. "Where is it to?"

"Oh. Frankfurt."

"Frankfurt, huh?" This was on a plate. "I love Frankfurters." I licked my lips. "I could wrap my tongue around one right now."

Okay, so maybe that was going a bit far, but he was falling faster than Marlon Brando from the Empire State Building.

"You're hungry?" Gavin croaked.

I let my eyes match his. "Starving." Abruptly, I let my gaze fall. "I've been working all day."

"Yeah. Me too. What time do you—"

"I was on all day yesterday as well," I said. "With all those belt failures." I stuck my fingers under my own belt for emphasis. I swear, Gavin's little piggy eyes nearly rolled out of his head.

"I was at home," he said in a strangled voice.

"Really? You weren't working overnight? I hear the problem happened overnight."

He shook his head. "I was asleep. Came on at six yesterday."

"You came straight here? Right up to the gate?"

"Check-in."

"You didn't leave the desk all day?"

He shook his head. "What—"

Shit. Losing cover. "I mean, I was on check-in yesterday. I'm surprised I didn't see you."

He smiled. "I saw you."

I blinked. "You did?"

"Yeah. You ran through yesterday." He frowned. "You weren't in uniform."

Double shit. No, I wasn't. "I, er, I was just coming off shift," I explained hastily. "I got changed then realised I'd left my uniform in the staff room. Silly me." I rolled my eyes.

He nodded. "You always get changed in your staff room?"

I shrugged and nodded. I'd heard what I needed and I wanted to go now.

"It's right next to ours. Hey, just think, you've been getting undressed next to me for months and I never knew."

Urgh. I so didn't need to hear that. "Yeah. Imagine."

"Oh," he was smiling wider now, "I'm imagining."

Triple shit. I swung around and started tapping on my defunct keyboard. Nothing happened and I had to restrain myself from slapping my own forehead.

"You want to hop on over here?" Gavin asked, and I nearly shuddered.

I managed a smile and leaned over him again, this time trying not to touch. "Well, won't you look at that? They changed the gate. It's in Sat 1. Gotta go!"

I tried to straighten up but was stopped by Gavin's hand on my backside.

Oh, quadruple shit with bollocks on top.

"So, what's the combination for your staff room?"

I leapt away from him. "I don't know," I stammered. "I, er, I have to go."

"Wait a sec," he squinted at my name badge—or maybe it was my chest, I could never tell—and grabbed my arm. "Sophie, don't go—"

I started staring around randomly, looking for some excuse. I was about to start yelling that there was a plane on fire outside when to my immense relief I saw Luke sauntering casually towards me.

"Luke!" I shouted. Bollocks, I mean, "Luca! The gate's been changed for Prague, we have to go..."

"You don't have a Prague flight for hours," Gavin murmured. "Spend some time with me."

I wrenched myself away and ran to Luke, much to his amusement. "I think you've got the wrong idea," I chuntered to Gavin, who looked very confused. Beside me, Luke was nearly cracking up. "I—I have a boyfriend. Right here. Luca is my boyfriend."

Luke stared. Gavin stared. Half a million Ryanair passengers stared. I hadn't realised I'd been *quite* so loud.

I glanced up pleadingly at Luke.

"That's right," he said eventually, sexy Italian accent in place. "Sophie is my girlfriend. We are in love," he purred, slipping his arm around me. Mmm. He felt pretty good. All warm, and hard, and warm...

I glared at Gavin.

"But—but you were coming onto me," he said forlornly.

"I was not! I was making polite small talk, one PSA to another."

Gavin glared at Luke. "She's a bloody tart," he said.

"Hey, don't insult my girlfriend. Is okay, baby, I'm here now," Luke said, and to my astonishment, kissed me.

I think it might have started out as a little closed-mouth kiss, but it very, very soon turned into a full-blown snog. Christ, he was a good kisser. Or maybe Pete-the-philanderer had been really bad. But I'd never kissed anyone and had sparks before. Not actual sparks. I swear, if it had gone on any longer we'd have blown up the satellite. We'd have been arrested for terrorist action. Standing there in the blackened rubble of the building, still making out.

And there were hands too. Actual hands. Doing rather naughty things under my jacket. Under my shirt, too. I forgot how to breathe when Luke's fingers brushed my bare skin, but that wasn't a particular problem at the time, since my mouth was glued to his and I'd given up on oxygen.

My God. His mouth should be illegal.

Probably is, in some Southern states.

"Jesus," I said when he let me go. I was shaking. An American family were applauding us.

Luke had his arms around me—just as well, since my bones had all turned to the consistency of custard. "We could get fired for this," he murmured.

"I'm the one with the payslip, remember?" I glanced around and my gaze alighted on Gavin. He looked mightily pissed off.

"I'm calling Ace," he said, and we both shrugged. He'd only get through to the check-in office, and Luke had said Paola was on today. She'd think it was hilarious.

"We'd better go," I said, grabbing Luke's hand—yes, just his hand, although other ideas did flash through my mind—and pulling him away from the gate.

In the lift on the way back down to the terminal transit, I couldn't look at Luke. My face was burning. I had to be professional about this. Yeah. We could be professional. I glanced at Luke.

"That was hot," he said, and I felt like dying.

"Ih," I said, trying to sound indifferent, "it was okay."

Luke lifted my chin so I had to look at him.

"Liar," he said, and I nearly stopped breathing.

The lift doors opened and I stumbled out into the cool air of the transit platform. It was full of passengers and I pushed through them to the front, Luke following me.

"Sophie," he said, catching my arm, "are you embarrassed?"

"No."

"You are." He grinned. "That's very cute."

I blushed even further and thought about throwing myself under the transit tracks, but they were bloody sealed off by hydraulic doors.

"I'm not embarrassed," I told him. "I'm professional. That was a professional action."

Luke got very close and said, so no one else could hear, "You wanted me."

Maybe I could go out onto the tarmac and get myself sucked into an aircraft engine. I heard that was a great way to die.

The transit train arrived and I hurtled into the furthest corner, tailed by Luke.

"Don't you even want to hear my news?" he said.

"No." Then, "What news?"

"About Ana?"

"Oh. Yes." I tried to settle myself. "What about her?"

Luke winked. "I can't tell you here."

The journey back was torture. I made sure I was in the middle of a crowd all the time so Luke couldn't tell me how much I wanted him again. Because I really did want him. He was sexy as hell and he kissed like it was life support.

But I was determined not to let him see. I knew his type. He knew he was gorgeous and he was just trying to get a rise out of me. Well, fuck him.

Not literally, obviously.

We got back to the terminal and I eventually had to turn and face him. But his face was blank. "Where now?"

"Home, James?"

I shrugged. "If we're done here. My car's at the office."

We walked back down to the car park in silence. Maybe Luke had forgotten about it. Why was he being so quiet?

"So, how'd you get on with the thug?"

I nearly tripped down the stairs. "What?"

"Did you get anything?"

I stared.

Luke laughed. "About the murder. Did you find out where he was?"

"Oh." I tried to recover myself, and failed. "He was at home. In bed. He came on at six, spent the whole day on check-in."

"Right." Luke nodded. "Well, he was just a fail-safe anyway. We found out he had a juvenile record. He wasn't on camera."

I glared at him. "So I got the dummy?"

"In more ways than one. Whereas I found out something extremely useful."

"I'll bet you did."

Luke grinned and held the door for me. “Ana wasn’t on the desk when I got there. They said she was off sick. I said I needed to get hold of her on a personal matter and they told me to wait. I told her I couldn’t wait, I was her boyfriend.”

“Lot of that going around.”

“And they said, you can’t be, her boyfriend was killed in an accident yesterday.”

I stared at Luke.

“Ana Rodriguez was Chris Mansfield’s girlfriend?”

“Yep.”

I shook my head. Pretty little Ana? God, she must be devastated.

“So why’d she go down there in the middle of the night?”

“Four a.m. Why’d you think?”

I shrugged, then it occurred to me. “No!” Luke nodded, and I whistled. “That is kinky.”

“Yep. It’d have been kinkier still if they’d pulled it off, but the tapes only have her going down there, not him.”

“So to speak.”

Luke laughed. “Yeah.”

“So what do we do now? Go and speak to her?”

“Bingo.”

We walked out to the car in silence. It was cold and the wind blew straight across the runway at us. I shivered, and Luke put his arm around me.

“Hey, cut that out.”

He looked amused. “You didn’t seem to mind at the gate.”

“I was acting at the gate.”

“Ah.” We’d reached the car now, and Luke dropped his arm to get his keys. “Acting.”

We got in, and I fastened my seat belt. My fingers were shaking.

“So, if I told you the thug was walking this way right now, what would you do?”

I started to turn my head, but Luke grabbed me. “Don’t look.” He kissed me again.

I have to tell you, I am fully prepared to back Jeremy Clarkson in his hatred of the Vectra, based on my own experiences. Those seats are bloody uncomfortable when you're trying to make out.

But then equally, I have to hand it to Luke. After about thirty seconds I no longer cared about the seats. Or the gear lever. Or the hand brake. Or *any* of it. Luke's hands were on me again, and it was magic. His mouth was hot, and he kissed me like he was in charge. I ought to have been bothered about that, but the Scarlett in me just swooned and let herself be dominated.

The only thought that entered my brain was how attractive my underwear was. Once I'd remembered it was perfectly presentable, I happily shut down all cognitive functions and concentrated on the heat of Luke's body under my hands, the sweep of his tongue against mine, the hot, sweet taste of him. I felt drugged. It was marvellous.

Eventually Luke pulled back into his own seat and extracted his hand from my shirt. "Your place?" he said, and I nodded. I knew there'd been no thug.

I swear, the journey home had never seemed so long. It was about five miles but it felt like fifty. Luke's fingers brushed my leg whenever he changed gear and I got so hot I had to stick my head out the window. Note to self: don't do this when there are trees by the side of the road. Having my head attached to my body could only be a good thing.

It took me bloody years to find my keys when we got to the flat, and Luke didn't help by running his hands over me and murmuring in my ear what he wanted to do to me. My hands were shaking at the mention of those things. I liked those things—okay, I liked the idea of those things. If he actually did them to me, I'd probably die.

But what a way to go.

We fell inside, still kissing, and I tripped over the mail.

"Dammit," I said, grabbing the bunch of bills. "Just let me—euw!"

"What?" said Luke, as I held up an envelope that was dripping all over me. It was dripping something red. It was dripping blood.

Suddenly all sexy thoughts vanished from my mind, and I could see they were vanishing from Luke's too. He raced over to the kitchen and grabbed my rubber gloves, took the bloody envelope from me and carefully opened it.

And withdrew a severed finger.

Chapter Seven

We both stared at it. Luke was standing there in my hallway holding a severed finger that was dripping blood all over the carpet. Thirty seconds ago I'd been about to have sex with him. Now he was holding a severed finger.

"Oh God," I said, clutching the wall for support. I reached out for the envelope but Luke held it away.

"Fingerprints," he said, and peeled off a glove for me.

It had been addressed to me in the most ordinary of writing, plain blue biro on a manilla envelope. There was a torn plastic bag inside which I guess had been to stop the blood leaking all over the place. Somehow it had failed.

"That's a finger," I said, staring at it. "That's a real live finger."

"Actually, it's a real dead finger," Luke said, going into the kitchen again and looking for something to put the finger on. He ended up with a plate, which I resolved to smash immediately.

I watched him get out his phone and speed-dial. "Lexy? Can you access the autopsy of that body? The Mansfield one."

How many bodies did they have on the go?

"Was it, by any chance, missing a finger?"

There was a pause. My heart was hammering. Someone sent me a severed finger in the post.

Someone sent me a fucking *severed finger* in the post.

"Several. And toes too? Marvellous. Did they check in the mechanism? Okay. Thanks."

He switched the phone off and looked at me.

"There are more to come?" I said, and my voice was rather shaky.

Luke sighed and stared at the finger. "He was missing all his toes and all but the last two fingers of his left hand. The police assumed they'd been ripped off by the mechanism but the autopsy says they were cleanly cut."

"But why only leave two?" I sat down as casually as I could, trying to sound like I wasn't about to pass out. I took some deep breaths. It wasn't that gross. It was just... Well, okay, it *was* that gross, but Tammy left dead things all over the place for me to find. Sometimes I didn't find them until they were mouldy. That was way grosser, right?

Someone sent me a finger. That was just... I mean, what kind of weird lunatic did that? It was gross, and I was officially offended.

Luke shrugged. "Maybe he got interrupted."

I love the way when people are talking about murders and stuff they always call the murderer a "he". Like a woman would never do such a thing.

Ha!

"Sophie," Luke was looking at me closely, "are you okay?"

I thought about it. I mean, I've never been sent a finger in the post before. I didn't really know how to react. Was I shocked? Was I scared? Was I mostly disgusted?

"I think I am," I said eventually, having pinpointed my uppermost emotion as dismay that I'd have to wait to sleep with Luke. "I don't suppose...?"

He already had his phone out. He didn't look like sex was the first thing on his mind, for once. "What?"

"Nothing."

Luke took charge, and not for the first time I wondered if he'd ever let me do the cool stuff. When would I get to ask Alexa about autopsy things? When would I call the police about severed fingers? When would I get a damned gun?

At the back of my mind, I started to form a plan.

"Okay," said Luke eventually, "we're going to take this up to the station and then..." He looked at me again. "Sophie?"

"Yes?"

"Are you sure you're okay? You don't want me to take you up to your parents' or anything?"

I made a face. I was a bloody secret agent now. I did not need to run to my parents every time something gruesome happened.

"I'm fine," I snapped. "Can you drop me at the office so I can get my car?"

We were silent in the car. I started to look around and notice things...things like the hands-free phone kit and the police radio that was currently switched off. I never understood how police kept up-to-date with those things. I mean, we had them at the airport, and occasionally if I got the supervisor's board or I was closing flights, I got the radio. And I found it impossible to concentrate on what I was supposed to be doing and listen out for the radio at the same time. People always had to call me twice and then usually phone me as well, and I could never clearly pick up what they were saying.

And I'm a woman, and we're supposed to be able to do several things at once. God knows how your average copper deals with it.

We pulled into the optimistically named airport business park and swung around the back to the SO17 office. Luke stopped the car and put a hand over mine as I started to unfasten my seat belt.

"Wait," he said.

"What? Why?"

"About what happened earlier..."

I felt my face start to get hot again. "Hmm?"

He gave me a tiny grin. "Maybe we should forget about it. At least until this is over?"

Forget about a kiss like that? Well, several kisses like that. I've never felt anything like that before in my life. I thought only Rhett and Scarlett kissed like that.

Those kisses would keep me going for a damn long time.

"Oh, that?" I said, as airily as I could. "I've already forgotten."

Luke opened the door, grinning. "Liar."

Alexa's office was empty, but Luke just walked straight through into One's office instead. I followed, slightly nervous. I didn't know why I should be in trouble for receiving a severed finger in the post, but it felt like being a receiver of stolen goods—really not your fault, but still a sure-fire way of getting police attention.

"Well, well, Miss Green," said One, straightening up from where he'd been looking over some paperwork with Alexa. "Second day on the job and already you've had one body and a severed finger."

"Call it beginner's luck," I said.

They stared at me. Okay, not funny.

"Um," I said, "technically, I think they're all part of the same body." Either that, or someone completely unrelated to this thing was sending me body parts. What a charming thought. "I can't see why it would be anyone else's finger. If it is, then that's a whole other mess of crap to be dealt with."

Probably I shouldn't have said "mess of crap" there. Why doesn't my brain intervene with my mouth?

"Also, if he was killed because he was involved in the Brown apprehension, then this is probably a threat to stop me becoming involved. I mean, more involved. It's probably from someone who knows I'm involved with SO17."

I sort of trailed off towards the end, because they were all staring at me. Or maybe because I used the word "involved" four times there in three sentences.

"I mean, maybe," I said, and Luke shook his head.

"Told you," he said to One.

"What?" I said.

"Smarter than she looks."

I preened a little at that.

"Okay," One said, "so who do you think it is?"

It was my turn to stare.

"I have no idea! I mean, I guess... Someone inv- er, connected to the Brown brothers?"

Alexa nodded. "We have a list of contacts."

Of course we do.

"Alexa," I said, sensing a day ahead of looking through meaningless names and guessing at things randomly—at least, on my part—"do you have a copy of the BAA footage from Monday night? I mean, Tuesday morning—you know what I mean."

"When Chris was killed?"

"Yes."

She nodded and pulled One's keyboard over to her. She hit a few buttons, pulled up a window blind, and there on a large pull-down screen in front of me was a grainy shot of the undercroft. So that was what the projector was for.

"This is 0155," she pointed to the time in the corner, "we have the death narrowed down to somewhere between two and four in the morning."

"But you have the rest of the footage?"

She nodded. "Basically I've got access to all the BAA cameras and all their archived footage. Here," she tapped the computer screen, "I'll show you how it works."

The way it works is this—I don't have a problem with computers, but they have a problem with me. A brand new machine will happily go into nervous meltdown the second I touch the keyboard. Most of the system-wide computer failures at the airport have been on my watch. I can barely check an e-mail at home without the screen suddenly going blank and error messages appearing all over the place.

I have, therefore, become something of an expert at rebooting a computer in less than the time it takes for someone to notice it's all gone wrong. I can find and dismiss a Help file in seconds and I know just where to go online for PC dilemmas. I'm on first name terms with quite a few of the forum hosts at www.helpmycomputerisdead.com.

So it didn't take me long to find my way around Alexa's computer system. I discovered, to my utter delight, that she hadn't just downloaded the BAA files, she had complete live access to them.

And—yippee!—she had Broadband.

For the rest of the afternoon I was, if not a happy little bunny, then at least a busy one. Luke watched about ten minutes of footage with me, then shook his head, waved the repackaged finger and said he was going to speak to the police who'd been at the crime scene.

I barely noticed he was gone.

I watched hour after hour of footage. I watched it live. It watched it from different angles. I replayed bits over and over. I felt like my dad watching *Ford Super Sunday.* I totally understand how men can watch the same goal over and over again. Every time you see something different.

Or in this case, I saw something the same.

By the time Luke came back mid-afternoon, I was sure of it.

"Watch this," I said as he walked in, having shown it to One about five minutes earlier. One, I might add, had done little all day but read the papers, check my horoscope for me, make a phone call or two to people called Bunty and Monty and Toffee (I think, although it may have been Tuffy) and ask me if I understood any of this computer crap. Alexa had long since wandered back to her own desk.

Luke stood behind me as I found the time segment I wanted and played it on the big screen. The time index said 0236, and I played it through to 0237.

"Did you get that?" I asked, rewinding, and Luke gave me a quizzical look.

"Help me out here."

"There," I pointed to a shadow skidding across the floor. "A mouse, maybe a rat."

"So? Could have got in anywhere, the undercroft is open all across the back. There are mice in the Ace staff room, Sophie."

"I know," I said. "I found one in the kettle once." I opened another clip, this one from three months ago. It had taken me bloody hours to find, hours of endless downloads and Please Waits from the computer, time I had utilised trying to explain to One why texting was a valid form of communication. He hadn't got it.

The three month old footage was the same footage, the same mouse, the same route across the deserted concrete floor. Even the time index was the same, 0236 to 0237.

"You see?" I said excitedly. "It's just been spliced in! Someone has copied and pasted this bit of footage into the archives."

Luke was silent, just as One had been a few minutes ago. I expect they were trying to think of suitable words of awe for my achievement. Maybe I'd get a medal or something. An OBE. Maybe I'd be a dame.

No, they always sound really old. Or transsexual.

"Sophie," Luke said eventually, pinching the bridge of his nose, "it's live footage."

"No, this is archived—"

"I mean, it's transmitted live. There's a big room under the terminal where people sit and watch these monitors all day long. It can't have been spliced."

"Well, then, it was looped in or something! Like on *Speed*. This is the same footage. Someone has played this over what we were supposed to see. They're trying to cover up the actual time-frame when Chris was killed."

Come on. I thought I'd been pretty clever. But Luke and One didn't look convinced.

"It could just be coincidence," One said. "I mean, looping footage? No one does that any more."

"Which is precisely why someone might have done it this time," I said. "You know, like on *The Sting*, where they use the wire because it's so old fashioned no one will suspect it?"

Another silence.

"Seriously, Sophie," Luke said, "do you really sit around watching films all day?"

I made a face and saved the files. "No, I get up at three-thirty in the morning because the TV's really good," I said, standing up. "Come on. At least admit it's a possibility?"

Luke and One exchanged glances.

"It's a possibility," Luke said eventually. "Now come on. We have to go and see Ana Rodriguez."

"Now?"

"Yes. Now."

I ripped off a salute, which Luke seemed to think was funny, and stomped out to my car.

"We're taking mine," Luke said.

"No."

"Yes."

"Why?"

"Because yours sticks out like an ostrich in an aquarium. Time you thought about changing that car."

"No!" I wailed, throwing my arms over Ted's scabby green bonnet. "Ted's family."

For a few seconds Luke just stared. "You named your car?"

"Of course. You don't name yours?"

We both looked at the Vectra. You could never get attached to a car like that.

"I don't keep my cars that long," Luke said as I gave in and opened the Vectra's silver door.

"Get bored easily?"

"No, they're just...sort of expendable."

I didn't ask what he meant by that. I had a feeling I didn't really want to know.

Ana Rodriguez, like a lot of airport workers, especially the foreign nationals who didn't have cars or UK driving licences, lived in town where there was a semi-regular train and bus service to the airport. We parked on a busy road outside the little house she apparently used to share with Chris, and stood on the pavement for a while, looking at it.

There was a To Let sign outside. I almost welled up at the sight of it. God, poor Ana. Stuck in a foreign country, boyfriend murdered, and now getting evicted 'cos she couldn't pay the rent by herself.

Then sense kicked in. He died less than forty-eight hours ago. Not many landlords are that... Well, I was going to say cruel, but what I'm really looking for is *efficient.*

Luke knocked on the door. Ana didn't answer right away, and I turned to him and said, "What if she's out?"

"She'll be in. She's got family coming in this evening."

"Who are we going to be?"

"Plainclothes. CID. Whoever you want. A warrant card's a warrant card."

I supposed it was.

Ana looked awful when she opened the door. Her clothes had chocolate stains on them, her face was puffy and spotty and her hair was greasy. She looked nothing like the gorgeous girl who gave people information in her sexy Spanish accent.

"Ms. Rodriguez?" Luke said, and his voice was kind of soft. He showed her his warrant card and I started searching for mine, but she'd already opened the door to let us in.

"You want to know about Chris?"

"Actually, we want to know about you."

She looked up tearfully. "What, you think I did it?"

"No!" I said before Luke had even opened his mouth. "We don't think that at all. We just need to talk to you."

She nodded and led the way through to the living room, where the curtains were closed and the carpet was covered with tissues and a film was frozen on the screen. The box for it—*Abre Los Ojos*—was sprawled open on the floor. Ana zapped the TV off and looked up at us. "Would you like some coffee?"

Luke shook his head and I, reluctantly because I did want some, shook mine too.

"We don't want to put you to any trouble. You're probably aware, Ms. Rodriguez, that the BAA cameras saw you making your way down to the undercroft early on Tuesday morning."

Ana started blinking and sniffing, but she nodded. She sat down and we followed. I was horribly aware of how close to Luke I was sitting.

"Could you please tell us what time?" Luke was asking Ana.

She shrugged. "About four a.m.?"

"You don't know precisely?"

She shook her head.

Luke nodded and asked gently, "Could you tell me why?"

She started crying again. It was awful.

"It's okay," I said, and I sounded pretty professional. "Take your time."

Luke glanced at me, and I couldn't read his expression.

"I know we shouldn't," Ana said, "but we were going for…we were going for…"

It was too painful. "Was it a romantic liaison?" I asked.

She looked slightly puzzled over "liaison", but she nodded. "Romantic, yes. It was my idea. Is all my fault!"

She started sobbing and she looked so miserable I got up and went over to her and put my arm around her. She clutched at me and wailed into my shoulder, "There is reasons why you not supposed to go down there. I kill him, is all my fault!"

I looked up at Luke. He looked uncomfortable.

"Could you maybe go and get her a glass of water?" I said, and he leapt up.

"Look, Ana," I said, no Ms. Rodriguez for me, "it's not your fault. You just wanted to do something exciting with your boyfriend." She was still crying, but not as hard. I went on, "Was it all secret?"

She raised her face to me. "You mean me and Chris? No one at the airport knew we were together. We were just…" she waved her hand, "flatmates. No, *house*mates. You know."

"How long have you been living here?" I asked as Luke came back in with the water. I gave it to Ana.

"Two years. Since I came here."

"How long have you and Chris been together?"

She started sniffing again. "A year. No one knows. His family don't like me…"

I nodded. Racism in Britain is alive and well. And it wasn't like Ana came from somewhere far off, with strange customs and strict ideals. She was Spanish. They were only an hour ahead of us. But you still see it a lot at the airport, this sort of generalisation. A lot of the foreign nationals have trouble finding places to stay. People think they're untrustworthy.

"I'm sorry," Ana apologised, brushing at the wet patch on my leather coat. "I can't stop crying. All day, I cry. Everything makes me cry."

"It's okay," I said, stroking her back. "Cry all you want. You've been through a lot."

I felt so awful for her, I really did. I mean, the closest I've come to personal loss is when my grandmother died, but I never really was what you might call close to her. She was just this distant old lady, and it sure as hell hadn't affected me like this.

"Ms. Rodriguez," Luke interrupted. "I'm sorry to go on, but we have to know a few facts. Did you see Chris when you got to the undercroft?"

She shook her head. "I thought I was in the wrong place. I never been down there before. I waited maybe ten minutes and I try to call him, but he didn't come."

"So did you leave?"

She nodded. "I heard someone coming. I know sometimes they start early. So I left."

This concurred with the video footage. Ana had stepped out of the lift at 0356 and got back in at 0411. It was hard to see exactly where she was, because not every part of the undercroft was aspected perfectly, but she explained that she'd gone round to the back of one of the Ace belts, where she and Chris had arranged to meet.

Except Chris never turned up. Because Chris was dead.

We left Ana with her small collection of Spanish films and a lot of chocolate, and walked back into the sunshine. It was one of those clear, lovely spring days when you just know that as soon as you take your jacket off and put your sunglasses on, it's going to start tipping it down.

"What do you think?" Luke asked as we got back into the car.

"About Ana?" I shrugged. "I think she was genuine. I don't think she's guilty. Besides, it would have taken more than ten minutes to open up the belts and get the body inside."

Calling it "the body" was easier than calling it Chris. If I looked at things objectively, it wasn't quite so hard.

Hey, look at me! I was coming over all Dana Scully. Maybe I should learn about pathology and stuff.

No. That was just too gross. Besides, Alexa could do that stuff.

"Unless she was the one who messed with the CCTV footage and spliced in more than we thought," Luke said idly, starting the engine. "She could have covered up loads and just added in a bit of her coming and going."

I gave him a sideways look. “I thought no one did that stuff any more?”

“An amateur might,” Luke said, and I rolled my eyes.

Chapter Eight

We went back to the office and Luke asked me where I was planning on staying tonight.

I paused. Was this a veiled proposition? Was he asking if I wanted to stay with him? Did I?

Hell, yes.

But there was something very smug in those dark, contact-lensed eyes of his, something that said he knew he'd got me.

So I said I was staying with my parents and regretted it all the way home.

When I was a little girl, I was the most stubborn creature on earth. I never did anything I was told and the only way my mother could get me to cooperate was by reverse-psyching me into what she wanted. But pretty soon I got wise to that, too, and no one could ever get me to do anything.

I didn't go to the school my parents wanted me to go to. I didn't go to the university they thought was best, even when I was supposed to be transferring. I was quite surprised when they condoned my choice of career (such as it was) but now I have the feeling they were hoping I'd give up a lot sooner than I did.

So I'm perverse. I'm a woman.

I got home and put *Buffy* on again and watched her and the Scoobies dance and sing their way around Sunnydale. I ate a whole load of junk food (told you I was showing off about the healthy stuff. None of it counts when I'm depressed) and thought about calling my parents to say I was staying with them again.

And then I felt pathetic, defeated. Wasn't I supposed to be a secret agent? Did I have to go and stay with my parents whenever I got scared?

When I first moved in here on my own, I hardly spent a night alone for weeks. Angel or someone, Ella and Evie who I went to school with, would come over and watch videos with me until the small hours, and then like as not fall asleep on the sofa. It wasn't until my very first night when I had to cook my own tea, clear up (that habit didn't last long), lock the door and switch the lights out all by myself, then get into my very big, cold bed and lie there listening to all the homicidal rapists right outside my front door, that I realised quite how alone I was.

But it passed. Now I liked my solitude. Now I loved the fact that I lived alone and took care of myself.

Or at least I did until someone started sending me bits of a corpse.

I got all my new secret agent paraphernalia out on the floor and looked at it. The stun gun I was starting to like. It didn't look like a weapon, it looked like the sort of thing my mother uses to curl her fringe, but maybe that was the cool thing about it. It was in disguise. But there was still a niggling doubt in the back of my mind. If it was illegal to have a knife in my bag, surely this would be illegal also?

I had handcuffs. But they were legal, right, because they sold them in Ann Summers. The defence spray—it wasn't anything damaging, it just sprayed a green foamy stuff on the attacker so he'd be stained for a while. Not very exciting. I also had the rape alarm my mum had got me when I was fifteen and went on a school trip to London. I set it off once by mistake and Norma Jean nearly left home.

Then there was the Kevlar. But it was huge—I'd tried it on in the privacy of my bathroom where no one could possibly see me, and there was no way I was wearing it undetected. I looked like I was wearing a fat suit.

So, really, if the finger-sender turned up at my house, I was pretty helpless. I didn't even have Tammy to defend me.

I thought about calling Luke and asking him again if I could have a gun, but right now I wasn't in the mood to see him. This morning I'd been about to have sex with him, and then...

Then the finger. Then the footage. Then Ana. Then the realisation that I just really couldn't get involved with someone I had to work with that closely. If it was Sven that'd be different. Loads of people at the airport are going out or sleeping together or even married. There aren't any anti-fraternisation rules. The hours and the stress generally do a good enough job of killing romance.

But SO17 consisted of six people, and I had a feeling I was going to be working very closely with all of them. I couldn't get involved with Luke. I couldn't.

I stared at my new phone, at the phone book which listed One, Two, Three, Four and Five as my work contacts, and called Two.

She answered straight away. "Sophie, hi!"

"Hey, Maria," I said, feeling a little uneasy. This woman was awe-inspiring. "Um, am I interrupting you?"

"I'm painting my nails," she said. "So, no. Are you all right? I heard about the finger..."

I wondered how she'd heard about the finger. Did she get bulletins from One or Alexa? Or did Luke call her a lot? After all, they'd been partners before.

Maybe they were still "partners" now.

Oh, God. Now I felt sick.

"Um," I said eventually, "yeah, I'm fine. I just, I needed to talk to someone and..."

"And you've had enough of Luke for now," she laughed. "Understandable. He's a lot to take. Look, you don't live far, right? You want to come over?"

Did I? Better than sitting around in my flat, feeling scared. "Sure," I said, and wrote down directions.

She lived in town, not far from the shops, and if I'd got it right in my head then it was a road full of very large, old, gorgeous houses.

I'd got it right.

Maria's house was a buttery yellow, maybe Georgian, maybe earlier. Most of the places around had been taken over by smart solicitors and their offices. All the houses had window boxes full of bright flowers. The cars were all expensive.

I patted Ted's flank nervously and crossed to Maria's house, hoping I'd got it right and she wasn't playing a prank on me.

She answered the door with a cordless phone clamped between shoulder and ear, foam separators between her toes, and a bright green face.

She gestured for me to follow her in, saying, "...you know he's a wanker anyway, though, right? No, he always was. Well, look—no, I have to go, I've got company—*no*, fuck him. No, he has no rights. Put marigold seeds on his lawn. What?" She paused, and laughed. "No, just a friend. No one you know. I'll—I'll see you later, 'kay? Bye."

She clicked the phone off and gave me a tiny smile, feeling at the green face mask. "Sorry," she said, "that was my sister, she's having neighbour problems."

"Ah," I said wisely. I'd lived in my flat for two years and still didn't know my neighbours' names.

"Come on up." She started up the beautiful staircase. "I have to take this stuff off before it tints me permanently green."

Wouldn't that be a shame?

No, stop it, Sophie. Maria is nice. She's been nothing but nice to you. She's on your side. Just because she's completely flawless and she's allowed a gun doesn't mean you have any licence to be nasty to her.

Dammit.

She left the bathroom door open as she scrubbed off the face mask. "So, how're you doing? Settling in okay?"

I shrugged, looking around the landing, which was as beautiful as a landing could be. "Okay. Maria, did you ever..." How to put this? Did you ever get off with Luke? Ever want to? "Did you ever get a finger sent through your door?"

She appeared in the doorway, towelling her face. "No," she said, "although I once found a stiff in my bunk. But that was accidental."

"Accidental?"

"Yeah. Got the wrong bed."

I blanched at this. What was I letting myself in for?

"But that was before SO17," she added, going through into a bedroom that was perfectly, beautifully furnished in shades of blue. She picked up a hooded sweater, pulled it on, and started down the stairs again.

"What did you do before SO17?"

She shrugged. "Two years in the Navy, three in the SBS."

"The...?"

"SBS. Special Boat Service? The less famous and much wetter version of the SAS. Then I got hauled out to do this. But SO17 was a lot bigger then."

"What happened?"

"Lots of things. Not so much work to do—security got a lot tighter and left us twiddling our thumbs. A few people retired, a few sort of had retirement thrust upon them." She raised her eyebrows at me. "The government withdrew funds, we got sort of stranded."

Withdrew funds? "I will still get paid, right?" I blurted, and Maria laughed.

"Of course you will. And aren't you still getting something from Ace? You'll be fine."

As fine as Maria in her beautiful house? Boy, the SBS must pay damn well.

I followed her into a big, messy lovely kitchen, with a conservatory and a big squashy sofa and a couple of huge lazy ginger cats, who I ran over to immediately. "What are their names?"

"Laurel and Hardy. When I got them Laurel was all thin and weedy but now they're both so fat they hardly get off the sofa except to eat more."

I grinned, sitting there stroking both of them. Laurel got up, stretched luxuriously and settled in my lap.

"I think you've made a friend," Maria said, and I knew she wasn't talking about the cats. I loved anyone who was kind to Tammy. "So," she started opening cupboards and getting out crisps and chocolate and Jelly Babies, "what did you want to talk about?"

I played with Laurel's tail. "It's not really that important."

"Spit it out. Is it a work thing?"

I shrugged. "Sort of."

Maria put down the junk food she was carrying and gave me a shrewd look. "Is it about Luke?"

I gulped nervously, and Maria laughed.

"You're going to have to work on your acting if you're going to be a spy," she said. "What's he done? Did he make a move on you?"

I bit my lip.

"Oh, Jesus. Well, look. He does that a lot. It's sort of like habit to him. I wouldn't expect a whole lot to come of it."

Should I tell her a whole lot nearly had come of it? That if it hadn't been for the dead finger, a whole lot really would have come?

No. Perhaps better not.

"Luke's a really good bloke," Maria went on. "He's good at what he does."

Hoo boy. I knew that.

"But he's not exactly stable when it comes to relationships."

How did she know that?

"It's hard to have a normal relationship when you have so many secrets to keep," Maria explained, shaking Doritos into a bowl and handing me some cheese and chive dip. "I can hardly remember the last one I had. You want my advice, avoid relationships. Stick to casual sex."

I blinked at her.

"Luke has it down to a fine art," Maria said wryly, scooping a Dorito into the dip. "Don't think he's been emotionally attached to anything since he got his SIG."

Marvellous.

Maria had an excellent sound system and she slotted a DVD of the Cranberries into the player. We watched for a while on the wide screen TV, eating lots of crisps and dip (saving the sweet course for later), and then Maria looked over at me and laughed.

"What?"

"You, eating junk. Luke said you were all holier-than-thou about additives."

"Only between the hours of three and five on the third Tuesday of every month." I scooped up a fat blob of dip. "And only in public."

"Amen to that. I did wonder why you had crisps in your house if you only ate pure things."

"Everyone has their vices."

I suppose they do. Looking at Maria, it was hard to figure out what hers were. Doritos, maybe? She had eaten about three.

She got up and went into the kitchen, and when she returned had a bottle of wine and two glasses.

"I'm driving," I said reluctantly, and she shook her head.

"Hasn't Luke told you the rule?"

I narrowed my eyes. I had a feeling there were a lot of things Luke hadn't told me.

"One unit a day. Stops you from becoming a complete lightweight and means you can still get in a car and drive if you need to." She poured some out and I was instantly seduced by the thick glug, glug from the bottle.

Just one, then.

"And you know how to spit-back, don't you?"

"With a shot and a bottle of beer? Like in *Coyote Ugly*?"

She grinned and nodded. "Exactly." She put her head on one side and looked at me. "I think we'll make a secret agent of you yet, Sophie," she said, and I wasn't sure if I was flattered or insulted.

She jumped up and ran into the immaculate dining room. "I almost forgot," she said. "I have something for you. Went and raided Boots today." She handed me a large carrier bag and I peeked cautiously inside.

It was full of hair dyes. What was I expecting, that Boots the Chemist had opened up a hand gun section?

"Great," I said, trying and failing to sound enthusiastic. Maria reached out and fingered a wisp of hair that had fallen out from my scrunchie.

"Is this real?"

"No, it's all a wig."

She rolled her eyes. "The colour. Are you a natural blonde?"

Not since I was about twelve. "Mostly."

"But you can still dye it, right? It won't go green or anything."

"No. I've dyed it before." I picked out the bottles. Mostly they were shades of brown, a few reds thrown in for variety. No Sydney Bristow pinks or blues, then. Damn. "What's this?" I lifted out a smaller box.

"Coloured contacts. Very useful. If someone describes you as a green-eyed redhead and you turn up with blonde hair and blue eyes, you'll walk straight by."

Clever. I made a mental note to keep some in my bag.

Maria showed me how to use the contact lenses. It took hours, and I nearly blinded myself several times, but I still drove home with newly violet eyes. I could get used to having violet eyes. They were cool.

My mobile rang as I walked in. "Why don't you ever answer your house phone?" my mother wanted to know.

"I was out."

"Hmm. Are you staying here tonight?"

I looked down at the bag full of hair dye, at my slightly illegal stun gun (Maria said you needed a firearms licence to carry one, so I'd better keep it hidden), my defence spray and my drawer full of kitchen knives, and told myself I was a highly dangerous secret agent. Tomorrow I was going to go out and enroll in a self-defence course.

"Sure," I said. "What's for tea?"

Everyone poured out glasses of wine at dinner. This was one of those things that was supposed to be all sophisticated, oh, we always have wine at the table, but it didn't quite work when it was the coffee table. We eat breakfast at the kitchen table, but never all at the same time. We eat lunch and tea in front of the TV. We always have done. If we ate in the dining room, there'd be two problems. One, we'd have no TV to argue over, and two, my dad took the dining room over as his office about five years ago. The dining table is covered with files and printer cables now.

I thought about the dead finger, which Alexa had told me she had got back so she could analyse it herself, and desperately wanted to pour out a lot of wine. But I'd had my one glass. I might have to leap in Ted and go screaming off to another crime scene at a moment's notice.

But that was kind of cool.

My mother can drink for Britain, but she's the self-denying sort when it comes to things like crisps and chocolate. So she'd bought a tub of Ben & Jerry's for dessert and sat there smugly with an apple while we all tucked in.

"Sure you don't want some?" Chalker waved the pot under her nose. "Cookie dough, mmm..."

My mother made a face. "Raw cookie dough? I can't think of anything more disgusting."

But she never took her eyes off my spoon.

My parents were happily bickering over football versus Jamie Oliver when my Nokia rang. Chalker gave me an envious glance, having no such excuse to escape, as I legged it and tried to figure out how to answer the damn thing.

"Couldn't find the 'answer' button?" came Luke's voice when I eventually did.

"Oh, piss off."

He laughed. "Thought you might like to know we have another suspect for you to come on to."

"Marvellous."

"Name of David Wright. Businessman with some rather dodgy connections."

I sat down on the stairs. "What's he got to do with Chris's murder?"

There was a pause, and it occurred to me that it could be absolutely nothing.

"It's complicated."

"And I'm not important enough to know."

"No, it's..." Luke sighed. "Okay. He's a big businessman. New York, Sydney, Hong Kong, London, Frankfurt. Owns Wrightbank...?"

"I think I've heard of him," I lied.

"People have speculated for a while that not all of his rather vast fortune was earned by entirely legal or morally correct means. He has been known to buy up ailing banks, sack everyone and merge the money into his own account."

"Nice."

"It is for him. He's also really stingy. Never travels first class, loves to use low-cost where he can."

I had sneaking suspicion I knew where this was going and laid my head down on the stair above. "He's flying Ace tomorrow, isn't he?"

"Oh, you're so *smart.* Yes. The 348 to Rome. And the reason he's flying out there, we think, is that he's going to buy up a huge stake in Ace Airlines."

I waited, but Luke didn't say anything else. "I don't get it," I said. "Why am I following him?"

"Following who?" Chalker asked, sneaking up behind me. "Hey, Soph, new phone?"

I glared at him. "Fuck off."

"Since when did you get a picture phone? I thought you had that cheapo thing."

"It's not cheap," I said, and I could hear Luke laughing down the phone. "I spend a fortune on texting..."

"Who are you talking to?" Chalker and Luke asked at the same time, and I paused deliciously.

"My boyfriend," I said to both, and legged it outside.

Luke was silent for a while. "You have a boyfriend?"

"Didn't I tell you?"

"No. It wasn't in your file."

"My file?"

"Your Ace file. How do you think I knew where you lived or what your school results were? I'd never have hired someone who failed all her GCSEs."

I took in a deep breath and let it out. Of course he'd investigated me. There wasn't anything to get mad about. Especially since it was his job. And now mine, too.

"I don't think they keep notes on people's romantic lives," I said.

Luke made a small noise that seemed to mean, "Well, they should."

"Are you jealous?" I asked slowly, with great glee.

"Jealous? Hell, no. You're a nutcase. People send you dead fingers."

I grinned and hugged myself. This was great.

"I didn't think you'd be jealous of the finger."

Luke was silent. Through the window, Chalker started making faces at me. I ignored him and turned to the windy garden instead.

"Look, can you just keep an eye out for this guy tomorrow?" Luke said eventually, sounding annoyed. "I'll send you a photo of him. No baggage belt stuff this time."

And with that he was gone, and I felt very pleased with myself.

Chapter Nine

Next morning I was woken again by the combined forces of Tammy and Norma Jean. I got up, got dressed and went back to my flat to take a shower and sort out my Ace uniform. I always hated going back to work after my days off. Hated it. I seemed to spend the whole time going, “Only two days ‘til I have to go back. Only one day. Only twelve hours.” It was like the end of a very short, unfulfilling holiday.

Still. There were no more bloody envelopes on the doormat and no one had disturbed the tapes I put on the door (roll over James Bond), so I figured the day was starting reasonably well. Now for a little bit of slight illegality.

I dressed in my most scary outfit of leather jeans, heeled boots and ripped punk T-shirt, added a biker jacket and lots of eyeliner, and dragged Ted up to Smith’s Guns.

“I need a hand gun,” I said to Joe, who looked me up and down twice. “Something small and discreet. A silencer, too.”

I was pleased with myself for adding this. It made me sound like I knew what I was talking about.

“Sure,” he said. “Where’s your licence?”

“I don’t need a licence,” I flashed my warrant card, “I have this.”

He took it, looked it over and sniggered at the photo, which Alexa had screen-captured when I signed all my confidentiality things.

“This is a warrant card,” he said. “It’s not a right to bear arms.”

"It says I am a government agent," I said. "I can carry whatever I like and use it in whatever means I see fit to halt the, erm, disruption of, uh, evil." Eh?

Joe looked me over again. "No," he said.

Oh, for fuck's sake. "Look," I said. "I'm a spy. People shoot at me. Someone I worked with was found in a baggage belt the day before yesterday. I'm getting dead fingers in the post. *Give me a fucking gun.*"

But Joe said he couldn't, not without the proper paperwork and authorisation, and I snarled at him and swung back to Ted, who growled sympathetically when I started him up.

"Bloody men," I said. Joe stood in the doorway, shaking his head at me. I thought about running him over, but decided against it. Too much paperwork.

My phone bleeped with a text message, and I picked it up to find a booking number and flight details for David Wright. *I'm on check-in*, Luke had added, *go straight to gate 13. DON'T let him on flight.*

I stuck my tongue out at the phone. If Luke was in check-in then probably this Mr. Wright wouldn't even get past security. Ha, as long as he didn't go down the baggage belt.

Still, it was nice to see Luke could spell properly. Since the advent of predictive type, I've started to get really annoyed at txtspk.

I went home to get changed and eat something before I started my shift. I passed the postman on my way up the drive, and he scowled at me. Hey, it's not my fault someone sent a bloody envelope to me yesterday. If the Royal Mail had handled it more delicately then it wouldn't have burst and gone all bloody.

Still, I opened the door with some trepidation. The post lay there, looking innocent. A bank statement. A pre-approved credit card offer (this from the people who turned down my first credit card because I didn't have a rating). A special order code from La Redoute offering me free post and packaging if I placed an order within forty-eight hours. A free pen from a children's charity (surely they have better things to spend their money on?).

No finger.

I dropped the lot, unopened, on the kitchen counter and started looking for something to eat. Bread, but no butter. Cheese, but no Ryvita. Pasta, but no sauce.

Damn it, it'd have to be crisps again. This time it was clearly not my fault.

I checked the answer phone. Depressingly blank. I charged up both my phones and the stun gun, changed into my uniform and checked my watch. Luke had said I only needed to be there for the Rome flight, which was due to depart at 1410. This meant I had to be at the gate by 1310. This meant I had to leave the house at 1250 if I had a chance in hell of parking anywhere within ten miles of the terminal.

It was 1245. Already? I got my keys and Ted and I rolled off to the car park.

It's a depressing truth that the ratio between how far you have to park from your destination and the number of minutes you have to get there, is inverse. If I have fifteen minutes to walk up to the terminal, I can park in the first row, so close to Enterprise House I can wave at the office workers. If, on the other hand, I should have been there two minutes ago, I'll be parking within ogling distance of the control tower, and have to leg it the entire length of the car park.

Today was the other hand. It's a really big car park.

I didn't even go to the office to sign in and flirt with Tem, but rushed straight through to the transit train and tried to stop my face from looking like a beetroot that was about to explode. Not a sexy look.

I got out my Nokia again and checked the photo Luke had sent me of David Wright. Mid-forties, brown hair, slightly large build. Exactly like every other businessman who travels with Ace on an hourly basis.

To my surprise and delight, Sven was partnering me at the gate. I hadn't even glanced at my roster to see if he was in or not. I'd hardly thought of him at all. Which showed what an empty life I had before, spending precious wake-up minutes checking to see which cute blokes were on shift with me.

"Sophie! Are you all right?"

I grinned and nodded. "I'm fine. Sven, you never go to the gate."

He shrugged. "You always said the gate was better. I think you're right."

I preened slightly at that. Hey, I was right!

Something chirruped in my bag. I searched through it, careful not to let Sven see what was inside. Stun gun, cuffs—oh Christ, imagine if I have to cuff Wright at the gate!—defence spray, Siemens phone (silent), Nokia... flashing and bleeping. The screen said Three. Luke.

"Just five seconds," I said to Sven, who nodded.

"Are you there?" Luke asked.

"Yes. Completely dead."

"Well, the flight's full. Booked at 148."

"Shit!" That was maximum capacity. "Have you seen him yet?"

"No. Only half checked in. We've got a school party."

"Fantastic."

"And they're Italian. All those big, heavy suitcases." He sounded really pissed off, and I had not a shred of sympathy for him. He'd tried to sleep with me yesterday, tried to add me to his list of emotionless conquests. Well, ha! He wasn't getting me.

"Give me a ring if he turns up, okay?" I glanced at Sven who was listening casually. Well, he probably wouldn't understand what I was saying anyway. I looked over at the gate phone. "I'm on 3223."

"Speak to you later."

I turned round to Sven as I switched my mobile off. We're not really supposed to use them in public. In fact we're not supposed to use them at all.

"That was my brother," I improvised. "We're having some furniture delivered."

Sven nodded. "I put the flight on Open," he said, gesturing to the computer.

Great. Even Sven wasn't flirting with me. Did I put eye shadow on my cheeks or something?

People started turning up and asking us questions. A lot of them didn't speak English. Quite a few weren't even travelling on our flight. I kept having to remind myself that I was working for the government now, doing something very important and exciting, although it would have been nice if I could have known what it was.

All the time I kept scanning the crowd for Wright, turning my head left and right. Sven must have thought I had a neck problem. The phone rang and I pounced on it, but it was just Lissy, the dispatcher, telling me we could send them down now.

I looked over at Sven. "Can I just check the loads first?"

He shrugged and opened up the flight for me, but with him looking over my shoulder I couldn't start searching for Wright. I made do with checking the manifests, but I didn't get as far as the Ws before another person asked me if we were going to be boarding soon, and Sven said yes and picked up the microphone.

So I pulled boarding cards and kept my eyes peeled for a middle-aged businessman with brown hair.

I must have sent thirty of them through, still scanning Sven's queue for Wright, when I came to the large group of Italian kids, all passing through in three and fours, giggling over each others' identity cards and passports.

I didn't see Wright at all. The phone hadn't rung. My Nokia, safe in my bag beside me, kept silent.

So I pulled the last boarding card wrong, waited until the passenger had disappeared, then said to Sven, "I got the wrong half of the card. I'll just go down and give her her luggage receipts." Then I grabbed my bag and legged it before he could ask me anything.

I pulled out my phone as I ran and tried to call Luke, but got nothing. Damn! I got all the way to the plane, waved the ticket stub at Lissa and ran up into the aircraft. The card belonged to a woman taking her seat halfway down the plane and I sauntered down there, keeping an eye out for Wright.

Yes! There he was! Sitting near the back in the middle of the group of school kids, looking pissed off. I wondered what he'd done at check-in to deserve that.

Then I wondered why Luke hadn't stopped him.

Then I wondered why everything suddenly got more closed in and quiet, and I looked around and realised in amazement that they'd shut the doors. Why hadn't they told me to get off?

Because I was in Ace uniform, I'd over-sprayed my hair that morning so it was in a hostess-style helmet, I wasn't wearing my hi-vis (which I should have, but it was still in my bag), and I was just about to say something to a passenger.

They thought I was cabin crew. I was on my way to Rome.

The flight to Rome is two and a half hours long, the longest two and a half hours of my life, excepting my Philosophy exam, which I snuck out of early because my head was going to explode from boredom. I convinced the crew that I was a newbie, not hard since they were—miraculously—expecting one. I also, and totally without effort, convinced the passengers that, as it was my first day, I'd fuck-all idea of what I was doing.

I dropped things. I spilled things. I forgot things. I was a bloody wreck. I was insanely grateful that I still had my passport in my bag from when I took it in for One to see, so I wouldn't get chucked out of the country before I could follow David Wright and...

And what? What the hell was I supposed to do? Tail him to his hotel? Disguise myself as room service and spy on him from there? Why was SO17 even interested in him anyway?

"Are you okay?" asked a pleasant American voice as I prepared to spill tea down my tenth victim. They make it look so damn easy when you're flying. Being cabin crew is really hard!

"Yeah, I'm sorry." I looked up from the tray into lovely hazel eyes and a perfect, all-American smile. "It's my first day."

He grinned. "Gotta start somewhere. Well," he peered at my chest, and I realised he was looking at my name-badge (hell cannot know how much I hate that badge and the trouble it gets me into), "Sophie, I think you're doing just fine."

I gave him a tense smile. "Thanks."

He offered me his hand. "I'm Harvey."

Like the cocktail? "Nice to meet you." I handed him his tea, dripping slightly, and moved away. But every time I passed him, he smiled at me, and I started smiling back, feeling like I had a friend on board.

Which was more than I could say for the crew. Ace hired the biggest bitches—male and female—there ever were, and locked you in a tin can with them. Cruelty! They never said anything nice to me, never helped me out at all, just told me to do stuff and laughed at me when I said I couldn't.

"Didn't you have any training?" one of them asked. He had peroxide hair and could not have looked gayer if he'd been wearing pink and flopping his wrist. He gave me an up-and-down that took in my frazzled hair (no amount of hairspray will hold it), melted make-up, sweat-patches under my arms, and tea stains on my trousers. He sneered, and I snapped.

I reached past him for my bag and withdrew my wallet with my red pass and warrant card.

"No," I said, flashing the card at him, "no training. I'm undercover. I have had a long day, people have been sending me fingers through the post and I found a dead body the day before yesterday. Be nice to me or I'll show you what kind of weaponry a government agent carries."

God, I wished I'd had a camera.

In fact, I did, and I took out my Nokia and snapped a picture of his face.

"For my files," I said, and after that, they couldn't have been nicer.

We landed at Ciampino airport and I abandoned the crew, rushing away after Wright. He had no luggage to collect and strode ahead out of the little terminal to the taxi rank, where he stood talking to the driver in rapid Italian.

Shit. There were a lot of other taxis around but I didn't know the Italian for "follow that car"!

I stood staring at him as he got in. "Double shit!" I hissed, stamping my foot.

"Are you okay?"

It was Harvey, the all-American boy. Out in the sunlight he was tall and sparkling, looking perfectly refreshed after the flight, jacket slung over his arm, tie perfectly in place.

I let out a sigh. "Do you know the Italian for 'follow that car'?"

He grinned, shading his eyes and looking after Wright's taxi, now waiting to turn off the concourse. "That car?"

"Yes. There's a passenger in there who left his camera behind. I want to give it back to him."

Harvey stared at me. "You're a full service airline, aren't you?"

"I surely am." I looked up at him, pleadingly, and he shrugged. "Okay, hop in," he said, opening the door for me. "I'll come with you."

I stared.

"We had a chat at the gate," Harvey said easily. "We're staying in the same hotel." He said something to the driver, who nodded. Harvey gave me a little push towards the car.

I had no choice but to get in, one hand inside my bag, searching for my stun gun. Illegal, hell. Thank God for my red pass which had let me through security without being scanned.

Though fuck knew how I'd get back through Italian security.

"So," Harvey turned to me, flashing his perfect white teeth again, "how are you finding the aviation industry?"

I hated it. I hated every part of it. People should go back to ships and trains.

"Oh, I'm loving it," I said brightly. "Especially the people. They're all so kind."

He nodded. "I guess it takes a special kind of person to do that kind of job."

Yes. A complete sociopath.

"Of course. It takes a lot of patience and understanding, and you have to love working with people."

"Have you always wanted to do it?"

No. Even when I was a little girl and there was still some sort of glamour to flying, before the days of the low-cost airline, I always thought being an air hostess must be the worst job. Like being a waitress in a tin can.

"Always," I said with as much sincerity as I could muster. "Ever since I was a little girl. It always looked so glamorous."

"I guess it still does," Harvey said. "So, do you get to fly long-haul? Weekends in Maui, that sort of thing?"

Oh, the bliss. But your average Ace crew went to Belfast and back five times a day and slept nowhere but at home. Alone.

"Well, not so far with Ace. But I have my sights set on BA and Malaysian. I just adore their uniforms."

Harvey gave me a quizzical look. "Don't you have to be, um, well, Asian to do that?"

Do you? I had no idea. "Well, this is the twenty-first century," I beamed. "So tell me about you. What are you doing here in Rome?"

"Oh, business," Harvey said with an easy smile.

"What kind of business?"

"I work for a cell phone company."

"Oh, really? Which one?" That reminded me. I needed to get out my phone, start praying I got overseas coverage, call Luke, and give him hell.

"It's a division of Eurotel. We're setting up links with Europe, wider coverage, that sort of..."

I listened politely as the taxi sped at a truly alarming rate through the pretty Roman streets. I swear, they drove like lemmings. Put your foot down and aim for your destination. Ten points if you hit an old lady. It's a good job this is the HQ of a world religion, so none of the prayers have to go too far. Our driver seemed to consider a red light to be an advisory signal. Shall I stop? Eh, no, don't feel like it today.

We swung round the Coliseum like something out of *The Italian Job* and roared past some rearing ancient columns.

"Wow," I said, like *Pretty Woman* in that hotel.

"It's cool, huh?" Harvey said. "I think that was the Roman forum or something."

"Where Caesar was killed?"

"I think so."

"So where's this hotel?" I asked as the driver took another bend at about a hundred and twenty miles an hour. My palms were nearly bleeding from digging my nails in.

"The Piazza Trinità di Monti. Just off the Via Tritone?"

I nodded like I understood.

"It's not far from the Trevi Fountain."

I nodded again.

"You have no idea what I'm talking about, do you?" Harvey said, laughing, and I blushed and shrugged.

We pulled up and Harvey paid, which I was glad for, because I don't understand Euros. I made a vague promise to pay him back and went rushing inside to the desk.

It was all very grand.

"*Inglese*?" I asked hopefully, and the immaculate woman at the desk nodded and smiled.

"How can I help you?"

"I'm looking for someone. A friend. He's staying here... David Wright?"

She nodded. "*Si.* He has just checked in. Would you like to leave him a message?"

I shook my head. "No, I just..." Damn it, Harvey was watching me and he'd be expecting me to hand over a camera. "Could you tell me his room number?" Probably I'd get told no, for security reasons.

She flicked through her computer. "Twenty-seven."

So much for security.

I nodded gratefully, then looked around for a second. I could never afford a place like this. There was marble everywhere.

Harvey, meanwhile, was happily checking in, in fluent Italian, ordering English and American papers for the morning (I think, although he could really have been commenting on the weather. My Italian is pretty much limited to a Pizza Express menu), and taking his key. He glanced at me.

"Where are you staying?"

I shrugged. "I don't know yet."

"Don't the crew have a hotel?"

Actually, the crew were probably taking a return trip. Or possibly sleeping in the plane. Damn them. Damn Wright. Damn Luke.

Yeah. It was all his fault.

"Yeah, but I have to find my own. It's a newbie thing, it's like a, like a, an initiation thing."

He frowned. "What, are they like the Freemasons or something?"

I gave a weak smile. "Yeah, something."

"Why don't you stay here?"

I'm afraid my eyes boggled.

"I, uh..." I looked down at my rather shabby-looking uniform. How could I tell him there was no way on any of my salaries, real or fictional, that I could afford a place like this?

"I can lend you some money," Harvey said softly.

It was a tempting prospect. But then how would I pay him back? I'd have to give him surety. I'd have to give him my address. He'd probably expect me to sleep with him.

Although that wouldn't be so terrible a prospect.

"No," I said, summoning a smile from the depths of my ancient Ace training, "thanks. That's what credit cards are for." To the receptionist I said, "I'd like a room, please. Just for tonight."

Harvey had a suit carrier, the sort I wasn't supposed to allow as hand luggage but usually did, out of boredom. It was the sort of bag that could carry everything for an overnight stay. I had my Ace bag with a hairbrush, lip gloss, body spray and handcuffs. Not what you call overnight essentials.

Well, depending on what kind of overnight you had in mind.

I said a reluctant goodbye to the handsome American and went to find my room. It was gorgeous. There were toiletries and everything. I just really wished I had some spare clothes. I could hardly wander around in just my uniform, could I?

Unless they had a laundry service. I checked the room service card. They had a damn laundry service! Yes! If I just stayed in my room, I could get my clothes washed and go home in them in the morning. Easy.

I called Reception and they said they could have it done in half an hour. I started running a bath. Things were not as bad as they seemed. I had to remember that. Things were never as bad as they seemed.

I switched on my two phones and used one to send a text to Chalker that I'd be staying at Angel's tonight. That would stop them from calling home. At least Tammy was being looked after. Then I used the other phone to call Luke.

"You let him through," I said.

There was a pause.

"Sophie?"

"Yes?"

"Where are you?"

"I'm in Rome," I said. "I'm in Wright's hotel. You let him through. Sven let him board. I followed him like a good secret agent and they thought I was crew. So now I'm spending next month's grocery bill on getting my uniform washed in a ludicrously expensive hotel because I'm fucking stuck here until the next flight out tomorrow morning. And if you tell me to stay in Rome and trail Wright I'll be forced to improvise a weapon on you."

Luke laughed. I hung up.

He called back in a few seconds. "I lost the connection," he said.

"No. I hung up."

"Look, Soph, I'm sorry. He slipped through."

"Slipped through? *Slipped bloody through*? Luke, remind me in words of one syllable just what you do for a living?"

"Erm," he said. "I'm a spy."

I suppose he thought that was clever.

"So how could you let a dangerous criminal just slip onto a plane? He could have been armed."

"I doubt it. Security isn't that bad. And I don't really think he's dangerous."

"How do you know? You haven't even told me why I'm following him."

Luke sighed. "Promise not to get mad?"

I said nothing. I had a feeling I knew what was coming.

"He's not a dangerous criminal. That we know," he added quickly. "But he's interested in buying Ace. He already owns WES," Wright Engineering Services, of *course*, "and there's a suspicion he's hijacking Ace planes to bring the price down."

I opened my mouth to tell him that was ludicrous, then I thought about all the delays we'd been having. All those planes off tech.

Having to borrow from Titan because we didn't have enough to cover for our own. Low-cost carriers don't have spare planes.

"Suppose you're not lying to me," I said eventually, "tell me what I'm going to do out here?"

There was another long pause while Luke came up with something.

"Well, since you're there and all, I sort of need you to get into his room," he said.

"His room?"

"Yes. Do you know where it is?"

"It's on my floor."

"Great. Get yourself in there, have a look around, check for papers and things. Use the camera in your phone to take pictures."

"I don't get it. Why is this so important?"

"Sophie. The future of your employment hangs in the balance," Luke said severely, and I knew he wasn't going to tell me the real reason. Well, fine, then. I wasn't going to snoop around Wright's room.

"You do this for me," Luke added in Luca's voice, "I take you out for dinner."

I sniffed. "That better not be an empty promise."

"No, sure, I'll take you out. What do you like? Tomorrow's Friday, I could—"

"Tomorrow's Friday?"

He hesitated. "Erm, unless they changed the calendar. Today's Thursday."

"Oh, God! Luke, I need you to do something for me. This is really urgent. Life and death stuff."

"You didn't forget your medication, did you?"

"I need you to go over to my flat and—"

"How am I supposed to get into your flat?"

How am I supposed to convey a sarcastic look down the phone?

"I'm sure you'll think of something," I said heavily. "This is really important so I'll take you through it step by step. Are you writing this down?"

Luke sounded puzzled. "Tell me."

"Okay. The video control is the large grey one. It says Philips on the top. You need to—"

"Wait, Sophie, are you telling me to set your video?"

I shrugged. "It's very important."

"What, is your mum on TV or something?"

"No," I said, wondering how he could not know, "it's Thursday. Sky One. Eight pm...?"

Silence.

"*Buffy*," I said. "You have to tape it."

"I thought you said this was life and death," Luke said eventually.

"It is! Buffy's life and all the demon deaths... Oh, come on. I haven't seen this one and if I don't tape it, I'll never see it and I'll have to buy the videos and they're really expensive... It's award-winning TV," I added defensively.

Luke gave a great sigh. "Okay. I'll set the video. Eight o'clock?"

"Yes. And then set it for *Friends* as well."

"You really watch all this?"

"Only once a week. And then *Scrubs* is on at ten."

I could almost see him shaking his head. "I'll tape it for you."

I opened my mouth to tell him which tape to use, then decided not to push it. "Okay. Thanks. Now tell me how the hell I get into Wright's room without him noticing me? I only have my uniform and it's not exactly subtle," I looked down at the turquoise-ness of it.

Plus I was kind of conspicuous in it on the flight. I might have accidentally dropped a Danish pastry into Wright's lap.

"What time is it over there? About half six, right? Shops stay open late. Go and buy something."

"I've already got to pay for this hotel!"

"Should have got somewhere cheaper. I'll see you tomorrow."

"But—"

He was gone.

Swearing very colourfully, I sloshed around in the bath and used up all the free toiletries as I waited for my clothes to come back. When they did, I got dressed very gratefully, feeling dreadful for having no Euros to tip with, grabbed my bag and set off into the city.

Within seconds I was lost. I found the hotel again, went in to ask for a map and directions for the shops. And then I found an ATM and got some Euros—which was highly confusing, since the machine was all in Italian. And then I found the shops.

Jesus, it was tempting. Gucci and Missoni and Valentino. I didn't dare go in. Not in my uniform. I found some cheaper shops and started searching.

I'd noticed the hotel staff wearing navy suits with white blouses. Not hard to copy, although not cheap, either, for something I'd never wear again. But I did find an incredible Gucci dress for next to nothing, and bought that too. And then a small suitcase to carry it all home with. And some toiletries and basic make-up. And some shoes, because I might want to wear my dress, and it'd be a shame to have to clump around in my skanky work shoes. And a little bag, because it matched the shoes and because my Ace bag was huge and horrible. And then a pashmina, even though I know they're very last-millennium, but Rome in April is not as warm as you might think.

And then I lugged it all back to the hotel, and met Harvey in the lobby.

"I see you found the shops," he stared at all my bags.

"Well, I had to buy everything I could," I said defensively. "It took me so long to find them I may never get back there again."

He laughed. "Are you busy tonight?" he said. "Meeting up with your airline friends?"

Friends? I hoped they all got crabs.

"I haven't decided yet," I said, my all-purpose answer.

"Well, if you decide not to, maybe we could have dinner? You could tell me all about the airline business and I could bore you with cell phone frequencies."

What was the alternative? Sitting looking at my fabulous dress and cursing Luke for all eternity?

"That sounds great," I said, smiling warmly at Harvey, my saviour.

He beamed back at me. "I'll meet you down here at eight-thirty?"

I glanced at my watch in panic. It was already quarter-to.

"Can we make it nine?" I said. "I have some things to do first."

He shrugged. "Nine it is. I'll see you then."

I skipped upstairs, feeling much better already, and changed into my navy suit. I had my phone and credit card in my pocket, hoping I'd be able to jimmy open the door if I needed to.

I didn't need to. Wright answered the door, wearing a hotel robe and smoking a cigar. Oh, please.

"Room service?" I said. I hefted the towels I'd brought from my room. "I've come to make your room ready for bed."

He stood back to let me in. "English?"

"Yes, sir."

"What are you doing here in Rome, then?"

Hoping you'll go away.

"Studying, sir. Ancient Roman politics."

This stumped him, as I'd desperately hoped it would. "Right," he said, taking my towels. "I'll be in the bath."

Was it my imagination, or did he wink at me?

Bleurgh.

I clattered around for a while, until I was sure he was done listening to me, then I got out my phone and tried to remember how to take a picture with it. I messed around in Wright's briefcase, taking pictures of a lot of things—the camera was slow but the pictures were hella-good—but I didn't see anything I thought was very interesting.

However, I did see a magnificently placed wedding ring on top of a serviette with three girls' numbers scrawled on it.

"Room service?" Wright called from the bathroom, and I froze with my finger on the shutter to snap the ring. "Room service? Come and scrub my back."

I bolted.

Back in my own room, I found I had about ten minutes to get ready for dinner. I dropped the suit on the floor, wriggled into my marvellous dress (maybe slightly too small but at that price, who gave a damn) and shoes, sprayed on Impulse body spray in the absence of perfume, and ran my fingers through my hair.

There. Ready.

Sort of.

Harvey was waiting, looking handsome and indefinably American, and he smiled at me as I approached.

"You look brand new," he said. "You ready to go?"

Chapter Ten

We took a taxi across the river and wandered around looking for a trattoria in the Trastavere district. I had no idea a modern city could be so beautiful. Every road ended in a little piazza with the sort of topiary in huge terracotta pots that my mother would pay a fortune for from the garden centre. Soft, happy light and chatter and music flowed across the streets from every building. The people were beautiful, olive-skinned and charming.

One of the things I found so frustrating earlier in the day when I was running out of time to go shopping—I mean, complete my mission, ahem—was the way you can't follow a road to the end, then turn left or right onto the next road, as it appears on the maps. Oh no. Every road ends, as I said, in a charming little geranium-filled piazza with a dozen pretty little alleys leading off all over the place. Whichever one you take is guaranteed to take you completely the wrong way, and by the time you find a street with a street sign and locate it on your (by now very crumpled) map, you're halfway across the city in the wrong direction.

I minded very much when I was alone, but now I figured I was getting the hang of it. Of course, it helped that I wasn't getting quite so hassled by a lot of Romans who appeared to have never seen a blonde before. Now I was getting the same attention, but walking arm in arm with a handsome man seemed to subdue it somewhat.

"You're a hit," Harvey said as a wolf-whistle echoed down the street after us.

"It's the hair," I said. "They have a thing about blondes."

"You ever been to Asia?"

I shook my head, no.

"Man, they go nuts over a white skin there. If you're a redhead they practically worship you. Blondes too."

"My mother went to Sweden once with her friend who's Indian," I said. "They couldn't get over her. People kept touching her hair. My mother's blonde like me and she was kinda pissed off people kept ignoring her."

"People notice her a lot?"

I thought about it. My mother had never been like other people's mothers. She didn't look old. She didn't have scary-hair-in-the-air like my friends' mothers all had from when we were at primary school. She borrowed my clothes. She was attractive and made the most of herself in a growing-old-gracefully sort of way. She moved with the times, which I guess was the secret to avoiding old age.

"Yeah, people notice her a lot," I said.

"Must run in the family."

He was very sweet and charming, and he spoke perfect Italian, and he didn't act appalled when I told him I didn't eat meat. People have been known to stare at me like I'm an alien or something. I just smile and reassure them it's not contagious.

He asked me about being a stewardess and I told him we were now called cabin crew, which if you ask me is just de-glamorising it a bit more. I made up a load of stuff about the training and hours and things I had no idea about and asked him about the mobile phone industry.

"*Ti piace un piccolo caffè*?" the charming man who owned the trattoria asked us, and Harvey looked over at me and said, "Anything but cappuccino. It's just not Roman."

I thrive on an abnormal amount of coffee. I smiled sweetly and asked for *una espresso doppio*, which I learnt years ago in school and thought it sounded impressive.

It was impressive. A pure shot of caffeine so strong it made me dizzy, and I had to hold onto Harvey's arm as we walked back to the hotel.

Well, maybe it was also the wine that made me hold onto him. Maria said I should have a glass a day; well here I was bravely taking a week's worth.

And maybe it was also the fact that Harvey was very fit and cute and charming that made me hold onto him. It was certainly that which made me go back to his room and let him kiss me like the Prince Charming he was.

Although, seeing as he's a classless American, maybe that should be Citizen Charming. It doesn't quite have the same ring.

"Mmm," I said when he stopped kissing me. "*Ciao, bella.*"

"Isn't *bella* a girl?"

"Well, *bello*, then. Although that sounds rude."

He grinned and took off his jacket. He had lovely broad shoulders and shiny hair. He looked like exactly what I needed to cheer myself up.

He kissed me some more, and it was very pleasant kissing. Not the fireworks I got from Luke, nothing as scary as that. I wanted to put my arms around Harvey and let him protect me. I didn't want to shoot him, which I suppose made him a better contender than Luke.

Something vibrated in his pocket, and my eyes widened. "That could be fun."

He withdrew a sleek mobile and raised his eyebrows at me. "Damn," he said, reading the display. "I have to take this. Sorry." He disappeared into the bathroom.

Oh, great. So a call on a phone was more important than making out with me. I sat down on the bed, rubbing my arms which suddenly felt quite cold, and pulled off my shoes. Harvey was quite a bit taller than me, which is an interesting feat, but he wasn't lanky. He wasn't all lean muscle like Luke. He had brawn. A big hunk of American beefcake. Mmm.

And look at me! Making out with two men in as many days. Ella would be pleased. She said my talents were wasted as it was. I once asked her what she meant by my talents, and she blushed and said, "Remember when I came to visit you at uni that time? Well, the walls in those rooms are very thin."

See, I'm blushing now just thinking about it.

Harvey talked for ages. I spread myself out on the bed, feeling wanton, then quickly sat up, feeling stupid. I couldn't even go and freshen up, because Harvey was in the bathroom.

After a while I started to get really bored. What was so important that he'd rather talk about it than get naked with me? Unless I was that boring. God, maybe I was boring! Certainly Luke didn't seem to have missed me that much.

Miserably, I gathered up my shoes and pashmina and little evening bag and left the room. I had sort of lost the mood.

I got back to my room and stared at the perfectly made-up bed. My feet ached from my new shoes and all the walking I'd been doing, my head was fuzzy from the wine and I was feeling very unloved. I was so drunk I even half thought about seeing how powerful the vibrate function on my mobile was. I could ring one from the other.

I picked up my little Siemens phone. There were no messages. Nobody loved me. I picked up the Nokia. There were three texts and half a dozen voice mails, all from Luke, all demanding to know why I wasn't answering my fucking phone.

"Jesus Christ," he said when I called him, "why the hell didn't you answer?"

"I forgot my phone. Phones."

"Where were you? I thought—"

"I was at dinner," I cut him off. "With a very charming man. I've just come from his room."

Luke was silent for a few seconds. "Was it Wright?"

No, it wasn't right at all. "No. I went in there earlier. Dressed as a concierge. I took some pictures but there was nothing interesting in his briefcase."

"No, well, there probably wouldn't be. I think he's more of a puppet. This is bigger than just Wright." He was silent again. "So who did you go to dinner with?"

Hah! He was jealous! I did a little dance, sitting there on the bed.

"Just someone I met on the flight," I said.

"And what were you doing in his room?"

Oh, God, this is fantastic. "Investigating."

"Investigating what?"

"Whether he's a better kisser than you. And you know what, he is."

"Sophie, that's not funny."

"Yes, it is, it's funny because it's true." I stuck my tongue out at the phone.

"Are you drunk?"

"I have to be drunk to want to kiss someone else? Can't I pursue casual sex if I'm sober?"

Christ, I was drunk.

"Look," Luke said tightly, "just don't do anything stupid, all right? And set your damn alarm for tomorrow. I've got you booked on the 0625 flight out of Ciampino. Make sure you have enough cash for the taxi. Do you still have your passport on you?"

"Yes."

"Good. That makes it a lot easier. It's hard enough trying to explain special operations to someone who speaks your own language. I'll see you when the plane gets in, should be around seven."

And with that he clicked off, sounding pissed off.

Score!

The Nokia woke me up at five am. I pulled on my new civvies—the white shirt over the Gucci dress, which might have looked stylish on someone less hungover—found some ancient shades in the bottomless pit of my Ace bag to cover up my shadowed, bloodshot eyes and staggered down to reception.

"I need a taxi," I whispered to the perfect woman behind the desk. "To Ciampino airport."

She nodded, made a call, and five minutes later there was a car waiting for me.

I sat with my head back against the seat as we swung around Rome in the early morning and tried not to heave. I get carsick even when I'm dead sober. Seriously, it was like hitching a lift with Michael Schumacher.

Or Ayrton Senna.

I felt like month-old milk by the time we arrived at the airport. I checked in—having remembered to put my stun gun and things in my hold luggage—and stumbled through to the tiny airside bar.

At Stansted it's like a little shopping mall. There are clothes shops and shoe shops and TV shops and bars and restaurants and coffee stands and all sorts. You could live there. Some people practically do.

Ciampino airport's airside facilities consisted of a bar, which was closed, and a tiny tabaccheria. I bought a large bottle of water and some Soft Fruits and put my head on the table until it was time to board.

I slept my way through the flight, the last few days' sleeplessness having caught up with me, not to mention last night's wine, and dreamed of Harvey and Luke both turning me down. Bastards.

The plane was pretty much empty when I was woken by a (thankfully unfamiliar) stewardess. I grabbed my bag, trying to hide the Ace logo, and tripped off into the very cold, windy British spring.

We were off-jetbridge (stupid cheapo airline), so I had to walk across the freezing tarmac, keeping my head down so no one recognised me, and up the steps into the terminal.

Luke was waiting at the top, looking pissed off.

"Jesus," I said, "when you said you'd see me there I thought I'd at least get to Baggage on my own."

"You look like hell," Luke said, and swiped his pass to get us back into the terminal.

"Thanks," I mumbled. "Where are we going?"

"Back to the office. Quicker this way."

"I need to pick up my bag."

He stopped and closed his eyes and looked like he was counting. "What bag?"

"I had to buy some stuff! I couldn't walk around Rome in my uniform."

He ran his eyes over me. "So I see." He sighed. "Okay, let's go."

We went back through the normal route to the transit and baggage reclaim. I showed my passport, like a good traveller, and Luke flashed his pass. It was quite normal for staff to return from the gate through customs. It was great, like you're somewhere you shouldn't be, although it's perfectly legal.

Sometimes the whole airport thing just totally overwhelms me. I mean, there are all these rules about where people can and cannot go, and all these hidden tunnels and doors that are only used by staff, and if you open the wrong one and let a passenger in then it's unbelievably illegal. But if you have the right pass you can, in legal terms, wander in and out of the UK all day long.

And I swear, BAA must have acres of footage of me wandering around being totally lost in the bowels of the system.

We waited in silence for my bag, then walked out to the car park, equally quiet. Luke stopped by his Vectra, and I shook my head.

"Might as well get mine out of here as well," I said. "I'll see you there."

I walked down to Ted, incredibly relieved to see him again, and sat there for a few moments, feeling surreal.

So. I'd just done another handful of things that were not totally legal and, apparently, got away with them. I'd been somewhere exotic and beautiful. I'd kissed a total stranger in an unknown place. I'd taken photographs of documents in a suspect's room.

Was I like a great spy, or what?

Alexa wasn't there when I walked into the office, but Luke was standing talking to One.

"Ah," said my boss. "How was your trip?"

I looked between them cautiously. "Okay," I said. "Unplanned and exhausting, but okay."

"You found the shops," Luke said. "It can't have been that bad."

I glared at him. One laughed.

"It was admirable of you to pursue your quarry so far," he said. "We got your pictures. For reference, next time send them to my e-mail address...” he started looking around Alexa’s desk, “I’ll write it down for you...”

“I’ll just put it in my phone directory?” I offered gently, and he nodded.

“Ah yes. Much more sensible. It’s james_bond_95@hotmail.com.”

I blinked at him.

“1995,” he explained, “when Goldeneye came out. That’s my favourite.”

I blinked again, nodded and inputted the address. Was there anything about this place I was ever going to understand?

I could see Luke was nearly smiling, and I avoided his gaze. “Were they useful?” I asked. “The pictures?”

“Inasmuch as they told us he wasn’t the big man in this,” One said. “David Wright is something of a pawn, I fear.”

“A pawn in what?” I asked. “What is going on here? No one,” I glared at Luke, “ever tells me anything.”

“That’s because there’s not always a lot to tell,” One said, going into his office and motioning for me to follow. “Most of this job is pure instinct, Sophie. I’ve been watching you—” How? How had he been watching me? “—and I can see you work on instinct, too.”

Well, of course. Got to trust your instincts. Feminine intuition and all that.

“She certainly doesn’t work on logic,” murmured Luke from behind me, and I scowled. I hadn’t even realised he’d come in. So much for instinct.

One was seated at his desk. “What we have so far is this,” he said, looking up at me, and I tried to look alert and instinctive. “You’ve noticed that a lot of Ace planes have been having technical problems recently? That there have been delays, that passenger numbers haven’t been quite what they usually are?”

I shrugged. “Well, yes, things have been easier...”

“Airline profits have gone down drastically in the last few months,” One went on, looking at some figures on his desk. “The company’s losses are in millions. After September eleventh, of course, things took a bit of a dive but all the low-cost airlines rallied through."

This was true. A lot of the larger airlines had pulled out of Stansted, leaving it to holiday carriers like Air 2000 and the likes of Ace, Ryanair and Easyjet. For some reason, people didn't seem as afraid of terrorist attacks when they'd only paid fifty quid for their ticket.

"Ace was doing very well, making a lot of money. Now it's a PLC, of course, anyone can have a share of that money, but recently the shares have been going down in value. All these delays, inconsistencies, a lot of complaints have hit the news and there's been very little to counter that. David Wright has made no secret of the fact that he's interested in Ace in a big way. He already has a lot of shares in the company, but he's looking to buy more."

"And with share prices dropping so suddenly you think something's up," I said. "You think he's sabotaging the airline so he can get it cheaper." Clever bastard.

"Bingo," One said.

"But," I said, "he's not the one in charge of it all?"

"No. Wrightbank is owned by David Wright, but not controlled by him. Insiders have long speculated there's someone else pulling his strings, but no one knows who. We knew he had links with the Brown twins—he served a few months inside with one of them once."

I stared. "David Wright was in prison? What for?"

"Petty theft," Luke said. "A long time ago. His cellmate was one Neil Wilkes—the man you followed down the baggage belt."

"Brown Two."

"Yes. His brother is Thomas Wilkes. They're known counterfeiters. They can forge anything—money, credit cards, passports…"

"Hence their fake names."

"Yes. Now they're both safely behind bars, but neither will say a word about who they're working for."

"They could be working alone," I said. "Who says they have to work for someone?"

"They've never done it before."

"I've never pretended to be an air hostess before," I replied sharply, "but I did yesterday. First time for everything."

One smiled. "The crew were quite disturbed. One of them filed a report when she returned. The police brought it to us."

Aw, crap.

Luke was laughing. "She said she was never convinced you were a trainee and she was sure your warrant card was fake."

"Which one was she?"

"Her name was Kerry something..."

Ha! Kerry was the least helpful of the lot. And the stupidest. She'd told me she'd been on the crew for "seven months, since December".

It's April now.

"She was just jealous of my natural ability," I said loftily.

"Ace also had a record number of complaints about you from passengers," Luke said, grinning.

"Oh, well, passengers," I dismissed. But hey, at least they'd noticed me.

"Anyway," One said. "David Wright is booked on the afternoon flight back from Rome. He should be landing at 1745. Luke, will you see him off the plane?" Luke nodded. "And Sophie?"

I looked up helpfully.

"Go home and get some sleep. You look wretched."

Cheers.

Luke followed me out. "Guess you must be tired," he said, "all that travelling and shopping and socialising."

"I wasn't socialising."

"So you went back to your passenger's room on business?"

I couldn't help a smile. I wondered what Harvey had thought when he came back out and I wasn't there. Or if he'd noticed. Or if he was still on his bloody "cell phone".

"No, that was personal."

Luke scowled at me, and I turned away, grinning. I was just getting out my keys when another car pulled up, one of those special disabled cars, and Alexa opened her door.

"Hey, the traveller returns." She smiled. "Nice trip?"

"Not bad." I shot a look at Luke, who was still scowling. "You want a hand with that?" I gestured to the wheelchair she was reaching for.

"No, I'm good." I watched in amazement as she lifted the wheelchair over from a well where the passenger seat should be, set it on the ground by her door and opened it up. Then she moved a lever that rotated her seat outside of the car and tipped herself into the wheelchair.

"Very impressive," I said.

"Had a lot of practice." She grabbed her handbag from the footwell and pushed the seat back inside, locked the door and started wheeling herself up the ramp into the office. I marvelled at her upper arm strength.

As she disappeared inside, One appeared in the doorway. "Luke, Sophie," he said. "I'm glad you're still here. I just took a look at those photos you sent." He nodded at me. "You got one of his diary. I'm glad to see someone else uses a good old fashioned paper diary and not a bloody Palm Pilot."

I had to hide a smile. He sounded like my dad, the world's biggest technophobe. He wills his laptop to break down all the time so he can complain about how unreliable it is.

"He has the Buckman Ball written in for tonight," One went on.

Luke sighed.

"So you two are going to go. I'll get you some tickets and e-mail you the aliases."

Luke nodded and they both looked at me.

"What is the Buckman Ball?" I asked meekly.

"In London," Luke said. "A charity ball. Big celeb presence. Very boring. So far I've been every year for the last three years tailing someone. Why do they all go to the Buckman Ball?"

One did a palms-up. "Beats me. But you two are going. Get your tux out. Get," he looked at me, "your ballgown out. Luke, wear a wire. Sophie, this way."

Luke got in his car and drove off. I followed One back through into his office where he opened a filing cabinet and took out a collection of small, high-tech things.

"This has a long-range radio frequency so we'll be able to pick up what's going on from here," he said. "But you'll need to hide this away somewhere," he held up a bulky transmitter, "so may I suggest nothing too clingy? This here," he handed me a tiny grommet, "goes in your ear so you can hear Luke, and he can hear you. We can also break into the loop from here if we need to talk to you."

I gulped and took the device. "Exactly how posh is this thing?"

"The Buckman Ball? Gets coverage in *Tatler*. Madonna's on the guest list."

Jesus.

I drove home with my head whirling. I owned nothing suitable. Nothing at all. For the last charity bash Chalker's band had played at I'd worn my Monsoon standby, but it was both dated and clingy, not to mention far too obviously inexpensive for such an occasion. I knew my mother would have nothing suitable. Her idea of designer was the Marks and Spencer "Per Una" range.

Angel, I knew, would have lots of stunning things which she'd lend me in a second, but I'd hardly be able to get my left leg into any of her dresses. It was a shame, because her mother used to have some fabulous stuff, and it would be very cool to turn up in something IC Winter wore thirty years ago. Vintage, yah?

I got home and stared at my wardrobe in misery. Then I got out my phone and called Angel, just to see if she had put on a few stones in weight and gained several inches in height and felt the need to go on a shopping spree.

"I need a ballgown by tonight," I said. "A real, proper Oscar frock, and I have nothing. I don't suppose you have any cousins my size?"

"Sorry, honey," Angel said with real regret, because she totally lived up to her name, "I don't have any cousins at all. I could give my friend Livvy a ring if you like? She's quite tall."

I'd met Angel's old boarding school pal Livvy, who's actually Lady Olivia Something-Toff. She was my height, yes, but she was also a size eight. She had a sort of permanent stretched look to her.

"No," I said dejectedly. "It'll never work."

"I could lend you some jewellery, though," she offered. "So long as you tell me where and why you're going and who with?"

I couldn't lie to Angel. Well, not a lot.

"I can't tell you," I said. "I'm really sorry, but I can't."

"Why? Is he married or something?"

Bingo.

"Erm, yes. So you can't tell anyone, either."

"Oh my God, Sophie! You bad girl!" Angel said, but she said it admiringly.

I think.

I put down the phone and my Nokia rang. Luke.

"Did One give you the wire?"

"Yes, although I don't know how to work it."

"I'll show you. You want me to come over?"

"No, I can figure it out. I'm quite capable."

There was a little silence, as if both of us were working out what was wrong with that statement.

"I'll figure it out," I repeated. "Look, I have to find a ballgown by tonight—what time does this thing start, by the way? And how do I get there?"

"I'll pick you up."

"Where is it?"

"South Kensington. Gray's Hotel. Just by the tube station—"

"Great! Then I'll get the tube."

There was another pause. "You're going to travel on the London Underground in a ballgown?"

"Sure," I said defensively, "why not?"

Luke sighed. Then he laughed. "Okay, fine, I'll see you there. Nine o'clock. *Don't* be late."

"I won't," I said, offended, and as I put the phone down wondered why I had turned down his offer of a lift.

Then I remembered making out with him in the car and thought about how good he'd look in a DJ, and decided I'd made the right choice.

I spent the rest of the day cleansing and exfoliating, and dying my hair—it wouldn't do to let Wright recognise me from Rome—and trying to think of what to wear. The only designer piece I had was my Gucci frock, and that was a short, cocktail kind of thing. Not a ballgown by any measure.

I'd almost given up and was just getting my Monsoon dress out when I got a text from Ella. *Wht u doin 2nte?*

Going somewhere I shouldn't with someone I shouldn't, I replied miserably (see, I have predictive text). *You got a designer ballgown I can borrow?*

She rang me immediately.

"Designer ballgown, someone you shouldn't be going out with?" she cried as soon as I picked up. "Honey, what are you not telling me?"

"He's married," I said (no point in making a lot of lies). "He invited me to some ball thing tonight, it's really posh and I don't have anything to wear."

"Blow him off! I can't believe you didn't tell me this!"

Ella is a nanny and lives vicariously through me and her other friends. She spends her days changing nappies and driving around in a pointlessly large Land Rover, picking her charges up from poncy schools and ballet lessons.

"I—well, it's all kind of sudden," I said, truthfully.

"Are you sleeping with him?"

"Not as such."

"Oh, come on. What's the point of seeing a married man if you're not getting sex? Jesus, Soph, did I teach you nothing? Anyway, can't you sting him for a ballgown?"

"He's sort of unavailable," I improvised. "I'm meeting him there."

Ella sighed. "Okay," she said. "How much time do you have?"

"I have to leave here at eight, very latest."

"Come over at three. Her Ladyboat's going to the spa. We can raid her wardrobe."

Ella's employer is a very nouveau bitch called Crystal who used to be a stripper but is now the wife of an equally nouveau shipping magnate who got knighted recently. They have two young children who rarely see their parents. Normally I'd say this wasn't good for the children, but I'd met Sir and Lady Tasteless and now believed that the very best thing for these kids was if they never met their parents.

Besides, their father probably wasn't Sir Darren anyway.

So I got in Ted and rolled up the zen-raked gravel of Sir Darren's awful mansion just after three. He was out of the country on business (trans, shagging his secretary in Mauritius) and she was at the spa (getting botoxed). Ella had just picked the kids up from school and set them to doing homework (the cruelty! I never had homework 'til I was at secondary school, and I never did it then). She pulled me upstairs to her Ladyboat's dressing room and I stared in wonder.

"Look at all the pretty colours!"

Ella grinned. "Half of 'em never worn. She still hasn't cottoned on to the fact that real celebs don't actually buy their clothes, they just borrow them. Anyway. Where's this ball thing, then?"

"Kensington."

"Oh, very nice." She paused, pulling the cover off a blue beaded thing. "Not the Buckman Ball?"

"Erm, yes. Why?"

"Jesus! Her Ladyboat's been trying to get invites to that for years. She donates bloody billions to the charity—"

"What is the charity?"

"I dunno. Some children's disease, or an AIDS foundation or something fashionable. No one gives a damn about the charity, Soph, it's all about profiling."

She kept badgering me about my married man, and I kept saying I couldn't say. "It's really complicated," I said about a hundred times. "I'm trying to break it off..."

"But he keeps inviting you to posh things. Hmm."

Eventually, terrified I'd get caught, I grabbed a luscious Donna Karan dress and scarpered.

"What will you say if she notices it's missing?" I asked through Ted's window.

Ella shrugged. "It's at the cleaners."

"She ever worn it?"

"Don't think so. I'll tell her one of the dogs got in there and peed on it. I'll think of something. I'm still mad at you for not telling me about this bloke before," she added. "At least tell me his name?"

"Luke," I said, without thinking, and Ella beamed.

"Good name. Biblical." She waggled her eyebrows at me. "I'll see you later, yeah?"

I nodded and drove away gratefully. Ella had also outfitted me with shoes and a gorgeous gossamer wrap. I figured I was good to go.

The hair dye hadn't taken well, so I redid it when I got home. I figure my blondness is too ingrained to be covered by one shot of Clairol. When I washed it out, my barnet was deep, deep brown. Jesus. I looked like a total goth with my pale skin. Time for some bronzer.

By the time I was finished, I felt like I should have been sprayed with fixative. I taped the fully charged transmitter to my garter (yes, I own a suspender belt) so it was hidden by the petticoats of the skirt and fixed the microphone to the underwiring of the dress.

It's worth paying for designer things, I guess, for how good they make you look and how confident they make you feel. I was mad a few years ago when backless tops came out because I simply couldn't wear them without a bra. Even those clear-strap ones never look right, and they don't do them in big enough sizes, which makes me really mad, because girls who can wear the sizes they do make them in *don't bloody need to*! But this dress had full underwiring, and needed it, because it was so low at the back it nearly gave me butt cleavage. I wriggled into my best La Senza (funds not stretching as far as La Perla) and doused myself in perfume.

Then Angel, God bless her, turned up with some serious rocks in a velvet case.

"Jesus," I looked at the light refracting a million ways, "Angel, this could buy you a small island!"

She smiled. "It's an heirloom."

"I couldn't wear it."

"'Course you can. It'll look good with that frock. Is it Donna Karan?"

I blinked. See, that's what I don't understand. Members of the rockistocracy like Angel can tell a designer at fifty paces. I have to have someone show me the label, then translate it for me.

I put the necklace on, feeling my shoulders start to buckle under the weight. God only knows how Angel manages to wear something so heavy. She handed me matching earrings and a bracelet.

"No watch," she said.

"I'm not stupid."

"I know, just checking."

She let me keep my little diamond ring, the one my parents bought me when I was twenty-one, but nothing else. She checked over my hair, exclaiming in delight over the colour, and stood back and smiled.

"You'll do," she said quietly, and that's great praise from Angel.

I waited until she'd gone to put brown contacts in, wedge the earpiece in my lughole and finish arming myself. Since bloody Luke wouldn't let me have a gun and stupid Joe Smith wouldn't either (maybe I could ramraid it? No, the owner of a gun shop would probably have good security. Sirens, dogs, a shotgun or two...and Ted would never forgive me), all I had was my defence spray and stun gun. The defence spray I left behind because I didn't want to accidentally spray myself, or the dress, with green gunk or set off the shrill alarm that accompanied it. I didn't want to electrocute myself so I left the stun gun at home too. That left handcuffs, which were not exactly good for defence and far too kinky, should they be discovered in my handbag; and the Kevlar, for which I had not yet found a subtle use.

I slung my old rape alarm in my bag, added some gum, a credit card, lip gloss, keys and my Nokia, and left the house.

I'd put on my wool trenchcoat over the dress, but you could still see the red skirts peeping out like Mammy's petticoat in *Gone with the Wind*. The dress, for all its bum cleavage, had a flattering boat neck that skimmed my collarbones, and an A-line skirt held out by petticoats that rustled as I walked. I'd thought about taking different shoes to walk in, because one doesn't let delicate Manolos like these touch the pavement, darling, but I'd nowhere to put them when I arrived.

To my astonishment, I arrived at South Ken on time, without missing a train, going in the wrong direction, getting lost or tripped over, tearing my dress or splashing through a puddle. I looked up at Gray's Hotel, squared my shoulders and walked anonymously through the paparazzi to the door marked "Ballroom".

"Name?" asked the big scary black man on the door. I wondered if he was related to Macbeth.

"Antonia Porter," I said, and he looked down the list. My heart was pounding.

"Go on in," he said eventually, and I nearly cried with relief.

"Is James Bannerman here yet?" I asked.

"He's waiting for you." The bouncer looked at a note by Luke's alias. "In the lobby. You can check your coat in there."

I nodded nervously and stepped past him into one of the most nerve-wracking experiences of my life.

Chapter Eleven

There should be a moment in every woman's life when she walks into a fabulous setting, looking like a movie star, people turning and staring at her as she glides past them to the man she's interested in, and has the fantastic experience of having his eyes glued to her.

"Jesus," Luke said, looking me over.

"Jesus never looked this good," I said, so pleased with myself it was all I could do to keep from skipping.

"You look... *wow.*"

I grinned. "Wow" was pretty good.

"Where'd you get the dress?"

"I broke into Donna Karan and half-inched it."

Luke looked like he believed me.

"I borrowed it." I nudged him.

"And the ice?" He reached out to touch the diamonds.

"Real. Also borrowed."

"You have some generous friends."

He was still staring at me and I raised a proud eyebrow.

"Had your eyeful?"

"No." He shook his head. "You scrub up well."

"Thanks." Then, feeling something else was needed, "You too."

"Are you wearing the wire?"

"Subtle, Luke, really subtle. Yes, I am. Give me a sec, I'll go and switch it on."

I made my way to the ladies, which was as terrifying and grand as the rest of the ballroom, and shut myself in the cubicle to switch the wire on.

"Can you hear me?" I whispered to Alexa.

"Loud and clear. Good luck!"

I had a feeling I was going to need it. Luke was looking at me like I was dessert.

He was waiting for me when we came out. "Have you seen Wright yet?"

It was weird, I could hear him right down in my ear as well as in regular surround. I checked the grommet. "I've only just got here!"

"You should be looking out." He put a hand to the small of my back to lead me into the ballroom. His hand was warm and my skin was bare. I had to concentrate on breathing.

This is business, this is business, this is business.

This is acting.

"You can dance, right?" he said.

"Well, sort of."

"Can you manage a waltz?"

I nodded, not quite trusting myself to speak too much. It wasn't just the wire. Luke looked really good in evening dress. His hair was a good deal lighter than the brown I was used to—in fact it was almost blond. If I hadn't been so preoccupied with myself when I walked in I might have noticed that. His eyes were their natural blue... I think.

"What?" Luke said when I peered at him.

"Are you wearing contacts?"

"No. This is me."

Jesus. He was tall, blond, blue-eyed and built.

This is business, this is business, this is business.

God, he's hot.

"We'll do a quick circuit," Luke said. "Keep your eyes open."

I did, but I'm afraid I wasn't looking at what I was supposed to be looking at. Luke's eyes were all over the room, constantly searching for Wright, but my eyes were on him. It felt so wonderful to be dancing in his arms.

I wanted to touch his cheekbones. I wanted to stroke them. Was that weird?

"Okay, I see him," Luke said. "One o'clock."

Which wasn't very helpful as we kept waltzing round in circles.

"Where?"

I wanted to *lick* his cheekbones. Someone help me.

"Over by the windows. He's alone." Luke let go of me and I stumbled slightly. "Go."

"Go?"

"Flirt with him. Draw him out."

I gave Luke an incredulous look but he was already gone.

Flirt with him. Flirt with a chubby, balding fifty-year-old who'd asked me to scrub his back in a Roman hotel room?

Bleurgh.

I was halfway across the room when I walked into someone and I was shaking so much I recoiled and nearly fell over.

"Careful! Are you okay?"

I looked up at the man who had caught me. Dashing and handsome, clean-cut, shiny hair... Oh, shit, it was Harvey!

"What are you doing here?" I asked him at the same time he asked me, and we stared at each other.

"I have a business invite," Harvey said eventually.

"Right, your mobile company."

He frowned, looking distracted. "Mobile?"

Jesus, his company was in trouble if he didn't know what we called a cell phone. "Yeah, mobile—cell phones," I said, trying to see past him to Wright. But he was all shoulder, Harvey was, all shoulder and jaw. It was like trying to see past a huge wall.

"Are you here alone? I didn't know stewardesses moved in such grand circles."

"No, I, er, I'm here with my, erm, my brother."

"The guy you were dancing with?"

"Uh, yes. He's, er, he's quite grand. Knows Madonna. Small country and all that. My brother."

"Yeah, you look like him," Harvey was nodding.

I stopped and stared. "I do?"

"Yeah. Except your hair is different..." He peered at me. "Did you change it?"

No, my hair routinely changes from blonde to dark brown overnight. Men. "Yeah," I said. "Fancied a change."

"It looks good. So."

I looked up nervously, suddenly remembering that I'd walked out on him in Rome. "So?"

"Where did you go? I came out and you were gone."

"Oh, I, er, I had an early flight, so I had to go. Sorry about that."

"You didn't even leave a phone number."

Fancy that.

"I'm sorry," I said, "but I really, really have to go. To the, erm, ladies." I picked up my skirts and ran away, and because Harvey was calling after me and watching me, I had to go to the ladies again.

The uniformed woman by the sinks gave me a curious look.

"Champagne," I said with a smile. "Goes straight through me."

I locked myself in a cubicle and lifted up my skirts to check the phone holster on my other thigh, but I didn't need to. Something whistled in my ear and I dropped the phone on the floor. It skidded under the partition into the next cubicle. Rats.

"Who was that?" Luke wanted to know, his voice sharp in my ear.

"He's just someone I met in Rome," I said distractedly, trying to reach under the cubicle partition for my phone and hoping it hadn't landed in anything unsavoury.

"Someone like the guy you spent the night with?"

"I did not spend the night with anyone!" I hissed, aware that not only could everyone else in the ladies hear me, but Alexa and One could, too.

"Yeah, well, stop socialising."

"Hey, he cornered me. I'm going back out there in a minute." I reached out, and the phone suddenly came skidding towards me. I grabbed it and holstered it gratefully.

"Do that. Ask him about his business. Try and get some names."

"How am I supposed to do that?"

"I don't know. Maybe you could get a room and seduce it out of him."

"Maybe I will." I flushed the toilet for appearance's sake and stalked out of there.

This time I made a beeline for David Wright, detouring only for a waiter and grabbing two glasses of champagne. I hadn't had my drink for tonight and I needed some Dutch.

Right. Sophisticated. Urbane. Suave. I could do this. I was trained for this.

Crap, I wish they'd trained me.

"Mr. Wright." I handed him a glass of champagne. "Allow me to introduce myself. I'm Antonia Porter and I work for Ace Airlines. I've been wanting to meet you for a while."

He looked me over and appeared to like what he saw, because he smiled a greasy smile and said, "Have you, my dear? And why is that?"

"There's a rumour in my company that you're going to buy a majority in shares," I said, hoping I sounded like I knew what I was talking about. "If I can speak frankly, I'd like to see it happen sooner, rather than later."

He looked surprised. "You want to be owned by Wrightbank?"

I'd rather be owned by Saddam Hussein. "I think it's what Ace needs," I said. "Since we went public there's been a lack of direction, and I'm sure you can see that's a bad thing for an airline." I gave him a cut-glass smile, and he beamed back, looking dazed. "What Ace needs is a good, firm hand," I looked him in the eye and knew I was getting to him, "in charge. We need someone who's going to be more than a sleeping partner."

"Jesus," Luke said in my ear, "you're turning me on."

I ignored him. "So what are you going to do for us, Mr. Wright? Can I call you David?"

He nodded, looking glazed.

"Will it be just the fifty-one percent majority you'll be buying? That's not a lot of control, David. Maybe you need some surety."

Gosh, I sounded like I knew what I was talking about and everything.

"Oh, I'll have surety," Wright said. "I have a partner who's interested in stock as well."

"Bingo," Luke said.

"You do? A business partner?"

"Oh, yes."

"I thought you owned Wrightbank and its subsidiaries outright."

"Well, yes, I do—"

"I thought you had no partner."

"No, well, I don't, but when I say partner I mean a personal friend. Not a close friend," he blustered, "not that kind of partner..."

I smiled. "Of course. You're well known for keeping your personal life private."

Was he? I had no idea. But it seemed to please him.

"Well, yes, of course."

"But is this personal friend trustworthy?" I asked, as Luke said in my ear, "God knows how this imbecile runs a company."

I thought it was pretty obvious that he didn't.

"Oh, yes, very trustworthy," Wright said. "She's been in it with me from the beginning."

"She?" Luke said, and then Alexa broke in with, "Ask him about Jane Hammond. She was his partner way back when."

"Your partner is a woman?" I said. "I thought after Jane Hammond you might have changed your mind about working with women."

"I know I have," Luke muttered.

"What do you know about Jane Hammond?" Wright asked.

"I know she was your partner way back when," I said, hoping Alexa would come up with something else.

"Bad break up," she said, and I repeated it. "Swore to work alone after that."

"So I'm sort of surprised you're working with someone else on this," I said to Wright. "She must be very special."

"Oh, she is."

"Is she a well-known figure?" I didn't want to ask outright for a name. Didn't want to push him too far. He didn't look too bright, but then, neither did I.

Hmm.

"No, no, she's very private. Totally unknown."

"But obviously she knows a lot about this venture, about the world of finance," I said. "I mean, I've been looking into this," I said, looking down at my miraculously empty champagne glass modestly, "and there are a few names I've become familiar with." I started randomly casting around. "I know Helen Shilton said she'd kill to work with you."

"Really?" Wright said, looking interested. "Helen Shilton?"

Jesus, don't tell me there really is a Helen Shilton.

"Who?" Luke and Alexa said at the same time.

"But then obviously it's not her," I added quickly. "Is it a name I might know?" I asked coyly.

Wright tapped his nose. "I'll never tell."

"But surely I'll find out sooner or later when she starts buying up shares in my company?"

"Oh, is it your company now?" Wright said teasingly, and I knew I'd lost him. "What did you say your name was?"

"Antonia, er, Portman."

"Porter," Luke hissed in my ear.

"I'm sure I know you," Wright said, peering closer.

"No, I just have one of those faces. Would you like some more champagne?" I trilled, grabbing another couple of glasses.

"Not for me. You have some," he said generously.

How kind. Especially since it was free.

"No more," Luke said firmly as I lifted the glass to my lips, and I nearly spilled it. Was he watching me? "Get him drunk."

"I can't have any more," I pressed both glasses on Wright. "It goes straight to my head. Must be the, er, bubbles."

"Airhead," Luke sniggered, and was ignored.

"Me too," Wright said. "Don't drink much."

Fantastic.

"Can I not tempt you at all?" I said, fluttering my eyelashes.

"Not with champagne," Wright said, and actually winked.

Ugh.

Luke was laughing in my ear. "I think maybe you should get out of there," he said.

Oh, God, please yes.

"I have a room just upstairs," Wright said, and I nearly gagged.

"Really?" I said. "Well, why don't you go up there and I'll, I'll get my things and follow you up."

"You won't need a thing," Wright said, leaning close. I leaned back.

"You won't say that when you see what I have in my bag," I managed, and I could hear Luke laughing.

Wright's piggy eyes were all lit up. "Room 305," he said. "Five minutes."

Jesus.

I watched him scamper away, little piggy that he was, and turned in disgust to see Luke standing about ten feet away.

"That was a hell of a show," he said, grinning.

"Yeah, thanks."

"So what do you have in your bag?"

"Lots of things that could be fashioned into weapons."

"Just weapons? You didn't bring the cuffs?"

"I'm sorry, I didn't know this was a bondage party."

He laughed. "Room 305 probably is. Right." He took one of my champagne glasses and turned away from the crowd. I had to stretch to see what he was doing, but it looked like he was tipping something into the glass.

"What's that?"

"Sleeping powder. Five minutes and he'll be out." He grabbed a waiter and presented him with the glass. "Could you take this to Room 305, please? Compliments of Miss Antonia Port*er*," he gave me a severe look, "who desires him to drink it straight away as a prelude to the party. Those words exactly."

The waiter nodded and went away with the glass.

"That's that," Luke said. "He'll think it's Viagra or something."

"From the way he was walking I don't think he'll need it," I muttered, and Luke laughed out loud.

"Right," he said. "Five minutes. Wanna dance?"

They weren't playing a waltz any more, but we danced one anyway, feeling foolish, giggling a lot. Or at least I was. Luke looked very amused and held me so close I could hear the squashed crackle of his microphone in my ear.

"I can hear you," I said.

"Well, I am right here."

"No, I mean here." I took my hand from his shoulder and placed it on his chest. "I can hear your heart beat."

Luke looked into my eyes and we slowed almost to a stop. I could hardly breathe. He was going to kiss me again.

"Time's up," he whispered, and released me.

Bastard.

We took the lift up to the third floor and the atmosphere was tense. Gray's Hotel was movie-set grand, panelled in gleaming wood with faded gilt everywhere and lots of dark, aged paintings. But I hardly noticed, because every sense I had was desperately attuned to Luke walking easily beside me.

"Knock," he said to me when we reached the door. "If he's still awake, go in and wait for him to sleep."

"What if he's not drunk the champagne?"

"Propose a toast."

I took a deep breath and knocked. Nothing. I knocked again. "David?"

"Oh, he's David now?" Luke mocked under his breath as I tried the handle, with no success.

Luke pulled something from his pocket, a little wire, and picked the lock.

"Please show me how to do that," I begged.

"You planning on breaking into a lot of places?"

No, I just got locked out a lot.

"Hey, if you know it, I should know it. Spy training and all that," I whispered as Luke pushed the door open and reached for the gun holstered under his immaculately cut jacket.

We were immediately hit by the sound of snoring. I couldn't keep a straight face.

"Oh, is that the welcome I get?" I said.

Luke grinned. "Wouldn't catch me sleeping," he said. "Oh, Jesus, look at this."

We stood and looked at Wright, who was flaked out completely naked on the huge four-poster bed.

"Oh, that's just not pretty," I said, holding up my hand to shield my eyes.

"Definitely not," Luke agreed, holstering his gun and going over to Wright. He slapped the sleeping guy's cheek, and Wright snored louder. "Right. You keep an eye on the door. You never know, he might have invited lots of revellers up here."

Charming thought.

I stood by the door, listening hard for footsteps, while Luke did a lightning sweep of the room. I was gratified to see he checked all the places I had the night before, in Rome. Suitcase, briefcase, drawers, checking for hidden compartments in each.

Then he went over to the laptop. There hadn't been one of those in Rome.

"This could take some time," he said.

"Why, computer illiterate?"

He gave me a withering glance and took a USB stick out of his jacket pocket.

What the hell else did he keep in there?

Every minute he spent searching and downloading I was sure Wright was going to wake up or someone was going to come in. I was practically hopping with nervousness when there came a knock on the door.

"Shit," I said to Luke, who nodded and quickly ejected the USB stick and pocketed it.

"Answer it. Make them go."

Heart pounding, I crossed to the door and when I opened it, I nearly fainted.

"Harvey?"

"Sophie?" He looked as amazed as me. "What are you doing here?"

"I, er, this is my room."

Harvey looked at the number. "Really? Your room?"

"I, er..."

"No," I felt a hand on my shoulder and another at my waist, "our room. Sophie, honey, friend of yours?"

Oh, sweet Jesus.

Chapter Twelve

I looked back at Luke, whose fingers were firm on my shoulder, then at Harvey, who looked speechless.

"You're sharing with your brother?" he asked eventually, and I could have kicked Luke. Hadn't he heard me say that?

"Is that what she called me?" Luke said easily. "Bad girl, Sophie, telling lies like that."

Harvey looked between us. "You're a couple?"

Looked like it. "Yes," I said. "But it's a secret."

"Sophie, could I talk to you a second?" Harvey said tensely, and I extracted myself from Luke and slipped out of the room before he could protest.

"What's up?"

Harvey folded his arms. "You didn't tell me about him in Rome."

"No, well, erm, like I said, it's a secret."

"So secret you came back to my room?"

I blushed.

"Is that why you left?"

"Sudden attack of conscience," I said meekly. "I'm sorry, Harvey. It's...it's complicated."

That was becoming my catch phrase.

Harvey shook his glossy head. "And I thought he was your brother," he said as the door opened and Luke came out.

"He's *not* my brother. My brother is in Essex. You remember, Luke, I was talking to him when we were on the phone the other day..."

"Oh, so you do have a brother?" Harvey said.

"I thought he was your boyfriend," Luke said.

"I thought *he* was your boyfriend," Harvey said, pointing at Luke, looking confused.

"Who? Chalker?"

"Who's Chalker?" they both asked.

"Yeah, who is Chalker?" asked Alexa in my ear. I'd forgotten about her.

"He's my brother," I said firmly.

"So who's your boyfriend?" Harvey asked.

"No one," I said.

"That's not what you told me," Luke said.

"You said it was him," Harvey said, pointing again. Didn't the boy know it was rude?

"You told me it was the other guy," Luke said.

"*What other guy*?"

"The one you were talking to. At your parents'."

"That was my brother!"

"You're sleeping with your brother?" Alexa said. "How Greek."

"Not this guy?" Harvey pointed at Luke, and I grabbed his hand to stop him.

"No. This is Luke. He's not my boyfriend. He's not my brother. He's just my... my tormentor."

"So who am I?" Harvey asked, reclaiming his hand and massaging it pointedly.

"Yes, who is he?" Luke asked.

"We met in Rome," I said.

"Oh, *you're* the guy." Luke folded his arms and leaned back against the wall, looking Harvey over.

"What guy?" Harvey asked.

"Yes, what guy?" Alexa asked.

"No guy!" I half yelled. "We had dinner. That's all."

"Not totally all," Harvey said.

"I love this," Alexa said.

I looked at Luke. "Can we go now?"

He shook his head, looking highly amused.

"We have popcorn," Alexa informed me.

"Is there a boyfriend?" Luke asked.

"No!"

"Then why'd you say there was?"

"To piss you off!

"Why?"

"Because you were being annoying."

"So why did you—" Harvey began, but I'd already had enough. I started walking away.

"Sophie, wait," they both yelled.

I suppose under other circumstances it might be nice to have two handsome men running after me, but I'd had a really long day. The week seemed about eight days long already. My feet were truly killing me—her Ladyboat's shoes were too small and not really designed to be worn this much.

"No," I said, determined not to cry although my eyes didn't seem to know that. "I've had enough. I'm going home."

"Can I take your number?" Harvey asked hopefully.

"No," Luke and I said at the same time. I glared at Luke and carried on walking. I was almost at the lift now.

"Sophie, calm down," he said.

"No, I will not."

"Look, I'm sorry—"

"But you're not, are you, Luke? This isn't funny. You keep laughing at me and none of it's funny. I've had enough, I'm going home, goodbye."

"How?" Luke asked.

"What?"

"How are you getting home?"

"Same way I got here."

"Last train leaves Liverpool Street in ten minutes. You'll never make it."

Shit. I hadn't realised it was so late. Damn Angel, making me take my watch off.

"I'll—I'll get a taxi."

"It'll cost you a fortune!"

"I'll manage."

"After Rome and everything? Do you even have any cash on you?"

I said nothing. The lift doors opened and I stepped in.

"I'll figure something out," I said.

"I'll give you a—"

"No," I said. Luke tried to follow me into the lift and I glared at him. "Go away."

"No."

He was just like Chalker. So I did what I do with Chalker. I gathered my skirts and planted my heel in his chest.

I just had time to see his astonished face as the lift doors closed.

I stared at my reflection in the mirror as I pulled out my earpiece and switched off the wire. I no longer looked gleaming and expensive. I looked tired and miserable. Luke and Harvey would probably be fighting over who didn't get me.

Well done, Sophie. Well done.

I stomped into the ladies, where the attendant probably thought I fancied her or something, and peeled the contact lenses off my eyeballs. They were making my eyes sting.

That's my story and I'm sticking to it.

As I left the hotel, I tried to figure out my route home. Maybe if I got the tube back to Liverpool Street I could get a taxi and it'd be cheaper. Or maybe a night bus. Or something.

I stood on the steps of the hotel, shivering, the wind blowing bits of my hair around, trying to think.

A car pulled up in front of me. A silver Vectra. Luke's silver Vectra.

"How did they even let that in the car park?" I said as he rolled his window down and leaned over to me. "Don't they have a fifty grand minimum?"

"I showed them my badge. Come on, Sophie, get in. I'll take you home."

"Who says I want to go home? Maybe I'll go and find Harvey and get a room." I started walking and he cruised along beside me.

"Because that worked out so well last time. Look, you need sleep."

"I'll make my own way."

"I have a CD changer."

I almost smiled at that.

"What's on it?"

"Led Zeppelin—"

I held up my hands. "I'll walk."

"Nickelback. Avril Lavigne. Madonna. S Club Juniors. Dolly Parton. Pavarotti. Use the radio. Just get in the bloody car, will you?"

I hesitated. On the one hand, giving into Luke, which I really, really hated to do. On the other, spending hour upon hour trudging around in someone else's deadly shoes, alone, unarmed, in London—all right, Kensington, but it was still dark and cold and lonely.

I let out a big sigh as if it was the biggest chore in the world and got in. The car was warm and quiet, a cocoon against the outside world. We slid out onto the road again.

"You don't really have S Club Juniors in here, do you?"

He grinned sheepishly. "I don't even have a CD changer."

See? I knew he was a liar.

I must have dozed off some time before we hit the M11, because the next thing I remembered was Luke shaking me by the shoulder and saying we were home. I looked at the clock on the dash. It was well after midnight.

"Thanks," I said as I got out of the car. "For the lift and everything."

"No problem. You want me to see you in?"

"I think I can manage," I said with as much sarcasm as my tired mind could gather. According to my roster, I should be on an early shift today. Starting in about four hours. I stifled a yawn.

"I'll call in sick for you," Luke offered. "You already had today off."

"They'll love me," I said.

He got out of the car and walked me to my door without me asking. It was very sweet of him, but if he was expecting anything more than me passing out as soon as I got horizontal he was going to be very disappointed.

"You'll be okay?" he said as I unlocked the door, and he looked kind of adorable in the light from the security lamp.

"I'll be fine," I said, opening the door and shoving inside. A wave of hot smell hit me. "Jesus, Tammy, what have you brought in?"

"Need to turn that heating down," Luke said, making a face. "Something's rotten."

"It's Tammy. When she's feeling unloved, she brings dead things in…" I trailed off. Tammy was still at my parents' house. So unless something had crawled through the cat flap and died…

I kicked off the torturous shoes and rushed over to the post I'd discarded yesterday, scooping up today's on the way. No manilla envelopes, but one fat Jiffy bag, and the free charity pen…

I got my rubber gloves out and tore into the charity envelope. There was no pen. I opened the Jiffy bag. Nothing pleasant there either.

Luke and I stared at the two festering fingers. Bile rose in my throat.

"Okay, this is gross," I said. "Get me a, get me a sandwich bag for them or something. This is disgusting."

I didn't know where to put them—I sure as hell wasn't messing with the sleepy village policemen at this time of night—so I ended up shoving them in the freezer, well away from anything I might ever want to eat again.

In fact, I was thinking I might clean out the whole freezer when something caught my attention. Luke had been studying the printed "charity" envelope as it lay on the counter. I picked up the Jiffy bag.

"This wasn't postmarked," I said. "There's no stamp. This was put through my door. Someone came to my house and put this through my door."

I started to shudder. I was past fear now. I was tired and, weirdly, I was hungry, and I was damn annoyed that on top of Luke and Harvey and Wright and the Brownie twins, someone was sending me the severed fingers of someone whose murder we were miles away from solving.

I jammed my feet into trainers, strode over to the door and glared into the yard, as if I thought I might see something there.

Then I did see something there.

At least, I saw something moving beyond the fence. Not thinking, I ran straight out there, Luke yelling after me, and saw someone—not a cat or a fox or anything small, an actual person—disappear into the semi-abandoned building site across the car park.

"Sophie, what the hell are you—" Luke began, but then he stopped. "Soph," he said quietly. "There's someone there. Come back."

"The hell I will," I said. Probably it was just some kids on their way back from the pub.

On a private driveway, two hours after last orders.

I held out my hand. "Give me your gun."

"The hell I will."

"There's someone there. Give me your gun."

He'd reached me now and held onto my arm. "Stay here. I'll go."

"No." I wrenched away, invincible with anger, and walked straight into the building site, picking my way over the rubble, Luke swearing behind me.

Then there was a loud shot, very close, echoing and pinging around my ears, and then a crack and a shudder, and then something smacked the back of my head and the world vanished.

Unconsciousness is nice. Dark, dreamy, restful. Like sleep, but without the dreams. A nice place to stay. All warm and comfortable.

But unconsciousness is like watching TV or reading a really good book. People never let you do it for long. Someone wanted me awake.

The next thing I heard was Luke's voice, urgent and distant, and the next thing I saw was a lighter kind of darkness as he lifted something off my face.

"Sophie? Jesus, Sophie, say something."

I stared up at him, winded. "I think the dress is fucked."

He pushed more bits of rubble away from me. "Can you move? Can you feel your fingers and toes? Can you move them?"

I worked hard to catch my breath. There was too much stuff on me, I'd fallen into a pile of rubble or something. Or...had the rubble fallen on me? "I can't move at all."

Looking really scared now, Luke started shoving bigger bits of brick off me. I was covered in pieces of timber and brick dust and bits of concrete. I freed one arm, then the other, and tried to sit up. That... Was it a shot? Had someone *shot* me? It had knocked down half the building site—most of it, or so it felt, onto me.

Luke heaved a bit of wood off my legs and grabbed my calf. "Can you feel this?" He ran his hand up and down my leg. "Sophie, can you feel it?"

Oh, God, yes. Probably this was entirely inappropriate, but I was feeling other things as well. What he was doing was starting to make me feel dizzy. Not that I was desperate, but it had been a pretty long time and, well, you should see him.

I nodded silently, staring up at him. He was a little bit blurry. He'd taken off his jacket and rolled up his shirtsleeves and he was dusty and frightened and he looked incredible.

"God, Soph." He pulled me against him. "I thought you were gone. I thought..."

I put my arms around him. "I'm right here," I said, and Luke kissed me. And then his hand went back down to my leg, moving up over the transmitter and garter belt, doing very inappropriate things that I begged him not to stop. And then he pulled the rather ruined dress off me and I pulled his clothes off him, and then we were naked and once we were naked we got pretty hot and pretty happy, and then...

God, I can't believe I had sex in the rubble.

Afterwards I clung to him, breathless and sweaty and absolutely filthy and not caring at all, and he raised his head and kissed my nose and said, "You okay?"

I smiled dreamily. "I'm *great*," I said. "How' you doin'?"

"Only, you are lying in the rubble, and a building did just fall down on you."

I'd sort of forgotten. It was that good.

"I'm okay," I said, and Luke frowned. He moved away from me, and I was weak as a newborn, trying to stop him. He got something out of his jacket—what, was it made by the Mary Poppins Carpet Bag Co.?—and flashed a bright light in my eyes.

"Ow!" I pushed the torch away. "What's that for?"

"I think you have a concussion." He hit himself on the head, which I thought was pretty funny. "Shit."

"I don't have a concussion. I feel fine."

"Sophie, tell me your postcode."

I opened my mouth, but I couldn't even think of the first letter.

"Yeah," Luke said. "Better get you to a doctor. Can you stand?"

I was sure I could, but no one had told my legs that and they buckled under me. Luke held me up, pulled the dress back over me and shoved himself into his clothes, then picked me up in his arms.

I was fuzzily impressed. I must have been dreaming. No man has been able to pick me up since I outweighed my mother. When I was fourteen. I'm tall, okay? My bones are heavy.

I'd thought he might be taking me inside so I could snuggle up in bed with him, but he put me in his car, locked the doors and told me he'd be back after he'd locked up my flat. How sweet. And car sex, too.

I must have dozed off again, because Luke kept shaking me and talking to me, asking me really stupid questions all the time instead of taking my clothes off. Actually, I got past feeling sexy quite quickly and just wanted to go to sleep. This time yesterday I was in Rome. Imagine that, a different time zone, only yesterday.

"...Which is the first episode Dawn turns up in?" Luke asked, having ascertained that *Buffy* trivia was my specialist subject.

"I dunno." I yawned.

"Yes, you do. No one knows who she is. It's when Buffy's mum asks her to take Dawn out with her..."

"The Dracula one? Series five."

"Yes. And what's the one after that?"

"Dunno."

"Come on, Soph, help me out here."

"Wanna go to sleep."

"Which episode?"

"Where Giles has his mid-life crisis car and the, the magic shop..."

He nodded and stopped the car. I hadn't even realised he'd started it.

"Where are we?"

"Princess Alexandra Hospital. Casualty, sweetheart. Come on."

He half carried me into the horribly bright room, full of pub brawlers and girls who'd walked on broken glass, and somehow got me to the front of the queue, x-rayed and checked over and sewn up. I think there was a cut on my shoulder. They kept me awake, the bastards, and I really wanted to sleep so much. But Luke was there, holding my hand, making me stay awake, stroking my hair and telling me he'd take care of me.

I wanted to tell him I could take care of myself, but the truth was it felt too nice to have him watching over me. Some feminist I am.

Then Luke took me back to the car and finally let me sleep. I drifted away, blissful, dreamless.

Chapter Thirteen

When I was seven my brother Chalker and I went around to the neighbours' house to play with their kids. I walked and Chalker came a minute later, on his bike. It was only around the corner, close enough that our parents let us go alone. We only lived on a cul-de-sac. Safe as anything.

On the way back, running because—well, I don't know why I was running. Because I was a kid and it was fun, I think. I haven't really run properly in years. I was running back and Chalker was right behind me on his bike, and as I cut in front of him to jump onto the pavement and run across the lawn to our house, he clipped me with his bike.

At least, that's what he says. All I remember is running up the road. I don't remember him clipping me, I don't remember falling, and I don't remember hitting my head on the kerb. Of course, if you ask Chalker, it was my fault for getting in his way. It's his word against mine. I don't remember it at all. I just remember waking in my mum's arms, inside the house, wondering how I'd got there and why everyone was looking so concerned and why on earth my head hurt so much.

I remember that look. The expression on my mother's face. Like she was frightened and relieved and angry, all at the same time. I don't remember her ever shouting at my brother for it. I don't remember if blame was ever apportioned. No one told me off for it either. Everyone was so relieved that I didn't have any serious brain damage (although Chalker still has his doubts) that the incident itself was largely forgotten.

But I remember the look. Luke had it too, when I opened my eyes in the rubble. At the time I thought I'd never seen someone look so frightened, but now I remember my mother.

Why was Luke so frightened? Because he thought it was his fault? Because he'd have to train a new partner? Because he cared for me?

He hardly knew me.

Maybe it was just normal concern for another human being. Maybe if I'd been a stranger he'd have looked the same.

Hopefully, he wouldn't have shagged me, though.

In restless dreams, I walked alone. I was in London and I was supposed to be meeting someone. I can't remember who. Only I got lost, I missed my train or something and the person I was with got whisked away, so I got on the next train and went to the wrong place. It was like being a child—I had no idea where I was supposed to be, and I was frightened, really frightened.

I walked around the streets, streets that looked like where I grew up, where I went to school. But it was dark, and there was no one around, and I had nothing—no money, no phone. I couldn't even call a cab to take me somewhere, because I didn't know where I was supposed to be going.

I felt like crying. I didn't know where I was and I didn't know where I was going, and even if I got there I didn't know what I'd do.

And then I looked around, and there was Luke, rolling his eyes and asking what I'd got myself into now.

"They said you were gone," he explained, coming closer, warm and solid and wonderful. "I came to find you."

"I was lost," I said, feeling helpless.

"I found you." He smiled at me reassuringly, and I believed him. "I'll always find you."

He put his arm around me as we walked, a companionable gesture that made me want to snuggle closer. He felt safe, secure.

"How do you know where we're going?" I asked.

"What makes you think I do?"

"You seem so sure."

"I'm working it out."

We walked a bit further. The streets all looked the same—leafy, pleasant, a bit blurry. It was like walking into a blue screen.

"I'm sorry," I said.

"What for?"

"Causing so much trouble."

"You're not trouble."

"Got lost, didn't I?"

Luke's hand rubbed my shoulder, and it tingled. I had a feeling that meant something, but I wasn't sure what. Everything felt sort of fuzzy.

"You weren't really lost," he said. "I found you."

He kept saying that. He found me. But how? And where were we going?

"I'm causing so much trouble," I said.

"No. You're doing fine."

"Where are we even going?" I tried to remember but it felt like my head was full of pudding.

"You don't know?"

"I..."

"I thought you knew." Luke looked at me in surprise. "You're leading the way."

"No, I..."

"I'm walking with you, Sophie. You know where you're going."

I stopped and looked up at him. "Luke, will you kiss me?"

He smiled and stroked my face. My cheek tingled, just the way my shoulder had when he'd touched it there. "I already have."

"Kiss me again. I don't remember."

Luke sighed, a soft sound, and I closed my eyes. But when I opened them, he wasn't there and I was alone again.

For a second I was lost, frightened again. What was I doing? Where was I going?

Why wasn't he there to show me?

I looked up the street, looked down it. I didn't know which way we'd even come. But I wasn't going to get anywhere just standing here.

I turned left and started walking. Surely I'd end up somewhere.

I didn't feel so lost any more.

I woke in a strange place, comfortable and white, and for a second was truly frightened. I'd died. I'd been shot—it was like in *Ghost*, where Patrick Swayze runs down the road and doesn't realise his body has been left behind. I had never had sex with Luke. I'd not been to the hospital or anything. That's why I was in this marvellous white cocoon, with a high, dark-beamed ceiling...

Heaven is a loft apartment?

I managed to move my head to the accompaniment of severe pain from the unlikeliest of sources. I was in a big white bed between high-thread-count sheets. There were pieces of dark oak furniture around the pale walls. A door. A window with heavy linen curtains drawn.

Heaven had good taste. Stark, but not bad.

I tried to sit up and immediately realised this was not a good idea. I felt like a building had fallen down on me.

And then I remembered that it had.

The Nokia was charging up on the night stand, next to my little evening bag. There was a note propped by the phone, addressed to me.

I used up most of my strength stretching over to get it, and lay there for a while, exhausted, aching. Then I managed to roll back on my back, and unfolded the sheet of paper.

Sophie, These are your painkillers. I looked over and realised they'd been behind the note. *Take two every four hours and no more or you'll pass out.* Didn't seem like such a bad idea to me. *Take a shower but don't get the dressing wet.* What dressing? Oh, yes, the dreadful pain in my shoulder. Stitches or something. Great. *Don't go outside, I really don't think it's safe for you. Rest and sleep. Drink some water. Make yourself at home, I'll be back this afternoon. There's a video for you on the coffee table. Call me if you need anything. Luke.*

That was it. Not *love Luke*, not *dear Sophie*. No kisses.

Had I imagined the sex? No. I couldn't have.

No power on heaven or earth could have imagined that sex. Oh, boy. I licked my dry lips. I'd be carrying the memory of that to my grave. I frowned. Maybe thinking about graves when I hurt this much wasn't a good idea. Still. It was a bit of a foggy memory, but it was still a good one.

Imagine what it'd be like if I wasn't concussed.

Oh, *boy*.

I put a painkiller in my mouth and realised I couldn't swallow it. The pill was huge and my mouth was totally dry.

Gagging, I stumbled out of bed and shoved through the door into a large open plan living room with a clean, shiny chrome kitchen. I stuck my head under the tap and chugged a load of water, and the pill went down.

Breathing deeply, every nerve in my body wailing in pain, I leaned back against the kitchen counter and looked around. Luke's flat was a big loft with high, apexed ceilings filled with lovely old beams. He had oak panelled floors—real oak, not the fake stuff I have in my flat—and a lovely leather chesterfield that I coveted immediately. His kitchen was new and shiny but all the other furniture looked old and loved. Faded rugs on the floor. A punch-bag hanging from the high beams.

The place was spacious and lightsome. I hadn't really pictured Luke's flat in my head, apart from figuring it'd be full of complicated locks and timers and alarms and red beams criss-crossing the floor. But this was a really cool place.

I stood looking around for quite a while before I realised I was completely naked.

Oh. Hope he doesn't have any flatmates.

As far as I could tell, there was only one bedroom, simply the smaller half of the loft, with a bathroom attached. I hobbled back through, looked at the bed which was streaked with dust and crusts of dried blood—eurgh—and at myself.

Huh. No wonder the bed was a mess. No wonder Luke told me to have a shower.

Briefly, I wondered where he'd slept. On the chesterfield? That leather probably wasn't too comfy. And there were no spare sheets or anything lying around. In the bed with me? That figured. I finally have sex with someone as delicious as Luke, and I'm concussed; I get into bed with him, and I'm unconscious.

Ha.

I hauled myself into the bathroom and looked longingly at the shower. Then an idea struck me and I found myself in the kitchen, wrapping cling-film around my shoulder. Genius.

I spent hours in the shower, half wishing it was a long, hot bath with scented bubbles, but it felt good to pummel my skin with the jets of water. When I moved into my flat my nannan had had one of those scary hose attachments on the bath, no proper shower. That was the first thing I bought. A big, throbbing power shower. Yeah.

I washed my hair, which left khaki streaks all over the bath, and soaped myself all over several times. When I eventually stepped out, I peeled off the cling-film—the dressing was slightly damp but okay—and carefully washed the skin there. I nicked Luke's razor and made myself presentable. I even found some Molton Brown moisturiser and slapped it on, making a mental note to tease Luke about it later.

I looked utterly dreadful, bruised and perplexingly pasty, like a battered wife. My dark hair made me look white and frightening. I couldn't believe nothing was broken and all I'd needed was a few stitches on my shoulder. There was a big bruise on my cheek and the back of my head had hurt when I washed my hair, in fact there was not very much of me that didn't hurt, but under the circumstances I reckoned I'd got off pretty well.

Next I started looking for clothes. Mine appeared to have run away—oh, Christ, her Ladyboat's dress!—so I borrowed some of Luke's, feeling very kinky in his underwear. I wrapped up my poor abused feet in layers of plasters and thick sports socks and cuddled into joggers, T-shirt and a hooded sweater. I had no bra—first time for everything—but that was the least of my problems. I looked like a homeless person as it was.

He'd said something about a video on the coffee table, and when I went out looking for it, half hoping for something cool about special agent training, I found a tape labelled *SOPHIE—Buffy*, and was more touched than I think I've ever been.

I used his phone to call home and check my messages. There was one: "Sophie, you'd better be listening to this from my house. It's not safe for you to go home. Three fingers and one bullet do not a happy house make. Stay in my flat and don't go outside until I get back, okay? I'll be back in the afternoon."

Git.

I looked at the clock on the state-of-the-art sound system (living with someone like Chalker you get to recognise quality audio equipment). It was just after ten.

Which gave me a couple of hours to look for a spare gun, figure out how to use it, get my bearings and—somehow—get home.

I know, I know. How stupid was I? There were so many things wrong with that plan. But I was on severe painkillers, in some kind of shock, tired and hurt and in a very confused state about Luke, and I really had to go and check that Ted and the flat were okay.

I was so glad Tammy was at my parents' house. When this was all over, she was getting a whole tin of tuna to herself. No, stuff that, a whole actual tuna.

And then I caught myself. This might never be over. I had to get used to the fact that Tammy was never going to be safe. That people might try to kill me all the time. And I had to get used to the fact that I might never figure out who they were.

Too fuzzy to try and think of anything sensible about who it might have been, I started looking around the living room. The bedroom I'd searched quite comprehensively when I was looking for clothes. I found *Top Gear* magazines, ski goggles, condoms and a copy of *The Count of Monte Cristo* (in English, thank God—I don't think I could have coped if he was smart enough to read it in French) by his bed, but no gun and no bullets. He had to keep that box of .40 Smith & Wesson rounds somewhere.

He had CDs and DVDs and videos in oak furniture by the TV and under the coffee table. He had books in large quantity and great variety on shelves that covered the wall by the bedroom. He had fairly decent taste—I mean, there had to be some horribly embarrassing Christmas singles or self-help books somewhere, but he'd hidden them well. There were skis and a bike and walking boots and what looked like diving equipment in a large walk-in cupboard by the kitchen, but no bullets.

And then I saw it, almost hidden in the panelling of the wall behind the big TV. A secret cupboard. I'd found some keys in the kitchen—not very well hidden, Luke—and one of them fit.

Hey presto, who da man?

I da man.

Well, you know.

I opened the cupboard, almost afraid of what I'd find, and stared for quite a while at the things I saw. An ancient, scruffy teddy bear, shoe boxes full of photos, an RAF cap, and lots and *lots* of guns.

Hello.

I felt like I'd opened the Pandora's box of Luke's personality. I itched to look through the photos, but after one or two I realised they weren't going to mean anything to me. Family, maybe. Friends. Comrades, even. All strangers. Although there were a few of Luke in RAF uniform, looking completely one hundred percent edible, that I thought I might like copies of. And one, very old and rather faded, of a man and woman with Seventies hair. She was sitting up in bed, holding a tiny baby, and he was beaming like the top of his head was going to fall off. She was gorgeous, blonde model good looks, and he was the spit of Luke, with darker hair.

His parents. Tears pricked my eyes, and I blamed the medication for my unstable emotional state. They looked so proud with their baby. Was it him, or did he have a brother or sister? I couldn't tell. There were no more photos of anyone with a baby, although there were a few of a very cute little blond boy messing with paddling pools and a black Labrador. Damn Luke, he'd been irresistible even then.

The family photos stopped when the little boy was about five or six. No more pictures of his parents—not even a graduation photo. Surely being in the RAF involved some sort of graduation, ceremony—something?

I frowned, and carefully put the photos back in their box, in the order I'd found them, and turned my attention to the other things in the cupboard. A few trophies and badges, all rather dusty. Hmm, a military medal, although I didn't know what it was for or even if it was Luke's. It might have been his dad's or something.

The RAF cap with its little silver wings was cool. The teddy bear was downright adorable. The guns...

Oh, baby. The guns.

The thing was, I had no idea what ammo went with what piece. There were boxes and boxes of bullets, all labelled, but the labels meant nothing to me. What did .40 Smith & Wesson mean, anyway?

Eventually I opened up the magazine of a revolver and found five little bullets nestling in place. The sixth, a dredged-up memory told me, was a safety chamber.

I found a shoulder holster and eventually figured out how to strap myself into it (I was on really strong painkillers, okay?), slotted the pistol in, and felt very, very cool.

I zipped up the hoody, concealing the gun completely, and felt even cooler.

As well as pretty scared. Knowing me I'd probably manage to shoot myself.

Two more pairs of socks made walking more bearable and also meant I fitted into Luke's trainers. I found a spare key taped inside a kitchen drawer—slack, Luke, really not good at all—and locked up after myself.

The door opened straight onto the outside world, on a metal staircase climbing the outside of what looked like a barn. There were vans and things parked in the concrete yard and piles of roof tiles all over the place.

Curiouser and curiouser. I ventured across the yard to the driveway and the main road, saw a sign announcing Pearce Roofing, and laughed out loud. I'd driven by this place pretty much every day on my way to my parents' house. It was maybe half a mile from where I lived. I didn't have to worry about dodging train fares or hitching lifts or anything.

Fantastic.

On my way back home, feeling much lighter than I had all morning, I passed the village cobbler's. It was completely irresistible. The cobbler was slightly surprised to be presented with a credit card by means of payment for one key copy, but I had no cash on me.

I found my flat, my lovely flat, intact at least from the outside, with Ted standing guard and a pile of rubble on the other side of the car park.

Actually, you could hardly tell it was rubble. Building sites sort of all look the same, don't they?

That's my story, and I'm sticking to it. Boy, I have a lot of stories.

I was slightly nervous when I walked in, especially since I'd had to climb over a large box outside that had apparently been delivered in my absence. I'd open it later, when I knew my flat was okay. I dreaded to think what was inside. Internal organs?

The flat was as I'd left it—chaotic, with clothes and make-up all over the place. It looked better to my eyes than it ever ever had. I only wished Tammy was here with me.

Yesterday's post was still on the floor and I didn't need to look inside the bulkiest envelope to know I'd got another finger. The freezer drawer with the other two fingers was full of ice cream, so I put the new arrival on its own with the chips. It was well wrapped. I hadn't even opened it.

There was a voice mail on my Siemens phone. "Hey, Soph, it's Angel. Says in the book you've got flu, poor baby! I'll try and drop round on my way in—I'm on nine-five overtime…"

That girl was mad.

"…don't worry if you can't get to the door, flu sucks. Drink lots of water and have some chicken soup. Damn, I mean golden veg or something. See you!"

Ahh. Lovely, lovely Angel. And lovely Luke, too, for coming up with a plausible excuse. Not that I'd never used the flu one before. Ahem.

I got a knife from the kitchen and stood in my doorway, feeling cold, staring at the cardboard box. It was all taped up and my name had been scrawled on it. It couldn't be a delivery, I thought, there was no address or invoice. Besides, I hadn't ordered anything.

Feeling slightly sick, I crouched down and slit the tape, expecting something vile to leap out at me. Nothing did. Instead, I found myself looking at seven gorgeous boxed sets of *Buffy* DVDs.

For a moment I couldn't speak. Darling sweet Angel, who shares my obsession. These are her prized possessions! If her house was on fire this would be all she'd save. This and her father's guitar, which is worth millions. And has sentimental value, of course.

I dragged the box inside, heated up some soup, grabbed a bottle of water, and curled up with my duvet on the sofa to watch endless hours of Californian vampires.

Several hours later, I'd watched the entire first series of *Buffy*, complete with commentaries and featurettes, six episodes of *Sex and the City*, last night's *Friends* and twenty minutes of *Alias*. And I'd cried endlessly. I cried when Buffy and her friends had to kill that vamped mate of Xander's in the first episode. I cried when Carrie cheated on Aidan. I cried when Monica thought Chandler didn't want to have a baby with her. I cried because Michael Vartan is gorgeous.

I don't know what was wrong with me. I must have really been in shock. How could Luke let me come home on my own like that? Why didn't he lock me in? I felt so unsafe, and unloved—because it was dark already and he hadn't called or come by or anything. Not even a text. I even went online to see if he'd somehow got my e-mail address and messaged me that way, but no. There was nothing.

Maybe Maria was right. Maybe he totally separated sex from emotion. Maybe I truly meant absolutely nothing to him. My memories of the night before were hazy, to say the least—especially after all my painkillers—but I couldn't remember any cuddling or nice, sweet words.

The bastard used me. I was concussed and he seduced me. He's an arsehole!

Eventually, at about eight-thirty, the phone rang, and I ignored it. I hardly ever pick up anyway—that's what the answer phone is for. And I was supposed to have flu, which, as I remember, traps you in bed for a week with a body that feels like a building has fallen down on it.

Hmm.

The message rang out, clear and pissed off. "Sophie Green, you had better not be sitting there listening to this. I thought someone had fucking kidnapped you. I'm going to try your mobile and so help me, if you don't answer in thirty seconds, I'll blow your bloody apartment up myself."

Uh-oh. Did I forget to lock the door or something? Had he found out about the gun?

Quickly—well, as quickly as my crippled body would allow—I ran to the bedroom and shoved the revolver under the mattress. Then I hobbled back into the living room and picked up the Nokia, which was shrieking madly.

Is it my imagination, or does it sound more frantic when the call is important?

"Where the hell are you?" Luke snarled.

"At home."

"Why the hell are you at home?"

I recoiled from the phone. I sure was glad Luke was on my side.

"I—I didn't feel safe at your house. I like my flat."

"My house is significantly bloody safer than yours! Jesus, Sophie, whoever it is that's been sending you those fingers knows where you live. They were there yesterday. They'll probably be back tonight. They will probably try to kill you. And I for one am half inclined to let them."

I glared at the phone. "What did I do?"

"How did you even get home?"

"I walked. It's not far."

"How did you—"

"I've lived in this bloody village since I was two, Luke, I know where things are."

He was silent for a few seconds, but I could hear him fuming.

"I'm sending Maria over to keep an eye on you. I have things to do," he said eventually, and then clicked off before I could reply.

I stared at the phone in my hand. What was all that about? He'd have mentioned the gun if he knew that was missing. Why was he so mad?

Maria turned up ten minutes later, looking as perfect as always, dressed down in gym clothes, her hair shiny and perky. I shuffled back to let her in, feeling like the Hunchback of Notre Dame.

"Bloody hell," she shook her head at me, "he wasn't kidding."

"What?"

"You look like shit," she said frankly. "Sorry, but you do."

"I'm fine," I said. "Just bruised. I'll be fine. Really, you don't need to be here."

"Either me or Macbeth," she said, slinging her bag off her shoulder, "take your pick."

Maria was looking like the better option. Nothing against Macbeth, but he didn't look like he'd appreciate Ben & Jerry's and angry girl music.

"Do you know why Luke's in such a bad mood with me?" I ventured as she kicked off her sparkling trainers.

She shrugged. "I guess because he's worried about you. He's been at the office all day looking up stuff on Wright and some American guy, bugging the hell out of his FBI contacts and all. He said he was going back there later. I'm surprised he didn't come here himself..."

I was beginning to get the feeling Luke hadn't come in person because he didn't want to have to fill in all the paperwork that would follow killing me.

"Hey," Maria said. "I like your hair like that."

I touched it, remembering that it was dark. "Disguise," I mumbled. "You want to watch some TV?"

She nodded and looked over the mess of videos and DVDs on the floor. "Whatever you want."

As always in times of emotional insecurity, I turned to *Buffy*. Series four, that glorious episode where you get Angel and Riley and Spike all in one juicy bunch. Man, I want to live in Sunnydale, land of fit men and perfect hair.

"So..." Maria said after a while, digging into the ice cream with her spoon, "this is after Angel's left, right?"

"Yeah. But he comes back for a visit."

"Right. And Spike's been chipped...?"

"Yes. And Buffy's sleeping with Riley."

"Which one do you prefer?"

I considered it. "Well, Buffy's really not my type. Too short."

Maria laughed. "I think I'd go for Riley."

"Really?" He reminded me of Harvey, all shiny hair and nice teeth. Oh God, Harvey. I'd forgotten about that part of last night. "I'd have to go with Spike. I need a certain amount of sarcasm in my life."

Maria went after a cow-shaped chunk of chocolate. "Hmm. Bad accent. If we're talking sharp teeth, I'd go for Angel. I like 'em dark and brooding."

"Well, I'm not saying I'd kick him out of bed," I took the ice cream from her and chased a white chocolate cow, "but I like blonds. Even peroxide blonds."

"He does have good cheekbones," Maria conceded, licking her spoon.

"Mmm."

We watched Spike strut around in some caves, all black leather and sexy sneer.

"He looks sort of like Luke," Maria said after a while.

I said nothing.

"Don't you think? With the cheekbones and the smirk?"

Luke looked better. "I guess," I shrugged.

Maria took the ice cream off me and gave me a sly look. "Sophie, what are you not telling me?"

I stared at the screen. "Nothing."

"Why is Luke so concerned about you? What happened last night?"

"Someone fired a shot at me and the building site collapsed on me. He probably just doesn't want to find another partner."

She had her head on one side and was considering me carefully. "Sophie," she said seriously, and I looked up at her guiltily. "When we were talking about Luke on Wednesday and you said he'd made a pass at you, that's all, right? He hasn't been trying it on since then?"

I said nothing.

"Oh Jesus," Maria sighed, putting down the Ben & Jerry's. "What happened?"

I mumbled it very quietly.

"What?"

"We sort of had sex."

She stared. "Sort of?"

"Well, sort of properly. Orgasm and everything."

She was shaking her head. "When did this happen?"

"Last night."

"Before or after the building fell down?"

"After."

"Bloody hell." We stared at the end credits of *Buffy*. "Well, no wonder he's angry."

I frowned. "What do you mean?"

"He's feeling guilty. He totally took advantage of you, Sophie, don't you see? God, I thought he had a bit more self control than that."

I felt compelled to defend him a little. After all, he taped *Buffy* for me. "Well, I didn't exactly protest too much."

"Well, no, you wouldn't. I mean, it's Luke. Who'd protest?"

I had to ask. "Did you?"

"Did I what?"

"Did you and Luke... You know. Were you ever..."

"Ever more than just professional?" Maria's eyes went distant, and her perfect mouth curved into a smile. "I'll never tell," she said serenely.

Bloody hell.

I eventually crawled off to bed, painkillers and exhaustion overwhelming me, while Maria curled up on the sofa under my sleeping bag. But I couldn't sleep. I kept thinking about what she'd said. If a building falls down on someone you fancy, you get them off to the A&E pretty sharpish. You check for concussion straight away. You don't stop for a quick shag.

God, now I felt like one of those Victorian heroines in the sort of melodramatic novels I have always despised, like they used to make us read at school. Marianne Dashwood. Tess of the d'Urbervilles. "Taken advantage of." Jesus.

I was a modern woman. I could take care of myself. I could go out and have sex with whoever I wanted. In theory, anyway. People did not take advantage of me.

Right, when I saw Luke I was going to kick him in the head. Hard. With stilettos.

When I wasn't so crippled, obviously.

I guess I must have eventually fallen asleep, my pillow wet (what was wrong with my hormones? Was my Pill malfunctioning?), because you have to be asleep to be woken up. And I was woken. Very rudely.

There was a smash, a crash, then Maria's voice—"Jesus fucking Christ!"

I stumbled out of bed, groggy and frightened, to see her stamping on my sleeping bag. It was smoking.

She looked up. "Do people often throw Molotov cocktails through your window?"

I'm afraid at that point I fainted.

When I woke up again, I was in a dark car going at lightning speed. "Maria?"

She was driving. "Nice to see you."

I wiped a bit of drool from my mouth. Very sexy. "What's—where are we going?"

"Luke's. He wasn't kidding about it not being safe for you."

Rats. Now I'd have to face him. And I really didn't want to face him.

And his revolver was still under my bed at home.

At least, I hoped it was.

She pulled up, and I realised I was cocooned in my duvet, a bag on my lap. "What's this?"

"Overnight stuff. Deodorant and toothpaste and stuff. I might have forgotten a few things. Come on."

She was brisk and swift, not like the companionable girl who'd been comparing *Buffy* beaux with me earlier. Before the firebomb.

Shit, someone firebombed my flat. My little flat! What had it done to anybody?

"What about Ted?" I wailed, and Maria looked at me.

"Ted?"

"My car."

She rolled her eyes. "Your car is fine. Come on, get out."

Luke appeared at the top of the steps to his door, blond hair tousled, wearing a faded T-shirt and boxers, looking like sex personified. Like really angry sex personified.

I wasn't sure whether to be turned on or frightened out of my wits. But I was too tired to be turned on and I seemed to have left most of my wits behind in that collapsed building site. I opted for weary haughtiness, and feel I failed somewhat.

He didn't say anything to me as he took my bag and slammed back inside with it, leaving me to shuffle up the stairs with my duvet, Maria following. She dumped a cardboard box on the table and lifted a hand in farewell.

"You two are as crazy as each other," she said. "I'm going back to check your place out, Sophie. I'll call you if I find anything."

And with that she was gone, the door was closed, her car sped away, and it was just me and Luke looking at each other.

"You bloody deserved it," he said.

"Don't tell me *you* threw that thing through my window?"

He threw me a sarcastic look. "No, but maybe next time I will. Jesus, Sophie," he stalked over to the door and started punching in a code on the control box, "what were you thinking?"

"I was thinking, I'm hurt and I want to go home and lick my wounds."

He paused and raised an eyebrow at me.

"Oh, fuck off," I snarled tiredly, clutching my duvet about me. "You'd have done the same thing. Why didn't you set the alarm when I was here before?"

He sighed. "The same reason I dropped off a box of DVDs at your house. I knew you'd go back."

I stared at him. He knew? Then why was he so mad? "Those are your DVDs?"

"Yes. You seem to have a mild obsession." He started poking around in my bag. "Do you have your stun gun and things?"

"I don't know. Maria packed it."

"What were you doing?"

Drooling unconsciously. "I passed out," I mumbled.

"Jesus. Sophie," Luke came over and lifted my chin. "Look. If you want out of SO17 then tell me. It'll be easier sooner rather than—"

"Out?" I stared at him. "Luke, before all this the most exciting thing that used to happen to me was getting two numbers on the lottery."

"You need three to win a tenner."

"I know. But I've never got three. God, *one* is cause for celebration. I never win anything," I said moodily.

"You don't want to get out?"

"No! Why would you think that?"

He ran his hands through his hair. "I don't know. You've been through a lot. People have flaked out before on less than this."

"Yes, well, not me."

"Aren't you frightened?"

I was bloody terrified. Of everything. "Not really," I said, and Luke smiled for the first time that night.

"Liar."

Neither of us could sleep, so we sat up watching all the *Buffy* featurettes and episode commentaries. Luke was quite the aficionado—he knew more about it than me. It was bizarrely endearing.

"So what were you doing all day that was more important than keeping an eye on me?" I asked as the sky started to get light.

"Checking out Wright and any possible partners. He was right when he said it was no one well known. He's got no history of working with anyone. He doesn't even need to link himself with a bank, since he has his own."

"It wasn't that Jane... no," I yawned, "that Helen woman?"

"You made up the Helen woman," Luke reminded me. We were sitting side by side on the chesterfield. I was still wrapped in my duvet and Luke had taken a corner of it. I could feel his leg through the fabric of my pyjamas. It was making concentration quite hard. "I checked out Jane Hammond. She's been running a shipping company in Seattle for years. Wright hasn't even been to the west coast since they broke up. I'm pretty sure it's not her."

"Then who is it?"

"Did you consider your friend Harvey?"

I stared at the screen. Buffy was crying about something. "Harvey? He works for a cell phone company."

Luke sighed. "I know you're on medication and in shock so I'm going to ignore that. I was checking Wright's records—hotels, plane tickets, that sort of thing—and everywhere he went, Harvey went also."

I opened my mouth but couldn't think of anything to say. On screen, the Scoobies all hugged each other tearfully. "Harvey?" I repeated eventually, because it was the only thing that got to my vocal chords. "He couldn't be the partner."

"He did turn up at Wright's hotel room."

"Maybe he's Wright's boyfriend," I said peevishly. "Did you think of that?"

"You kissed a gay man? Was he better than me?"

I felt myself colour. "I'm not going to answer that," I said, "on the grounds that you'll probably hit me."

Luke made a face. "Look, about what happened last night—"

"I've forgotten it already."

He looked surprised. "Liar."

He didn't cuddle you, I reminded myself. *He didn't come round to check up on you. He doesn't really care about you.*

Oh, but he did give you those DVDs.

"If you'd had any kind of respect for me, you wouldn't have done that," I said.

"'Done that'? I'm not a Victorian villain, Soph—" Luke began, starting to smile, twirling an imaginary moustache. Damn him for thinking of the same thing I did!

"You bloody acted like one. You took advantage of me, Luke Sharpe, when I was physically and emotionally vulnerable. And you didn't call me—"

"I did!"

"To have a go at me. You couldn't even be bothered to come round in person. You sent Maria instead. God, I deserve a little bit more respect than that."

Now, in the light of the last few days, I wasn't entirely sure if that last bit was true or not, but I was damned if I was going to give him anything.

"Maria is a highly trained government agent. Didn't she protect you?"

"Yes, but I—but..." To my absolute horror, I felt my eyes prick with tears. Oh, great timing, eyes. Fabulous.

"But what, Sophie?" Luke asked, his voice soft now, his eyes gentle, and I couldn't look at him.

But... But I needed you, *Luke. I needed you to take me in your arms and promise me you'd protect me. I needed you to tell me that last night had been wonderful and you hoped it'd be the start of a great relationship. I needed you to tell me there was something between us that wasn't sex or sarcasm. I was scared, and you were somewhere else.*

"But you weren't there," I said as strongly as I could.

"I was there," Luke said. "I stayed with you all night. I was worried about you, Soph."

"You left before I woke up," I said, trying not to be impressed by that.

"I had work to do, you know that. I couldn't stay home and baby-sit you."

Baby-sit me? First I was incapable of taking care of myself, now I needed to be baby-sat?

I hardened my resolve, and then my jaw, to match. "You yelled at me and then stayed away. That's so damn cowardly."

I saw his face change, saw the anger creep in, and knew I'd hit a nerve. RAF officers weren't cowardly. SAS operatives were not cowardly. And SO17 agents were definitely not cowardly.

With the possible exception of me.

"Cowardly?" Luke said, his voice carefully controlled. "Because I didn't come round to tuck you in and pat you on the head? Because I had more important things to do, like try and figure out who had shot at you? There are more important things in this job than mollycoddling, Sophie, and if you don't get that—"

"No, I get that," I snapped. "I get all of it. I know personal relationships have to take a back seat—"

"Back seat? They're out on the damn road—"

"Exactly. And you knew that, but you still—"

"Okay, so maybe I shouldn't have!"

"Yeah, maybe you shouldn't!"

We glared at each other, and I'd have felt a lot better about the argument if I hadn't still been wrapped up in my duvet with the little cartoon cats on it.

"Well, it won't happen again," Luke muttered, looking away. "I do have some sense of self-preservation. Unlike *some* people."

I ignored that. "If you hadn't locked me in, I wouldn't be here," I said. "Give me my bloody keys and let me go home."

"You're going to walk home in your pyjamas?"

"Yes," I said, sticking my chin in the air, and then I thought about it, and it was a really stupid image. And then I made the mistake of glancing at Luke, and his mouth was twitching with amusement too, and I had to look away before I started laughing.

Damn him. Damn him for making me angry, and damn him for making me laugh. And double damn him for sitting there looking so bloody desirable in the low light, strong and sure and everything I wanted, even if he wasn't everything I needed.

"Okay," he sighed. "Bed."

I stared. God, I hope I wasn't blushing. "Were you not listening back there?"

"I don't mean together. I mean to sleep. Separately. I don't know about you but I'm knackered. You are an exhausting woman, Sophie Green."

I'm not sure if that was a compliment or not.

Chapter Fourteen

I awoke, for the second time in as many days, in Luke's big soft white bed. Alone.

Dammit.

Everything was warm and cosy and I was really only half awake when I realised I really needed to pee. Don't you hate that? All I wanted to do was go back to sleep. Sleep was good. I didn't want to get up.

But I did get up, sighing, and stumbled into the bathroom. My toothbrush leaned against Luke's in the mug by the sink and I tried to tell myself it meant nothing. But my stomach still did a back flip at the sight of it.

I went back into the bedroom and looked at the crumpled bed. He'd put clean sheets on and they smelled of fabric softener. It was ridiculous. I was getting heartfelt over fabric softener.

Well, he'd taken the sofa, acting like a gentleman for possibly the first time since I met him. Not that I recall being particularly gracious about it. I think my exact words were, "You seduced me when I was concussed, Sharpe. Sleep on the sofa or sleep outside, but you ain't coming anywhere near my bed."

"It's my bed, Sophie," he reminded me, looking slightly amused.

"Well, I'm going to be in it. Alone," I said, and stomped off in as dignified a way as I could manage, given that I was wearing his sports socks and was still huddled in my cat duvet.

I fear this was not particularly dignified at all.

Part of me had expected him to come crawling under the covers in the middle of the night, and been quite disappointed when he hadn't. He was still asleep on the chesterfield, wrapped in my duvet. His hand was up by his face, his hair was tousled, and he looked adorable.

Jesus, Sophie, get a grip! Do not *fall for Luke.* That would not be a smart thing to do.

I sighed and padded over to the kitchen, looking for coffee. One of those filter things would be nice, but I'd settle for instant. I wasn't fussy.

Coffee made, I went and stood by the chesterfield, watching Luke sleep. There was no harm in looking. Didn't everyone want to look at things that were beautiful? Like art and stuff. It was human nature.

Yeah. Human nature to stare at someone who *hadn't bloody called.*

Bastard.

Then the bastard spoke, and I scalded my hands with spilt coffee.

"Sophie," he said, "why are you standing there staring at me?"

How did he know? *How* did he know? His eyes were still closed! Did he have see-through eyelids or something?

No, he probably did. With bionic X-rays or something. Bet he could tell what colour my underwear was.

I blushed, because I was, um, still wearing his underwear.

"How long have you been awake?" I asked as coolly as I could, fetching kitchen roll to wipe up the coffee, keeping my flushed face turned away from him.

"Since you put the kettle on." He yawned and stretched and opened his eyes. "Make us a coffee, will you?"

I made a face. "What am I, your housekeeper?"

He rolled his eyes. "Okay, fine, I'll do it." He pushed back the duvet and stood up. He was barechested and golden all over.

Hello.

Get a goddamn grip, Sophie. He's doing this on purpose.

And it's bloody working.

Bastard.

Luke pulled on his T-shirt, which I suppose was probably for the best, and wandered into the kitchen. "Sleep well?"

"Like a log." It was nearly midday. I couldn't believe we'd stayed up so long.

"How's your shoulder?"

I shrugged experimentally. "Not too bad."

"Can I see?"

This would mean I'd have to take my pyjama top off. Not a good move, the way I was feeling. "Erm, you know what, I'm going to take a shower first," I said. "Freshen up."

"How are you going to take a shower without getting the dressing wet?"

I held up a finger in a "wait" gesture, and retrieved the cling film. Luke stared.

"You're kidding."

I shook my head. "Worked yesterday."

He laughed. "You're unbelievable. Okay. Shower's yours. I'll help you change the dressing when you come out."

I looked him over, leaning against the kitchen counter in his T-shirt and boxers, sipping his coffee, his hair tousled, looking sleepy, and took a deep breath.

"Luke..."

"Hmm?"

Can we share the shower? Can we please have sex one more time? Just so I know it's still good when I'm not concussed?

"Can I borrow your shampoo?"

He frowned, and nodded. "It's by the shower."

Dammit. I was such a coward.

I turned the shower water to cold, but it didn't help much. All I could think of was Luke and his bare chest and his sleepy eyes. I was pathetic. I was like a horny teenager. Although, come to think of it, I wasn't that horny when I was a teenager, so maybe I was making up for it now. Yeah. That's what it was. Not my fault at all.

He was waiting for me when I came out, making me jump. "The dressing," he said, holding up some gauze and scissors. I went and sat on the bed, clutching my towel very tightly, while Luke inspected the stitches and cut a clean piece of gauze to cover them. He was dressed, more's the pity, and somehow managed to smell really good without having gone anywhere near the bathroom.

"Look at you, all serious," I teased, trying to distract him from my rapidly rising pulse rate.

"Combat medical training. If you make a mistake early on, it can make for serious problems." His face was grim, and I didn't want to ask about it any more. Luke was scary when he went all professional.

Then he looked up, and his face was neutral again. "Breakfast?"

I found some clean knickers in my bag, but no bra and no other clothes, so it was either pyjamas again or Luke's clothes.

He looked me over when I came out in joggers and a T-shirt, and his eyes fixed on my chest. "No bra?"

"Maria didn't seem to think I'd need one."

"I like Maria."

I rolled my eyes. "I need to go home and pick some things up."

"I'll do it."

"No, I need to go."

"No, you don't. Unlike some people in this room, I'm quite good at following instructions."

I made a face. What I needed was to somehow get that revolver out from under my bed and back in Luke's secret cupboard before he noticed it was missing.

"So, what are we doing today?" I asked as Luke handed me a plate of toast.

"*I* am going to see if I can find out who chucked a Molotov cocktail through your window. *You* are staying here."

"Nice try."

"I mean it, Sophie. You need to rest and stay away from people who want to firebomb you. That wasn't an idle threat. If Maria hadn't been there you could have been killed."

If Maria hadn't been there. "So, what, you think I'm totally helpless? You think I need to be locked away from danger? I'm a bloody secret agent, Luke, and you won't even let me have a gun."

"You need a licence—"

"So get me a fucking licence!" Aware that I was shouting, I tried to lower my voice. "How am I supposed to protect myself if all I have is a green dye defence spray?"

"You have the stun gun."

"Maria didn't pack it." I drummed my fingers on the counter. "I mean it. I need weapons, not bubble wrap."

"A weapon makes you a target," Luke said calmly, finishing his coffee and rinsing out the cup. "You're not getting one."

I scowled at him as he sauntered away from me into the bathroom and locked the door.

"What if I just upped and left?" I said. "I did it yesterday. You can't keep me here."

"There's a keypad alarm on the inside and outside of that door," Luke said from inside the bathroom. "All the windows are laser-sensored. *I* couldn't break into this place."

"Doesn't tell me much," I grumbled. "You can't keep me here," I repeated in frustration.

"I can. I'm your superior and I can."

"You're such a bastard." I kicked the door and flounced out to watch TV.

I was checking the news when he came back out, shaved and dressed and smelling even more divine.

"You'll be fine on your own," he said. "I have steak knives if you want self defence."

"Thank you. Now I have something to attack you with."

He sauntered over and pulled me to my feet. "Sophie," he said, stroking my face, "don't be mad at me. This is for your own safety. As soon as I have a handle on this, I'll let you know."

"I'm coming with you."

"Out in public without a bra?" He traced the outline of my breast. "You wouldn't."

"Try me."

He grinned and took my hands in his. "I'll call you if I get anything," he said, and pretty much before I'd realised what he was doing, he'd whipped out a pair of handcuffs and locked one bracelet around my wrist, and the other around the standard lamp by the chesterfield. "Stay where you are," he added, stepping back quickly, and I lashed out at him, the lamp swaying alarmingly.

"You bloody, bloody bastard!"

Luke laughed and dropped the key in his pocket. He went over to the door and tapped in a code, shielding it with his hand so I couldn't see, and slipped out. "See you later..."

"Wanker," I yelled, and I could hear him laughing as he set the external alarm. "Bloody arsing bollocking fucking *wanker*."

My phone was on the kitchen counter and I stretched as far as I could, but I couldn't reach it. I glared at the lamp. The lamp stood there, looking heavy.

I picked it up, my aching body protesting, and carried it over to the kitchen. A modern ball and chain. I suppose he thought this was funny.

It took me most of the morning to free myself. The lamp was heavy and my back was killing me by the time I located a screwdriver in the cupboard by the door. I unscrewed the top and bottom sections of the lamp and presto! I was free.

"Stupid bloody lamp," I glared at it, then put it back together. I didn't want Luke to figure out how I'd got free so easily. I put the screwdriver away and made more coffee while I thought.

So. All the windows had laser sensors on them—he hadn't been kidding, I could see the thin red lines. Good job he didn't have a cat. There was the keypad inside the front door, and apparently one outside it as well. I could get one of his guns and shoot the damn things, but they were all unloaded, and I'd probably set the alarm off anyway.

I could get the phone book out, call the roofing place downstairs, and get them to break in for me. No. No broken windows. I didn't want to leave this place vulnerable and then get chewed off for letting it get broken into.

I could call the fire brigade or the police, but that would bring me to the same place.

I could call Luke and beg.

I could try to disable the locks.

Of all my options, the last one seemed the most appealing. But I had not got a clue how to. I told you I'm anathema to computers. Just when I think I'm starting to understand them, they shut down or reboot or do something incomprehensible.

Then I had a brain wave. I got my phone, and dialled Five.

"Sophie Green?"

I took a deep breath. "Macbeth. I need a favour."

He laughed when I told him I needed to break out of somewhere, and laughed even more when I told him where.

"So wait a minute. He's got you locked inside his house without no clothes—"

"I have clothes, but they're his."

"Too bad it ain't the other way round. I'd love to see him in a dress."

"But can you do it?" I asked. "Can you disable those alarms?"

"Are they just alarms, or are they really locks too?"

I looked at the one inside. "I think this one's just an alarm. I think the one outside is a lock, like the ones we have at the airport."

"Windows?"

"Laser sensors. I don't know if they're triggered to an alarm or if I'll get shutters clanging down on me."

"Hmm. Where are you?"

I told him, and he said he'd be there in ten minutes.

I washed out my coffee cup, put all my things back in my bag and looked at the bunch of keys Maria had thrown in. There was Luke's front door key—in duplicate—much good it had done me. I needed to learn the code from his front door before I could break in now.

Macbeth knocked on the door nine minutes later. "I think I got this one," he said, and the door clicked open.

"I'm impressed. What did you do?"

He held up a little gadget. "Scanned it. You want the code?"

"Yes, please."

I wrote it down in my little diary, then the inside code too. I taped Luke's original key back inside the drawer where I'd found it, slapped a little note on the kitchen counter and beamed at Macbeth.

"I owe you big time," I said. "Massive. Anything you want."

He looked at me speculatively. "Take off your shirt."

I gaped. "Anything but that."

He grinned. "I ain't gonna do anything, I just want to see you."

"That's all?"

"Then we're even."

He got me out of a securely locked house. Sure I could flash him.

Closing my eyes, I pulled off Luke's T-shirt.

"Oh, baby," Macbeth said.

I pulled it back on. "That's your lot."

"Honey, I'll unlock a door for you any time." He grinned. "You want me to set the alarm before we go?"

"Please."

I waited at the top of the stairs. It was cold outside and I was glad I'd half-inched a sweater from Luke's drawer.

"So what were you doing locked in there?"

I rolled my eyes. "He thinks it's unsafe for me to go out."

"Is it?"

"No! One firebomb doesn't mean I'm not safe."

Macbeth shook his head. "Maria told me. You gotta pick the right bottle for a Molotov cocktail."

I'd bear that in mind.

He offered me a lift and led me to a blue Corsa. "Tell me this is not your car."

"Course not. I'm undercover."

I hated to tell him, but the only place he'd be convincing undercover is in a cell block.

"You got a bondage thing going on?" Macbeth glanced at the handcuffs I was still sporting.

"No. I think this is Luke's idea of a joke."

"So are you really not sleeping with him?" he asked, and he looked disappointed when I shook my head violently.

"Luke? No. I'm not nuts."

Macbeth said nothing.

We pulled up at my flat and I stared at the kitchen window which had been broken yesterday but was now fixed. "You want me to check the place over for you?"

I started to say no, then I nodded. "Thanks."

"No problem." He got a gun out of his jacket and advanced on the door. "You gonna unlock it?"

I tried, and then I found that the key didn't fit.

"Son of a bloody bitch changed my locks!"

Macbeth grinned. "No problem." He aimed the gun at the door and shot the lock off. "I just changed them, too."

I added "call locksmith" to my mental to-do list and followed Macbeth inside.

"No bodies," he said, coming out of the bedroom. "Nothing broken. You got your TV and shit. You're fine."

"Thanks," I said again. "For everything."

"Hey, we're comrades now. If I ever need to, you know..." he waved his hand as he apparently tried to think of something I could do better than him, "accessorise or something, I'll give you a call."

I tried not to smile. "And I'll be glad to help."

He left, the Corsa trundling away, and I looked at my door in despair. Right. First clothes—I never thought I'd miss a bra that much. I put one on, revelling in the support, and then put a spare in my Ace bag.

Also on my to-do list: buy a Mary Poppins bag. I really couldn't carry the Ace one around out of uniform without looking like an idiot.

I called an emergency locksmith. I checked on yesterday's finger. It was there, but the other two, which had been in a different drawer (I had a lot of ice-cream to fit in that compartment, okay?) had gone. So Luke definitely had a key to my flat.

Or at least he'd had one before Macbeth shot the lock off.

I had to start looking up security firms in the Yellow Pages. I wanted Luke-style alarms on my front door and all my windows, especially since they were all on the ground floor. Maybe shutters, too. No more firebombs for me.

I needed to get Angel's jewellery back to her—I was hoping quite desperately that Luke had locked it away somewhere safe—and see what sort of state her Ladyboat's dress was in. I also needed to haul ass up to my parents', get the leftover flooring from the garage, and replace the burnt floorboards in the living room.

And when I'd done all that, I needed to work out who had caused the wood to be burnt and who had shot at me the night before last.

The first thing I did was make some more coffee and take some more painkillers. I brushed my hair and put some make-up on, grimacing at the bruise that had come up on my temple. My whole body was a collection of bruises and grazes but they were all covered up. No wonder Luke hadn't made a move on me this morning.

Then I got out my toolbox (yes, I have a toolbox. I am a Modern Woman. Look upon me and tremble) and sawed off the dangling bracelet from Luke's handcuffs. I was stuck with the other one for now, but maybe I could pretend it was a new line in jewellery.

The locksmith turned up, frowning. "I already came out here once today," he said.

"Yes. Erm. Well, you see, my *friend* thought it would be great fun to get the locks changed on my flat. So I couldn't get in."

"So you shot the lock off? You've been watching too many American cop shows."

"Can you repair it?"

"You'll probably need a new door."

"If I get a new door can you fit a damn lock?"

He appeared taken aback by this. "Well, yes, but—"

"But?"

"I can't wait here while you go—"

"Yes," I said, "you can. And you will. Because I still have the gun that made that hole and I've been having a really bad couple of days. So either you sit here and wait while I fetch a new door, or—"

He held up a hand. "I'll wait! Only fifteen minutes to get to Homebase, anyway," he added with a weak smile.

I was glad he'd interrupted, because I had a feeling if I'd finished that sentence, *I* might have called the police on me.

"Make yourself at home," I mumbled, and rushed out to Ted. Lovely, solid, dependable Ted.

When I got to Homebase, I realised that there were a million different kinds of door and a million different sizes. Swearing, I called my home number and snarled at the answer phone until the locksmith picked up and told me what size I'd need.

I grabbed a solid wood door and commandeered an assistant to take it to the check-out and put it in my car. This spy stuff was costing me a fortune.

When I got back the locksmith was watching Sky News, but he hurriedly leapt to his feet and started to fit my new door.

"What happened to your floor?" he asked.

"What? Oh, firebomb," I said, glancing at the TV and then double-taking. They were showing the Ace desks at Stansted. Ooh, Sven looking hot. I turned the volume up.

"...a massive dip in confidence for this airline, which has been steadily losing business since November. Passenger numbers are down and many people are trying to cancel their flights. But Ace's policy, like that of most low-cost airlines, is not to offer refunds, which is further angering many worried passengers."

I stared. What the hell had happened?

"You want the handle on th—" the locksmith began, and I waved a hand for him to shut up.

Then the TV started showing pictures of plane wreckage. Numbers scrolled across the screen—missing, injured, trapped.

Dead. Times and places. Weeping relatives. Cardboardy executives.

Ace flight 128 to Glasgow had crashed in North Yorkshire, destroying a primary school and instantly killing seventy-eight children, five teachers, two pilots, three crew, and fifty-five passengers.

I watched it scroll across my TV. *A hundred and forty-three people are dead, and it's all your fault, Sophie Green.*

"You got a letter box?" the locksmith called out, and I marched into the bedroom, retrieved the revolver and aimed it at him.

"Shut the fuck up," I said. "This is important."

I tried to digest the details but I couldn't take it all in. Flight recorders, safety checks, radio transmissions. There were half a dozen survivors, all in ICU. I was finding it hard to breathe.

Eventually I managed to pick up my mobile, one hand still aiming the gun somewhere in the vicinity of the door, and dialled Luke.

"Have you seen the news?"

"Sophie?"

"*Have you seen the news?*"

"What? No, I've been—"

"Switch on the TV, or a radio or something. Go online."

"What's happened?"

I told him.

"Shit," Luke whispered. "Seriously?"

"Yes, Luke, seriously. A hundred and forty-three people."

"Jesus."

"I know."

Both of us were silent for a bit. Then Luke asked, "What the hell is that noise?"

The locksmith was drilling. Luke thought I was still at his place.

"I don't know," I said sweetly, "if I look out of the window I'll set off the lasers."

"Sophie—"

"It's okay. I'm all right. But, Luke, this crash. Don't you think it's suspicious?"

"You think Wright's desperate enough to make a plane crash? You think he's bright enough?"

"I think Wright is being manipulated," I said. "I think he has someone very nasty in partnership."

"Your friend Harvey?"

"Why do you think it's Harvey?"

"He's been wherever Wright's been. Do you know his name isn't even Harvey? It's James Harvard."

"How do you even know it's the same person?" I asked incredulously.

"I Googled him. Found a picture."

Bloody hell. I can Google for hours and get nothing. I bloody hate people who can get precisely what they want from the Internet.

"I think you're clutching at straws," I told him. "And I don't think it's Harvey."

"Why the hell not?"

I sighed. I didn't really want to tell him. It sounded like an excuse.

"This partner? Wright said it was a woman."

"That doesn't mean—"

"He's not bright enough to do that on purpose," I said. "And besides, Luke, think of all the most vicious people you know. I bet most of them are female."

There was a silence. I'd dug myself into a hole here.

"The lady has a point," Luke said eventually. "Right. I'm going to see what I can get from Ace on this."

"You're just going to call them up?"

"No. I'm going to hack into their communications. I'm going to email you all the reservations we have for James Harvard. Every one has a different phone number. See if any of them are live. The password to get online is Sunnydale. Oh, and I'll see if I can get a manifest for the 128. See if anything looks suspicious."

With that cheerful request he signed off, and I was left with a bewildered and frightened locksmith, a new door with a mortise lock, and a lot of calls to make.

I paid the locksmith double, really hoping I'd get some nice cash from SO17 for this and knowing I probably wouldn't, and booted up the computer.

James Harvard had travelled all over the world with Wright. Every reservation gave a different address and phone number.

I hate making phone calls. The Internet was a revolution for me because I could keep in touch with relatives I didn't like and school friends I hardly talked to, I could order things and learn about things without having to talk to people. But this time I knew I was stuck.

"Hello," I said when the first number picked up. "Can I speak to Harvey, please? You don't know anybody called Harvey? I'm sorry, I must have dialled wrong. Thank you. Bye."

I then repeated this about a million times. Probably half the numbers I dialled weren't the numbers on the computer. I hardly cared. Harvey wasn't at the end of any of them.

I mean, really. Luke was talking crap. How could sweet, clever, clean-cut Harvey be involved in killing a hundred and forty-three people?

The computer bleeped to tell me I had new mail. I looked at the sender—Luke (LS17@aol.com, how original)—and the subject: *Now who's innocent?*

Dreading the message, I opened it up. It was the passenger manifest for the doomed AC128 to Glasgow. James Harvard had booked a ticket online, but he hadn't checked in.

Oh God.

I sat back in my chair, trying to put it together in my head. Harvey was in this horrible plot with Wright. Together they were sabotaging Ace Airlines so share prices would come down and they could buy it cheaply. It all seemed so overblown. If Wright wanted the airline that much then why didn't he pay full price for it?

I opened up Google and typed in David Wright. I got a million matches, half of which were irrelevant. I tried again with David+Wright+Wrightbank. This narrowed it down but mostly to press releases and financial advice sites.

I thought for a bit, then searched within the results for Ace Airlines.

Bingo.

There was a five month old interview from a dull business mag where Wright said he was interested in branching out into the aviation industry. "I think this is the most important part of the travel industry," he said. "Even more important than cars. People are flying where they would have driven or taken a train. Domestic flights all over the world have taken off—no pun intended. And since September eleventh, fares have plummeted. Passenger numbers have hardly diminished, but fares have gone down drastically. The low-cost sector of the market is incredibly interesting."

Not as incredibly interesting as you, I thought. This article had been published at about the time things started going wrong at Ace. I'd hardly noticed the change—there were always delays and tech problems, and over the summer things had been as frantic as ever. Around September, things started to quiet down. End of summer. I hoped.

But if I thought about it, then there had been increasing numbers of problems. Ace rarely cancelled flights but it had happened a few times. There were ATC strikes and delays. Little things, like an increase in the number of credit card payments that hadn't gone through. The wrong flight booked by mistake. Passenger numbers gradually easing off. Last week's Titan plane for Edinburgh, because ours was off tech.

And it had all been happening since last November.

I downloaded the interview and went back to Google. This time I searched for James Harvard. I got nothing—or rather, I got a lot of irrelevance. I tried James+Harvard+David+Wright. Still nothing.

I stared moodily at the computer screen, but that didn't help, either.

I was halfway through looking up next week's *Buffy* when my mobile rang. Not my Nokia, but my little old Siemens. I didn't recognise the number.

"Hello?"

"Sophie?"

The voice was familiar. “Yes?” I said doubtfully, trying to place it.

“It’s Sven. From Ace?”

Oh, yes, and there’s me thinking you’re the other Sven I know.

“Sven! How—how did you get this number?”

“From Angel. She said you’ve been ill.”

“Erm, yes. Flu, or something.”

“Are you all right?”

Still the same grave tone of voice. “I’m better. Still not quite right,” I added hastily, in case I was expected to go back to work, “but getting better.”

“I was thinking if you’re well enough maybe I could come and see you?”

Jesus.

It never rains but it pours.

Sven? Sexy Sven? You know, with everything that had been going on I’d hardly even thought of him. And I used to, all the time, my idle brain bringing up an image of his Caribbean blue eyes or his white-toothed smile.

My eyes travelled around the living room. There were videos all over the floor, plates and glasses piled up in the sink, the hole in the floorboards...

“I tell you what,” I said, staring at the monitor which was starting to blur, “I think it’d do me good to get out for a while. Why don’t I meet you somewhere?”

We arranged for Funky Joe’s in town in half an hour. I could get the train in and not worry about drinking and driving.

Oh, though. What about my one a day? What about emergencies? What about my painkillers? I might pass out.

So I’d not have much to drink. Just one unit. I’d tell Sven the truth. I’m on painkillers.

Well, it’s *part* of the truth.

I started to get dressed in something pretty, but then I remembered about my bruises and scratches and realised with a sinking heart that I’d have to cover up. I found a flimsy little cardigan in the back of my wardrobe and teamed it up with jeans and a strappy top. At least my hair was clean and being reasonably well behaved. And I could wear lipstick, if not eye make-up, because the bruise on my temple had broken to a cut and it hurt to touch that side of my face too much.

I locked up with my new keys, set bits of tape on the door, and drove into town.

Funky Joe's was an American bar and pretty much the only decent place to drink in town. Mostly it was full of airport workers who went in at odd hours and paid no attention to weekday protocols. I spied a few people I knew on my way in. It was surprisingly full.

And then I heard a burst of sound, and realised why. Sunday was Live Band Nite. And this Sunday, Chalker's band was playing.

I stood for a while, trying to remember if my parents were supposed to be coming to the gig. I didn't think so, but then you never knew. I saw more and more people I knew, school friends, people who lived in the village, other mates of the band. The same people I saw at every gig. Plus airport people. The place was packed with people who knew me.

And I had a massive bruise on my face. And one handcuffed wrist.

Marvellous.

I saw Sven by the bar, getting chatted up by the waitress, and stood for a while, taking in the beauty of the scene. This handsome man, glowing and gleaming like a golden god (can I alliterate, or what?) was waiting for me. Had asked me out.

He saw me and waved. "Sophie!" he cried over the sound of the music. "Are you all right?"

"I'm okay," I said.

He touched my face and I shied away, wincing. "What happened?"

"Oh, I, er, I walked into a door. The flu. It made me dizzy."

He nodded sympathetically and handed me a pint of lager. I hate lager, but since the last time we all came out for a drink and I switched from halves of cider to pints, because it took so long to get served, I've been known as the Girl Who Drinks Pints. And I guess cider does look like lager from a distance.

We found a table by a banquette, empty because the band was invisible from there, and smiled at each other for a few minutes.

"Do you like the band?" Sven asked after a while, seeing me mumbling along with the words.

"My brother's the bassist." He looked confused. "The bass guitar? With four strings? He plays that."

Sven looked impressed. "Oh, cool. So you know them all?"

"Went to school with them. They're pretty cool."

This is my practised speech for when the band get famous and I get interviewed as the gorgeous younger sister of the cool bassist. "Yeah, they're all really cool. Always in and out of the house, coming to see Chalker or just chill. We get on really well. We're like family."

Convincing? Cool? I think so.

The set ended and the band disappeared from the stage, reappearing in seconds at the bar. I saw Tom, waiting for a pint that was bigger than him, and flicked a beer mat at him.

He turned, saw me and bounded over.

"Soph! Thought you were ill."

I blinked. "Who told you that?" I hadn't spoken to my family in days.

"Chalker. Ran into that fit mate of yours, erm, Angel, in town. She said you'd got flu." He scrutinised me. "You don't look like you've got flu."

"I'm a genius with make-up."

"What happened to your face? Get in a fight?"

"Yeah. You should see the other guy."

We smiled at each other. Tom's like the little brother I never wanted.

"And who's this?" He looked Sven over and didn't seem impressed.

"Sven. We work together. Sven, this is Tom. He's the singer in the band," I added, realising a bit late that it was rather unnecessary.

"I like your music," Sven said politely. "What are your influences?"

Tom looked blank. "Pretty much whatever I'm listening to," he said.

"You sound like this Norwegian band I know, called Eek! They're a rock band..."

I tuned out. Eek! didn't sound like anything I wanted to hear about. And from Tom's expression, he felt the same way.

I let my gaze roam over the room. Kids I did my A levels with. Kids who borrowed my GCSE notes. Kids who I played hopscotch with at primary school. Kids who peed their pants at playschool. It felt like I knew everyone in the bar. Including...

Oh, Jesus. Oh, bloody hell.

"Can you excuse me a minute?" I said, and Tom gave me a murderous look. I ignored him and slipped away across the room, to where a man with green eyes was propping up the bar and glaring at me.

"I got your note," he said. "Very funny."

I bit my lip. I'd torn out a page from my diary and scrawled, "Shame I wasn't in *The Great Escape*," and added a winker.

I said *winker.* Like an emoticon? Don't be filthy.

"Oh, come on, Luke." I nudged him. "It was a little bit funny."

"I thought you'd been kidnapped. Again."

I put my head on one side. "How long were you in the flat before you saw the note?"

He scowled and didn't answer. I grinned.

"You were worried about me."

"You're a liability. I should fire you."

"For escaping from a securely locked flat? You should promote me."

Luke stared moodily at the empty stage.

"Anyway," I said, "what are you doing here?"

"Following you."

"Why?"

"Thought I'd get into the mindset. Trouble follows you all the time."

"You think of that all by yourself?"

He said nothing.

"How did you know I was here? I didn't see you following." I'd been careful to check my rear-view all the time. I was like driving school fresh.

"No, well, you wouldn't, because I was three cars behind all the time. Your car is like a sore thumb in fit finger land."

It was my turn to scowl. "Ted's a great car."

"And I still can't believe you named it."

"So I have an emotional attachment to my car."

"Is that wise?" Luke sipped at his pint. Proper dark beer, not lager.

Show off.

"Anyway," he went on, "what are you doing out here with Sven the Stuffy?"

"He's not stuffy."

"He's really boring. He has no conversation."

"Not with you. And he is speaking a second language."

"I can sparkle in several languages—"

"One of which is obviously not English." I glanced at Luke. Green had been an appropriate choice of eyewear. "If you must know, he asked me out."

"You're on a date?" Luke asked incredulously.

"It's not illegal, is it?" It probably was. Section 12, paragraph 16: Government Agents shall not date cute Norwegians. That would pretty much be my luck.

"You do have work to do."

"I have been Googling all afternoon. I found something on Wright but it wasn't very interesting. Just that he said in November he wanted to buy up an airline. I 'mailed it to you."

"Did you find anything on Harvard?"

"You mean Harvey?" I teased. "I still don't think it's him. I mean, I don't think Harvey is Harvard."

"I think he is. You've seen how he tends to turn up a lot. I don't believe in coincidences."

I made a face. "I tried all those numbers. They've never heard of him."

"Then isn't that suspicious?"

"Maybe he just wants to protect his privacy."

"Yeah. Maybe he doesn't want to be found."

I sighed and looked around. Sven was alone, apparently having failed to convince Tom on the merits of Eek!

"I should get back," I said.

"Try to sound happier about it."

What did he expect? "My head hurts. You keep trashing my friends—"

"Harvard is *not* your friend."

"I got another finger."

Luke sighed. "What'd you do with it?"

"Freezer. And by the way, who gave you permission to break in and have my locks changed?"

I may have said that a little loudly. People were giving Luke looks of disgust.

"I was trying to keep you out."

"You failed." I gave him a brittle smile. "Are you going to follow me home?"

"Probably."

"I'll see you then."

As I walked away, Luke called out, "Did he notice your hair?"

I ignored him and walked back over to Sven, whose face lit up. "Who were you talking to?"

"Old friend. Mate of the band." How could he not see that Luke was Luca? It was blindingly obvious.

"He didn't look happy to see you."

"Hmm. Yeah. We used to go out."

"But you finished with him?"

"Er, yeah."

"Then he must be sad. I would be." Sven gave me a puppy-dog look, and I smiled. He was really sweet.

The band started up again, and I turned to listen. Tom was singing "Don't Listen To Him", which is an old one of theirs and one of my favourites. He kept looking over at me.

How sweet! He knows I love this song. Everyone was being very sweet to me today.

Apart from Luke, that is. He was watching me and scowling. I raised my glass in salute and tried not to grimace at the lager.

Sven put his arm around my shoulders and I snuggled up to him, giving Luke a smug look. But Luke wasn't listening. He was talking on his phone.

Hmph.

They finished the song, and Tom looked around the room.

"How is everybody?"

There was a babble of noise as people yelled stuff back.

"Yeah, the same to you. Good to see so many old faces…and so many new ones…" He looked over at me again. I'd brought a new face. I beamed back at him. "Don't nobody go nowhere."

The next song started, and Sven stood up. "Excuse me, I have to go to the bathroom."

So polite. Most of the Ace boys would be like, "I'm going for a slash. Back in five." Not Sven. He's so polite.

Even if he is a little boring.

But politeness is important. We can't all be entertainers.

Luke loped over. "Got rid of him?"

"He's gone to the bathroom."

"Let's hope he locks himself in, eh?" He waved his phone. "Just got a call from Lexy. James Harvard checked into the airport Hilton half an hour ago."

Alexa had access to hotel records? Put paid to any ideas of a dirty weekend.

Although, if it was with Sven, it'd be worth it to piss Luke off.

"So what does that mean?" I asked. "Is Wright there too?"

"No." Luke frowned. "But that means we can check out his room easier."

"We?"

"Yes. We. I need you to get in there."

"And how am I supposed to do that?"

"I don't know, you did it before. Play your cards right, you might even get to sleep with him this time."

I slapped him for that, and it felt *good.*

Luke put his hand up to his face, and slowly brought it back down again, his eyes on mine. I was partly horrified to see a handprint appearing there. And partly proud.

"So now we match," he said, touching my cheek, and I flinched.

"You're such an arsehole."

"Says she, going out with someone who doesn't even ask her what she wants to drink."

I opened my mouth, but Luke got there first.

"You've hardly touched it. I saw your face when you drank some. You hate lager."

I said nothing, but my face felt tight and my nostrils flared.

"Come on, Sophie, we have to go."

"Right now?"

"Yes. Right now."

"What about Sven?"

"Leave him a note. Isn't that your style?"

I nearly slapped him again for that. "Two things, Luke. Fuck. Off."

"You're funny."

"I've hardly slept in two days. I had to break out of your flat two days in a row, and I got another finger yesterday. There's probably another one on its way right now. I have a bruise on my face and a big headache—" to my horror I felt my eyes start to sting, "—so just piss off and stop bloody following me."

Unfortunately at that moment the song ended and Tom stopped singing and everyone heard the last bit I said. I glared somewhat tearfully at Luke.

"I think we should leave," he said quietly, and I nodded.

"Just let me say goodbye to Sven."

Luke looked at his watch. "How long has he been gone?"

"Since you came over."

"Too long."

"Maybe there's a queue."

Luke gave me a look.

"Maybe he's ill."

"We can only hope."

"Do you want me to slap you again?"

"That's such a girlie thing to do."

"I am a girl!"

"Can we just go?"

I folded my arms. "No."

"I could carry you out of here."

"Not unless you want me to beat the snot out of you. I will, you know," I added when Luke started laughing. "Look, can you just go and see where he is?"

"You want me to go and tell your boyfriend you're leaving with me?" Luke put his head on one side. "Okay."

"You're such an arsehole," I said again.

"I don't have to tell him."

"You do if you want me to go with you."

Luke sauntered off, grinning.

The band hadn't started the next song yet and I looked up at the stage to see what was taking so long. Tom was missing. Probably gone for another pint. He said his voice needs lubrication. He'd yet to come up with an excuse for the cigarettes.

And then Tom was beside me, grabbing my arm. I winced as his fingers dug into a bruise.

"Why aren't you singing?"

"I tried to get your attention earlier but you were all snuggly with your boyfriend."

"He's not my—what did you want?"

Tom lifted up Sven's drink. "He put something in this. I saw him drop it in. Like a pill or something."

"But that's his drink..."

"No," Tom grinned, and picked up my untouched pint, "this is his drink. I switched them when he wasn't looking."

I stared.

"Is he on drugs or something?" Tom asked.

"Sven? No, no, he's...he's Norwegian..." I said vaguely. "Just a sec." I needed to find Luke. "Keep an eye on these for me. Don't switch them or drink anything."

"I'm not stupid," Tom said, fiddling with his lip ring.

I dashed over to the toilets and saw Luke coming out of the gents.

"Where is he? Where is the little—"

"He's in there." Luke caught my arm before I could rush in. "He's out cold."

I stopped in my tracks like a cartoon character. "He's what?"

"Passed out on the floor. In a puddle of vomit." Luke shook his head happily. "It seems there is a God. How much did he have to drink?"

I stared at him. "That was meant for me," I managed.

"What was?"

"The vomiting and the passing out. Tom saw him put something in my drink."

"Tom?"

I grabbed his arm and pulled him back to my table. Tom was sitting there, looking bored.

"The things I do for you, Soph," he said.

"This is the first thing you've ever done for me," I said. "Payback for all those times I've picked you up from the pub and kicked your girlfriend out at her brothel. Tom, tell Luke what you saw."

"Saw?"

"What Sven did."

Tom looked Luke up and down. Apparently he approved of him more than Sven, because he said, "I saw him put something in her drink. When she was talking to you. So I switched the drinks. Then I had to go back on stage so I couldn't tell Soph..."

"So he drank whatever was meant for her?"

Tom nodded. "Pretty cool, huh?"

"Tom, you're a lifesaver."

"What did it do?"

"He threw up and passed out."

"Why not just give you vodka? I remember—"

"No reminiscences," I said firmly. "Come and give us a hand."

"What?" said Luke and Tom at the same time.

"To get Sven out of here. Don't you want to talk to him?" I asked Luke.

"I'd like to beat the crap out of him. Talking comes later."

"I second that," Tom said. "Where is he?"

Sweet little Tom. He's about four inches shorter than me and as skinny as a supermodel. He couldn't win a fight against Tammy.

I followed them over to the gents and waited outside. Then Tom trudged to the door, looking moody, and said, "He says you're stronger than me."

I bit back a laugh. He was right.

The gents was just like the ladies, only the ladies didn't have urinals. Still, it felt like alien territory. I was glad there was no one else in there.

Sven was indeed slumped on the floor and there was, indeed, a puddle of vomit all around him. And you know, maybe it was the scent of urine or the vomit in his hair or the fact that the fucker had tried to drug me, but suddenly he wasn't so cute any more.

I picked up Sven's feet and looked at Luke. "Just out of interest," I said, "are we going to carry him all the way through the bar?"

"Out this way," Tom said from the entrance, pointing to a side door. "The van's out here."

We shoved Sven in the back of the bandwagon and stood there looking at him.

"Now what?" I said.

"I have to get back," Tom said. "We're getting paid for two whole sets and Chalker'll kneecap me if he don't get his money."

I hugged Tom. "Thanks for your help."

He kissed my cheek. "Any time."

"We'll take him to the office," Luke said firmly as Tom disappeared inside and the door shut out the sound. "Sophie, go and get your car."

I did as I was told, and we hefted Sven into the back.

Luke looked at my wrist, where the handcuff bracelet still shone. "He didn't notice that, either. Have you got yours?"

"Is this appropriate?"

He grinned. "For Sleeping Ugly here. In case he wakes up. Cuff him to the seat belt and keep the doors locked. I'll follow you."

"How come I get him stinking up my car?"

"I have nicer upholstery." Luke chucked me under the chin. "I'll see you there."

I made a face and got into the car, revving far harder than was necessary, and sped out of the car park and off towards the airport. Sven was completely silent and still in the back. I wondered if he was dead. I wondered if I cared.

An hour or so ago, I fancied him completely. I couldn't believe he'd asked me out. This golden god, wanting me? Little old (well, okay, but big young doesn't have quite the same ring) me?

And then what? He drugged my drink. Was he a dealer? Was he going to rape me? Did I have anything in the car I could use to hurt him?

Luke pulled up behind me as I got out of the car and stood looking at Sven.

"Still think he's cute?"

"No. I'm going for 'vile' now."

"Right there with you."

I unclipped the cuffs from the seat belt, refastened Sven's wrists behind his back, and we carried him up the ramp to the office. Luke swiped his red pass, keyed in a code, and we were inside.

"Okay," he said as I blew bits of hair out of my face. "Remember how when you came in the first time and you were all disappointed it wasn't more James Bond?"

"I never said that!"

"Hell, I did when I first saw it. Anyway. We do have something here that's kind of cool." He dropped Sven's head on the floor with a satisfying thud, lifted a big file from the bookshelf by Alexa's desk, and fiddled with something on the wall.

Then the bookshelf parted in two, sliding away over the wall, cascading files and bits of paper onto the floor, to reveal a small elevator.

I gaped. Luke grinned. "Pretty cool, huh?"

"How is it possible you didn't tell me about this?"

He shrugged. "You didn't ask."

I narrowed my eyes. "I'm asking now. Where does it go?"

"Downstairs. The bunker."

We dropped Sven on the riveted steel floor and Luke swiped his card, keyed in his code and spoke his name into the microphone above the control panel.

There was a bleep, then we started moving.

"When we have a little more time, we'll set up your voice recognition," Luke said. "Lexy cannibalised an early voice recog phone to make this."

Clever Lexy.

The doors opened, and I looked out on the reason why SO17 had to hire someone as inexperienced as me.

There was money in here. Lots and lots of money.

Chapter Fifteen

"Jesus H," I said, stepping over Sven into the bunker.

"I know," Luke said.

"This is why SO17's broke?"

"Well, it has something to do with it. Alexa ordered it. Her own spec. We needed a lab..."

And a lab it was. The walls were steel and there were no windows, but a few vents that Luke assured me led to tanks with weeks of oxygen in them. There were racks and cupboards and microscopes and metal tables and the sort of scary stuff you usually only see in Frankenstein films.

"And then we have this," Luke said, picking Sven up by a foot and dragging him over to a cage on the far wall. "Maria and Macbeth have been down here working on this. Making it everything-proof."

I tapped the bars. They were set in inch-thick security glass. There was a small serving hatch with secure hinges and locks all over it, and a larger one, through which we shoved Sven. Luke swiped his card to open it, and again to close it. Both times he had to get voice authorisation.

We stood back and looked at Sven.

"I think he should be chained up," I said, and Luke grinned.

"Chains we can do." He opened a steel cupboard and pulled out some manacles. "Would you like to do the honours?"

"This is weird," I said as we chained Sven up to the wall.

"Not big on bondage?"

"You know what I mean."

"Never thought you'd have to chain up a co-worker, huh? Especially not one you fancy."

"Believe me, I've gone off him."

"Date rape'll do that."

"Do you think that's what it was for?"

Luke produced a bottle of the drugged lager from his backpack. "I'll get Lexy to analyse it tomorrow. But it was probably Rohypnol or something. Good job I was there."

We stepped out of the cage and Luke locked it up.

"Good job you were there? What did you do? It was Tom who switched the drinks."

"Could Tom have got Sven off you if you'd drunk the bad beer?"

"All beer is bad." I scowled and earned a smile from Luke.

"Yeah. Now, d'you want to stay here and prod him with one of these," he fetched something that looked like a cattle prod, "or do you want to go home and get some sleep?"

Sleep seemed like a very enticing prospect. "Where home?" I said. "If I go back to yours, you'll probably drug me to keep me there."

Luke gave me an indefinable look that brought me out in goose-pimples.

"You can't go to your place," he said quietly.

"It was fine when I got there. And I have new locks on the door. Lots of them. And I had bolts put on the windows."

"'Cos they'll stop another arson attack. Look. You can't go home alone."

"If you think you're staying—"

He laughed and took a step closer. "Would that be so bad?"

"It would be..." He was very close and it was getting harder to breathe. He still smelled really good. "It would be unprofessional."

Luke sighed. "Fine. Go home. Get blown up. See if I care."

Dammit. Wrong reaction. Plus there really was a possibility that someone might try to blow me up.

"I could go to my parents'," I suggested, and Luke nodded.

"Good plan. I'll stay at your place."

"Why?" Oh shit, the revolver.

"So I can look through your underwear drawer." He grinned, and amended, "So I can protect the place." He paused. "Do you have a fire extinguisher?"

I shook my head. "I don't even have a fire alarm. It kept going off at random and frightening Tammy."

"Jesus."

We stepped into the little lift. "How long do you reckon he'll be out?" I asked, glancing back at Sven before the lift doors swooshed shut. He was slumped very unattractively in the corner of the cell with vomit in his hair.

"Could be hours. He'll probably still be asleep tomorrow. If he isn't, we can always hit him over the head with something heavy."

I smiled. Luke could be okay when he wasn't yelling at me.

He locked up the office, having left a Post-it on Alexa's desk that we had a visitor who was to remain undisturbed, and we walked to our cars.

"So," Luke said.

"So." He looked good in the moonlight. Was he going to kiss me?

Did I want him to?

Oh, hell. When did my life turn into something so complex?

"So your car turned out to be useful for something after all." He gestured to Ted's back seat. "The vinyl, I mean."

God, I wish he hadn't said that.

"He's a very versatile car," I managed.

"Sure is." Luke tossed his keys up in the air and caught them backhanded. "Well, you officially have the day off tomorrow, despite your flu."

"Oh, yeah. But unofficially…?"

"Unofficially, you have to come back here pretty early to think of something to do with our Nordic friend."

"Not my friend," I said with feeling.

"Glad you realised that."

Luke went back to his place to pick up a fire extinguisher and his other overnight essentials, and I called my mother to say I'd be staying with her because they were starting building work again over the car park.

I really hoped that one wouldn't come true. And if it did, I really hoped I wouldn't be there when it did.

I got home and shoved some things into a bag. I wrapped the revolver up in my pyjamas and shoved it under my comfort copy of *Gone with the Wind*, heart beating fast, hoping Luke wouldn't turn up before I'd left.

But of course he did, standing there looking sexy while I rushed around trying to make the kitchen look as if a bomb hadn't exploded nearby. The fact that one nearly had wasn't much comfort to me.

"I'm going to follow you up to your parents'," Luke announced as I picked up my bag and keys. "Make sure you don't go anywhere you shouldn't on the way."

"What's that supposed to mean?"

"No sneaking off to Smith's Guns and trying to break in. Joe is strongly against people trying to break into his shop."

"Would I?" I tried to flutter my eyelashes but I was too tired.

Luke just grinned.

"Can you do something for me?" I asked, and he looked interested.

I held out my hand.

"Can you get rid of this damn bracelet?"

Luke looked vaguely disappointed, but he unlocked the cuff and I flexed my wrist gratefully, got in my car and drove off, Luke in my rear-view.

The ground was dry and he managed to follow me up the muddy drive to my parents' front door. There were lights on in all the downstairs rooms and I could see the TV through the window and Norma Jean was barking hysterically because there was someone outside.

Ah, home.

Then my mother opened the door, wearing a striped apron, a wineglass in her hand, and reached out to me.

"Love! What happened to you?"

I touched the bruise on my temple. "Oh, I just, I just walked into the bathroom door. It's nothing. Looks worse than it is."

The hell. It smarted constantly.

"Oh, love." She put down the wineglass and put her arms around me, and I nearly cried, because nothing in the world could make you feel as loved and protected as a hug from your mother.

Luke stood there in the darkness, holding my bag. "Where's your stuff?" Mum asked, and he held the bag up.

My mother gave me a look of great interest. "And who's this?"

"He's just a friend, Mum. Works at the airport." I tried to think of a reason why he might have followed me here but failed, and glanced back at Luke for help.

"Luke Sharpe." He held out a hand, and my mother shook it in delight. "Sophie's been a bit down, so I said I'd see her up here safely."

My mother looked very amused. "Well. Isn't that kind of him, Sophie?"

I nodded tiredly. "Thanks, Luke. I'll see you tomorrow?"

He nodded and, after a second's hesitation, kissed my cheek. He smelled really good. "Eight o'clock. Sleep tight."

After that? Fat chance.

My mother wanted to know all about Luke, but I said I was tired and ran off to bed, feeling mean. She was interested, and who wouldn't be? Here was I, treating her house like a hotel, turning up whenever I felt like it, dumping Tammy on her for nearly a week, and refusing to tell her anything.

I am never having kids. We're horrible.

Tammy ignored me when I came in, running away and being all catty and aloof, but half an hour after I switched out my bedroom light and lay there awake in the moonlight, the door opened. She slunk onto the bed, nosed under the duvet, and curled up in a tiny ball on my chest, purring loudly.

"Have you forgiven me, Tammy Girl?"

She licked my fingers and tucked her nose under her paw. Aww. Little baby Tammy. Sod kids, I'll have cats instead. Tammy's like a baby anyway—whiny, demanding, noisy and sometimes smelly, but ultimately adorable and loved unconditionally.

I must have finally fallen asleep, because I was woken up by Tammy's Pavlovian response to my dad's alarm clock, which is to leap out of bed, scarring me as she flies, and rush downstairs to be ready and waiting with her cute starved kitten look when he comes down to make tea.

I looked at the clock. Six-thirty. I'd said I'd meet Luke at the office in an hour and a half, but if I was clever...

I crept out of bed and got dressed quickly, slipped out of the house and into Ted. I'd like to have sidled quietly out of the drive, but there's a reason no one chooses a diesel as a getaway car. I could see my dad peering out of the living room window at me as I rumbled away.

Luke's house was closer than mine and the roofer's yard was empty as I parked on the road outside. Like I said, noisy car. I crept up to the front door, heart beating fast, and quickly keyed in the code on the keypad.

A long second while the machine thought about it, then a green light flashed and I turned the handle.

Nothing. Oh yeah, the key!

Once inside I knew I had twenty seconds to disable the alarm, but I also knew the code for that, and I did it without a sound. I disabled two alarms and broke into the most highly secure residence since Posh'n'Becks set up home, and *there was no one here to see me.*

Dammit.

I retrieved the right key and crept over to the hidden gun cabinet, not sure why I was being so quiet but also not willing to make any noise. Twenty seconds and the revolver would be hidden again and Luke would never have known I'd taken it.

Well, he'd never have known if I hadn't somehow set off an alarm when I opened the cupboard. Suddenly there was a cold metal gun pressed against the back of my head and Luke's voice was saying, "Stand up. Slowly."

I dropped the revolver and did as I was told, holding my hands in the air. Why the hell was he here?

"Now turn around. Keep your hands where I can see them."

I did and looked up guiltily at him. Luke stared back in shock.

"Sophie?"

"Um. Yeah."

"What the hell are you doing here?"

"I could ask you the same question. Will you put that bloody gun away?"

"Not until you tell me what you're doing breaking into my apartment."

"Aren't you supposed to be in *my* apartment?"

He raised his hands, and I relaxed as the gun swung away. "I came back to pick some stuff up. Jesus, Sophie, I thought someone had broken in."

"Well," I said, a little smugly, "they had. Me."

"How?"

"Magic."

"*How*?"

The gun was back. I made a face. "I disabled the locks."

He narrowed his eyes and I sighed. "Macbeth," I said. "How do you think I got out of here yesterday?" I pushed the gun away and stepped past him.

"Macbeth is here too?"

"No. He showed me how to do it. I learnt your codes, Luke," I said, going into the kitchen and switching on the kettle. I needed coffee to calm me down.

"Jesus Christ," he said, flicking a safety catch on the gun and tucking it under his belt. "You are a bloody menace."

I gave him a smile. "I'm using my initiative. You're supposed to be impressed."

"What were you doing breaking into my gun cabinet?"

"I was curious. Didn't know you had guns in there." Thank God he hadn't realised I'd nicked one. Shouldn't he have been more vigilant? Why hadn't he set the alarm when I was locked in?

"So what if I'd done that when I was locked in here?" I asked, searching for a teaspoon. "Would I have had to live with the alarm all day? I'd have gone mad."

"You already are," Luke muttered. "I switched off all the alarms when you were here. I knew you'd try and make a break for it. Didn't want to have the alarm wailing all day long. The guys downstairs complain about it."

"Nice to know you considered my hearing."

He glared at me. "Did I say you were welcome to coffee?"

"Yes." I paused. "Maybe not today. Anyway, you're always taking stuff from my place."

"I'm allowed."

"Yeah, and why's that?" I started looking for food and located some digestive biscuits in the shiny chrome bread bin.

"I just am." He looked irritable. "Look, today we have to go and think of something to do with Sven."

"Shouldn't we hand him over to the police?"

Luke rolled his eyes and sighed. "Sophie, what are we?"

I tried to swallow the biscuit but didn't manage. "Special agents," I said through a mouthful of crumbly digestive.

"Better than police."

"You mean we're above the law?"

"No, just above the police. They help us. We don't answer to them."

Cool.

"So can we do what we want to Sven?"

Luke cracked a smile and leaned back against the kitchen unit, his arms folded. "What did you want to do to him?"

I thought of starting by waking him up with a nice gentle bikini wax, but then it occurred to me that I didn't really want to get into his pants that much any more. "Something painful," I said.

"We have to be careful," Luke said. "He's a foreign national. Ultimately we have to return him to the Norwegian authorities and if he's in bad shape, they might not be very happy with us."

"Don't we have, like, privileges about that or something?" I asked through another biscuit.

"Privileges about beating up foreigners? Sophie, you ever hear of the Geneva Convention?"

I made a face and swallowed my biscuit. "So what are we allowed to do to him?"

He winked. "Things that don't leave marks."

I kept that happy thought in my head as I drove up to the office. I had my stun gun in my bag, fully charged, and was looking forward to seeing what I could do with it. Overnight Sven had turned from a gorgeous fantasy figure to a rather pathetic creature, and to be honest I didn't want anything to do with him any more. I wasn't even too bothered about torturing him.

Well, not too much.

It was still early and no one else was in the office as we made our way down to the lab. Sven was huddled in a corner of his cell, looking terrified. He stared at me for ages before finally gasping, "Sophie! What is going on here?"

"You tell me, Sven," I said, and I was surprised to hear my voice sounding perfectly calm. I folded my arms and looked down at him. He really did look pathetic. What the hell had I ever seen in him? "What was going on last night?"

He shrugged helplessly. "I don't know. I don't remember anything."

"Do you remember putting something into my drink?"

He shook his head rapidly. "No, nothing, I swear. Sophie, what is this place? Am I in trouble?"

"Yes," I said, "you're in trouble. You tried to drug my drink, Sven—" to my amazement I realised I didn't know his last name "—and knock me out."

"I didn't drug anything!"

"You were seen," Luke cut in, his voice icy, and once more I was glad he was on my side. He moved to stand just behind me, and I drew an inappropriate amount of pleasure from his nearness. Hey, I was a strong confident woman, I didn't need a man to back me up.

It was nice, though.

"We have a witness ready to state that you were seen putting a tablet into Sophie's drink last night," Luke went on.

"But—did you drink it?"

"No," I said. "You did."

Sven stared wildly around for a few seconds as if he was trying to take it all in. I turned to Luke and lowered my voice.

"Is it okay for him to see all the stuff in here?"

He shrugged. "It's just a lab. Everything's locked up. You need a pass to get in."

"He has a pass..."

"A proper pass. It needs to be put through the system." He glanced back at Sven. "You done with him?"

"I don't know."

"Leave him stewing. We need to go and get something concrete from your friend Tom anyway."

We left Sven crying out for help and I couldn't help my lip curling as the lift doors slid shut.

"I see the Florence Nightingale complex passed you by," Luke said, smiling.

"What?"

"You don't find him remotely attractive, all helpless like that?"

I made a face. "Kittens are cute when they're helpless. All animals are cute when they're helpless. People...need to get a grip. That was just pathetic."

"Remind me to never get hurt when you're around."

Because if he was hurt, I'd have to look after him. And unless it was minor and I ended up shagging him out of relief (he'd done it to me) then he'd probably die. I was not one of life's nurses.

Outside in the sunlight things were starting to come to life. People were parking up outside the other little offices and workplaces, the day was starting. I yawned.

"So where does Tom live?" Luke asked, and I tried to remember.

"I don't know the address. I know where it is... Chalker's always getting me to pick him up from there."

"So drive on."

I looked at my watch. It was eight o'clock. "You're kidding, right?"

"No."

"Tom is not going to be awake at eight o'clock. He probably didn't get home until about three or four and I doubt if he went straight to bed."

"So we wake him up."

Visions of fighting through the messy, smoky hole of Tom's room fogged up my brain, and I shook my head to clear it. "No," I said. "Anyway, then I'd have to explain who you are, and why we're there... I'll give him a call later."

We got back into the car and I pointed it homewards, counting the seconds of silence. "So, you and Tom," Luke began, and I burst out laughing.

"Eleven," I said, and he looked at me like I was deranged. "Eleven seconds until you said something... Never mind."

Luke was shaking his head. "You're a lunatic."

"There's that possibility."

"Is Tom a good friend of yours?"

I shrugged, enjoying the moment. Truth was, Tom and I had hardly spoken at school, but we got along okay where the band was concerned. Our relationship wasn't even brother-sister, it was sort of more like distant cousins.

"Yeah," I said, glancing at Luke, "we're really close."

He glared at the road, and I bit my tongue in self-flagellation. I shouldn't be encouraging Luke. Hadn't I already decided that it would be an extremely bad idea to fall for him? As a working partner, as maybe a friend, he was okay. I didn't need a complicated relationship with him. I especially didn't need him to fuck me over and tell me his work was more important than our relationship. I could get there before him. The work *was* more important.

Hell, I was doing important work! That'd *never* happened before.

"I had a thought," I said as we pulled up at my flat, and ignored Luke's snort of surprise. "About Harvey. I know we tried Googling him but maybe we could try one of those alumni websites. Like a Friends Reunited thing. If James Harvard and Harvey are the same person, it might be on there."

Luke blinked. "That's a very good idea," he said, and there was wonder in his voice.

"Yes, well, I do have them occasionally," I sniffed.

He grinned. "I checked all the people search engines. We have a couple of accounts online..."

"Do I get access to them?" I asked, wondering if an American search engine was really the height of sophistication in the modern spy world.

"Sure. I'll come in with you and log you on, then the cookies will be on your PC."

He then proceeded to complain about everything to do with my computer, from how clicky the keyboard was to how slow the dial-up connection was. "Don't you have Broadband?"

"I can't afford it. Not with all the spending I seem to be doing recently."

"No one made you stay in a nice hotel in Rome."

"No, but they did make me go out and buy something to sneak around in." I scrolled through the results the American engine had brought up for James Harvard. There was an alumni website that had a picture of him on graduation day. If you looked really hard and used a lot of imagination, then it could just about have been Harvey.

But then it could have been Tammy, too.

I rolled my eyes at Luke and searched for a database of old school friends. I found one that was free, logged on and searched for James Harvard. There were dozens, and I started reading through them.

Hi everybody at Jefferson High! I'm at UCLA studying Marine Biology and surfing loads...

Greetings and salutations. Since leaving Martin Van Buren High three years ago...

I've been working for the Third Bank of Kyoto for ten years and have not left Japan in that time...

"This is insane," Luke muttered over my shoulder.

"I know. Is there a single high school in America that's not named after a former president?"

"There was a president called Martin Van Buren?"

Hah! I found something he didn't know!

Oh, wait. Was Van Buren a president or just a congressman? Couldn't remember my A levels.

"Sure," I said. "Really famous president." I clicked on the next James Harvard.

In the twenty years since I left George Washington Prep...

"How old do you think Harvey is?" I asked Luke.

"Not old enough."

"No. Well, I didn't think he'd have been to a prep school."

"And what's wrong with prep school?"

I turned to look at him. "*You* went to prep school?"

Luke looked defensive. "Didn't you?"

"No! I went to the same school as everyone else around here. Which you should know as you've been checking up on my personal record."

"I thought it was a grammar school."

"Not for about thirty years. They just keep that in the title to fool people." I clicked on the next James Harvard. "So what, were you a public school boy?"

Luke mumbled something that I didn't quite catch.

"Did you say Eton?"

"Mmm."

"You went to Eton?" Did they allow anyone as sexy as Luke at Eton? "Don't tell me, you were head boy."

Glaring at me, he mumbled, "Prefect."

Jesus. I never even considered applying for prefect at my school. As far as I could see all it meant was reduced lunchtimes as you policed the dinner queue while the dinner ladies gossiped. My form tutor told me to apply and I remember asking her to tell me why without using the letters C and V. She shut up.

"Eton prefect." I was still shaking my head. "RAF, SAS, you must think I'm such a pleb."

"No, I don't."

"So, what, are your parents mega rich? Titled?" Hey, that would be cool.

"No," Luke said sharply. "I don't want to talk about it, okay?"

I shrugged. That was a back-off tone. "Okay." I looked back at the screen and started reading aloud to fill the silence. "'Hey to all in Temperance. I've hardly been back since I joined the army. I spent three years as a Ranger before leaving to work for a communications company. I now travel all over the world and hardly get back to America, let alone Ohio, although I sometimes see my brother in New York. But I have e-mail connections and would love to hear from anyone in Temperance, especially those who went to Temperance High with me. Harvey.'"

Jesus.

"Bingo," Luke said.

"He was a Ranger?"

"He could have made that up."

"He could have made all of it up! Harvey's got to be a pretty common nickname for someone with a name like Harvard, don't you think?"

I looked up hopefully. Luke was shaking his head. "That's him. He even told them the same story he told you, he's in communications. That's his excuse for travelling all over the world."

I stared at the screen. "It doesn't say anything about college," I said triumphantly.

"So?"

"If you went to—" I opened up the window with the alumni page on it "—Princeton, God, you'd tell people about it."

Luke frowned. "You ever been to Ohio?"

"No." All I knew about Ohio was that it was where Christian Slater killed people in *Heathers*, and Jennifer Crusie set her books. "You?"

"Yeah. Full of small towns." He grabbed my old school atlas off the bookshelf and flipped through it to North America. "Do you see Temperance, Ohio, on there anywhere?"

I made a face.

"If you went off to Oxford or Cambridge, wouldn't everyone in the village know about it?"

"No."

"Well, no maybe not, because this village is full of commuters who only step outside their front doors to go to work, but in a regular small town, like Ohio is full of, everybody knows everybody. Everybody would know that James Harvard went to Princeton. His mom would have told everybody. He wouldn't need to put it on the website."

I wrinkled my nose. "I still think it's not him."

"Well, I think it is him. And I think we need to go and check out his hotel room at the Hilton."

"Why?"

"Erm, because he might be Wright's partner?"

Oh, right. Wright. With all the stuff that had been going on I'd almost forgotten.

"Okay," Luke said, going into my bedroom and opening my wardrobe doors. "Harvey got distracted by you at the Buckman Ball, so maybe you can distract him downstairs in the bar while I search his room."

"Luke—"

"Come on. Pursuit of justice and all that."

"What about Chris Mansfield? Aren't we pursuing justice for him?"

Luke came out of my bedroom holding the Gucci dress. "Chris was killed because of his involvement with the Wilkes takedown. And that's also probably why you've been targeted."

Targeted. When he put it like that, I felt so much *un*safer.

"And the Wilkeses may or may not be involved with Wright..."

"Possibly as saboteurs. Or smugglers. Or maybe just as associates who were in the wrong place. The point is, we find Wright's partner, we might just find Chris's killer." He held the dress against me. "Does this fit?"

"I don't think it's your colour."

He made a face. "You're funny. You need to wear something that will make Harvard stay in the hotel bar."

"It's lunchtime!"

"So?"

"One, he's not going to spend that much time in the bar, and two, he could be out."

"So much the better."

"And three, he's already seen that dress."

Luke blinked. "You just happened to have it with you in Rome?"

"I bought it in Rome."

He stared at me.

"I needed something to wear—"

"A Gucci cocktail dress?"

"—and it was on sale... Come on. It was really good value. And it looked really good on me."

"I'll bet. Look, Harvard won't remember what you were wearing. A black dress is a black dress—"

"Not when it's designer."

"It is to a bloke."

"It's too short for daytime. And it'll show off all my bruises," I pointed to my shoulder.

"Okay, fine. You pick something out. Something sexy. Tight. Heels and cleavage."

Why is it that women have to show as much flesh as possible to be noticed by a man? You want to keep a guy's attention, all you have to do is flash a boob and he's yours. But men can get away with being totally covered all the time and still be considered sexy. If I covered every inch of my skin, I'd look like a nun.

"Look," I said, staring at my wardrobe while Luke picked apart my CD collection, "he thinks I'm a stewardess. Can't I wear my Ace uniform?"

"Not sexy enough."

I was feeling belligerent. "You think I don't look sexy in my uniform?"

He appeared in the doorway and gave me a very slow once-over. I felt my insides start to heat up.

"Yes," he said softly, "but I think you look sexier out of it." I threw a jumper at him and he ducked, laughing. "Oh, come on. That was a compliment."

Hmm.

Eventually I picked out a pair of tight jeans and a low-cut top, and spent half an hour covering my bruises with make-up. Then I tarted up my face and hair, added stilettos, and tottered out to face Luke, who was watching cartoons on TV.

"Will I do?" I posed.

"You look like a fashion victim."

That was sort of the idea. "Is it too much?"

"No. Very sexy. Can you walk in those shoes?"

"I can walk in any shoes."

"I'll bear that in mind. Come on. We'll get my car, it's more anonymous."

I got my bag, filled with all my useful crap, and stumbled after him, my heels clattering on the floorboards. Probably I was making dents. I looked behind me to see, and then walked straight into Luke.

"Sophie," he sighed, "did you check the post this morning?"

I shook my head. "There wasn't any when I left."

"And when we got in?"

"Let me think. You were complaining about how cold it was in here and then how slow my computer was."

He gave me a slow, sarcastic look, then pulled something out of the letterbox. "You've got mail," he said, handing me a pretty pink envelope with a teddy bear on it. I opened it resignedly, and sure enough, there was a finger inside. Along with a birthday card that matched the pretty pink envelope.

"This is new," I said.

"Is it your birthday?"

I shook my head. "I don't usually get fingers for my birthday." I opened the card. A printed rhyme was stuck inside.

One, two, three, four, five,

Once I caught a Chris alive.

Six, seven, eight, nine, ten

Quit or you'll be joining him.

"Nice," Luke said.

"I'm not sure if it's the finger or the bad poetry that's making me nauseous."

"What's with the numbers?"

"This," I held up the plastic-wrapped finger, which was yukky beyond belief, "is number five. I can only assume they'll be sending me the other five over the course of the week."

"He still had two."

"But none of his toes. So, actually, there are..." I added it up quickly—I'm crap at maths, okay?—"thirteen more digits to come." I put the card and the finger back in the envelope. "Do you want to go up to the office?"

"No. I had a text from Lexy, she's not feeling too good. I don't think another finger will do her much good. Or two fingers—did you say you had another one on Saturday?"

I nodded and crossed to the freezer. "Here. You missed it when you took the others."

"I didn't look in the chip drawer."

"Shame on you."

"I can't believe you have a chip drawer."

I stuck my tongue out at him.

I put the pink envelope in a bag, sealed it and added it to the collection. Then I disinfected my hands. Then I wrote *freezer bags* on my shopping list. If I was going to be getting more fingers, it was only sensible. Maybe I should call the post office and ask them to redirect bulky and/or bloody envelopes to Flight Services Inc. so Alexa could have the pleasure of examining them firsthand.

"Now are we ready to go?"

Luke was looking at a Mastercard envelope. "Don't you want to pay this?"

"Most certainly not. That's what credit is for."

We made a stop at Luke's house for his car and a few tiny electrical things. "Your wire." He handed it to me and clipped his own to the inside of his shirt.

"Oh, great, so if I have to seduce him, you can listen in?"

"I'm going to be in his room. If you seduce him, I can watch."

Pervert.

"Speaking of which," I said, "where's that red dress?"

"Why? You want to try it on for me again?"

It was obscene that I should find such a comment sexy. Totally obscene. "No, I have to give it back. It's not mine."

Luke made a face. "I wouldn't hold out much hope of that. It's at the cleaner's, but it's pretty manky."

Marvellous.

"What about the diamonds?"

"In the safe."

He had a safe? Talk about paranoid. "Where's that?"

He gave me a look. "I'm not telling you. You can have them later."

He's so *mean*. I sent a text to Ella to tell her the dress was a little bit of a mess, but I was having it cleaned and would bring it back soon (I hoped). She replied that her Ladyboat would hardly notice. She'd had the dress a few months, so it'd be old hat by now.

I have to admit to feeling bloody nervous when we walked through the lobby of the Hilton. Harvey's room was on the first floor and I walked along the corridor, Luke loitering in the stairwell, with my heart beating so hard I swear it must have been deafening him. I had the microphone clipped inside my bra, the transmitter in my bag, and the earpiece in place.

"How do I get him downstairs?" I asked Luke as I stood outside Harvey's door, tapping my feet nervously.

"Tell him they make a great Manhattan."

"Do they?"

"How the hell should I know? Actually, no, he's from Ohio. Tell him the beer is ice cold."

"Isn't that unfair generalisation?"

"Yep. Just knock on his bloody door, Sophie. I'm getting strange looks here."

"My heart bleeds for you." My fist knocked on the door. My knees knocked on each other.

There was no reply.

"Try again," Luke suggested, and I did, but there was still no reply.

"Okay," he said, "go down to the bar and wait for him. Keep a good view of the lobby so you can see him come in. If you can't stop him coming up then for God's sake alert me."

I was still shaking as I went down the stairs and I tripped and fell into Luke.

"Are you okay?" he asked.

God, it felt good to be in his arms. He was all warm and hard and, damn him, he smelled glorious. I really had to find out what brand of deodorant and aftershave he used and buy some shares in it. "I'm fine."

"You're shaking."

That's because you're the sexiest man I've ever met in real life, and I really just want to go back to your flat or my flat or break into Harvey's room and rip all your goddamned clothes off and bite you all over.

I blinked. This was not good. I had a job to do, I didn't need the distraction, I needed to prove myself and not act like a silly twittery cliché and I needed to get the hell away from the sexiest man I'd ever seen in real life before I did something really stupid.

Strong, independent woman. Strong. Independent.

I needed a drink.

"That Manhattan sounds like a good idea."

Luke grinned. "Atta girl. Only one, though, for Christ's sake don't get drunk."

"Would I?"

He raised an eyebrow but said nothing, chucked me under the chin, and sprinted off up the stairs.

I went to reception and asked if James Harvard was still in residence.

"Yes," I was told, "but he's not in right now. Would you like to leave a message?"

Déjà vu kicked in and I suddenly remembered the first time I'd met Harvey. He'd been so polite and charming. He couldn't be a bad guy. He just really couldn't.

"Um, yes," I said. "Tell him I'll be waiting in the bar for him. Sophie Green."

Then I tottered away to get my Manhattan.

Chapter Sixteen

Four hours later and I was learning all sorts of things about cocktails. A Manhattan was nice. A Cosmopolitan was pink. A Blue Lagoon made my tongue go all blue and the bartender thought I was a lush.

I switched to water a while ago, but I was still feeling sort of fuzzy. Luke had been up in Harvey's room all this time. He started telling me off for ordering so much so I took my earpiece out. It was making my ear hurt anyway.

Once or twice I wobbled over to reception to ask if Harvey had been by. They didn't know who Harvey was and I couldn't remember his real name, so I had to wobble back and wait. And while I waited, I experimented with cocktails.

Sex on the Beach wasn't all it was cracked up to be. And I think a Slippery Nipple was aimed at the men.

I mean... Oh, you know what I mean.

Truth is, I was so appalled at my body's blatant reaction to Luke that I needed to get drunk. Really drunk. I wanted to stop wanting him, because it could only be bad for me to get involved with a rat like him.

My body, however, didn't understand this, and it took a heroic amount of alcohol to quiet the steady thrum of "Luke smell good. Luke feel nice. Me want bite Luke's butt".

By the time my hormones shut up, I was seeing three of everything.

Finally, just as I was getting fed up of drawing patterns in the pink cocktail spillage on my table, someone tapped me on the shoulder and I looked up to see Harvey watching me with eyebrows raised.

"Howdy."

Boy, they sure made 'em cute in Ohio.

"Harvey!" I leapt to my feet, nearly breaking my ankle in the process. "Fancy seeing you here!"

"They told me at reception you'd been asking for me."

Shit. "I, er, one of the girls said she saw you here. I thought I'd pop by and say hello. Hello."

"Hello." He looked at the collection of cocktail umbrellas I'd amassed. "How long have you been here?"

"Oh. A while."

"Checking out the cocktail list?"

"Yeah. Making sure it's up to scratch. Sometimes people don't make them properly." What was I talking about?

"Is that so?" Harvey took a seat beside me on the banquette and signalled the waiter. "Budweiser. Sophie? Another cocktail?"

The waiter gave the umbrellas a long, slow look, then did the same to me.

"Mineral water," I summoned an angelic smile. "Still."

"So how'd you know so much about cocktails?" Harvey asked, smiling, as the waiter minced away.

"Oh, I, er, I used to be a cocktail waitress." Who was this woman inside my head and what was she saying?

"Really? Before you got the call to the skies?"

The what? Oh, right, the stewardess thing. "Yeah. It's a calling."

He nodded. "What happened to your face?"

My hand flew up to the bruise, slightly more enthusiastically than I'd told it to, and prodded my temple painfully. "Oh, I, er, I, er... you know those overhead lockers? Don't walk into them."

"I'll bear that in mind. It looks painful."

"Yeah. I'm on painkillers."

"Should you be drinking on top of painkillers?"

The waiter arrived and I pointed to my water. "I'm not drinking," I said.

Harvey blinked at the cocktail umbrellas. "Er, no," he said. "Of course not. So, how've you been? I haven't seen you since that night in London."

Oh, Jesus. *That* night.

"I've been okay." He was going to ask me about Luke.

"Did you sort things out with that guy? Uh, Lewis, Leo..."

"Luke. Yes. Sorted."

"So are you...?"

I stared. "Am I what?"

"Are you...involved with him? I was sort of unclear on that on Friday."

I took a long, contemplative sip of my water. I was still sort of unclear on that, too. Still, Luke wasn't here. Nothing had really happened since Friday.

"No," I said, looking straight at Harvey. "Not involved."

He nodded, smiled, and took a swig of his beer. "'Cos it looked a little like you were."

"What? No. That was just Luke messing around."

"He seemed jealous."

"Well." I looked him over. Nice teeth, kind eyes, good body under his suit. "Of course he is."

Like Kate Moss would be jealous of me.

"So you're single?"

I nodded.

"Can I..." He dropped his eyes and drummed his fingers on the table. Then he looked up at me. "Can I get your phone number?"

Deliriously happy, I reeled off my Siemens number. "How long are you staying here?"

He shrugged. "I'm not sure. I have to fly off up to Edinburgh tomorrow, but I'm back in the evening. Maybe we could have dinner?"

I nodded so enthusiastically my head nearly fell off. I was starting to feel dizzy.

"Great. I can't promise anything like the trattoria in Rome. Do you know any nice places around here?"

My head whirled. If I wanted to eat out, I went to Pizza Hut. “Erm, no,” I said carefully, “I don’t know the area well.”

“Okay, well, I’ll ask at Reception.” He peered at me. “Are you okay?”

The dizziness was starting to set in big time. I looked down at the pile of cocktail umbrellas and tried to count them but they all blurred into one smudgy blob. “Erm,” I slurred, trying to focus on Harvey, “yeah, I’m fine, but I, er, I think I could do with maybe freshening up?”

“My room’s just on the second floor,” Harvey offered, and I blurted out, “No, it’s not!”

He looked surprised. Shit. Bugger. “I mean, I asked at reception. It’s on the first floor.”

Harvey frowned, then he laughed. “Yeah, like this is the ground floor, not the first. I don’t get that about Britain.”

Me neither, I wanted to say as I stood up and wove after him through the bar, but I couldn’t concentrate on talking and walking at the same time.

We were halfway up the stairs when I realised that Luke was still in Harvey’s room. Oh, bollocks! And I hadn’t warned him! I’d taken out my earpiece!

“Oh,” I said, stopping. “I just need to, I just need to, erm, make a phone call.” I was swaying in place. These steps were awfully narrow. And very steep. A person could hurt herself if she wasn’t extra, super-duper careful. I clutched at the railing as I rummaged in my bag for my phone, feeling slightly sick. I got out the Siemens and stared at it.

“Something wrong?” Harvey asked, coming back down a few steps and taking my arm.

“This is the wrong phone,” I muttered.

“How many do you have?”

“I, er…” He was looking very blurry. Maybe I shouldn’t have had that second Blue Lagoon. And probably the pitcher of Margaritas was not a good idea.

“Sophie, are you sure you’re okay? How much did you have to drink?”

I had no idea. I could only remember the first half-dozen cocktails. The rest were hazy.

"Sophie?"

I looked up and the phone slipped from my hand. I stooped to pick it up, lost my balance, and then everything went sort of swirly and nauseous and black.

And when I awoke, I was alone. This bird had flown.

My head was in agony. I felt sick and dizzy even without moving. My eyelids felt like they'd been glued together. No, scratch that; they'd been lined with ponyskin, then stapled together.

I moaned.

"Sophie?"

I peeled open one eyelid and eventually focused on Harvey, looming over me, something white in his hand.

"How're you feeling?"

I thought about it. "Blegh," I said.

The white thing was a damp cloth and he pressed it to my forehead. "I think you had a little too much to drink."

Really.

I opened the other eye, because they were both starting to ache from the effort. "I know this is a really trite question, but where am I?"

He smiled a lovely gentle reassuring smile. "My room. You threw up on the stairs. And then you passed out."

How attractive.

"Have I... Have I been here long?"

"About ten minutes. You want some water?"

I thought about it. Right now my oesophagus only seemed to want to operate one way.

"I think I'm going to be sick," I mumbled, and stumbled from the bed.

Sick I was, but I at least managed to get into the bathroom and lock the door first. Huddled on the floor, wiping vomit from my mouth, I sat and shivered, feeling pathetic. I hadn't got this drunk since my eighteenth birthday, when I drank multi-coloured cocktails and threw up all over.

Hmm.

There was a knock on the door. "Sophie? You all right?"

Peachy. "I'm okay," I croaked.

"Your cell-phone's ringing."

I crawled to the door, unlocked it, and accepted my bag from Harvey. Then I locked the door again and shuffled back to my hideout under the sink to pull the phone from my bag. The Nokia. Luke.

Bollocks.

"What?" I mumbled.

"Several things. You have the James Bond theme tune on your phone?"

How the hell did he know that? "How the hell do you know that?"

"The wire. Remember? Sophie, did I hear that jockstrap saying you'd passed out?"

"Mmm." Where was the damn earpiece? My bag? My pocket? Christ, it was in my cleavage. Oh God, I was such a loser.

"And threw up?" He made a noise of disgust. "Twice?"

"I think I'm allergic to grenadine."

"Jesus, Sophie. What were you thinking?"

"I was bored."

"You were pissed. Really, majorly pissed. Are you still in his room?"

"The bathroom."

"Get out. Now. Get your arse down to the car. And put your fucking earpiece back in."

I ended the call, hands shaking, and hauled myself to my feet. I looked appalling. Worse than Sven had this morning.

Jesus, Sven! What if he'd somehow spiked my drinks here? Maybe he was working with Harvey! Maybe Harvey really was the bad guy.

Or maybe I'd really just had too much to drink.

I glugged down a lot of water and half a packet of Smints to try and take away the taste of vomit, and opened the door. Harvey was sitting on the bed, tie loosened, shirtsleeves rolled up. He stood up when I appeared.

"Hey," he said.

"Hey," I replied, quietly.

"Feeling better?"

You know what I felt like? One of those zombies on the "Thriller" video. At least there was no vomit on my clothes, although there was some on my shoe. And they were nice shoes, too.

I shrugged. "Ih."

"Never again, huh?"

"I have a blue tongue."

He grinned. "I know. Look, Sophie—"

"I have to go," I said. "I'm sorry."

"Go? Where? You can't drive like that—"

"I have a lift." I hefted my bag on my shoulder. "Thanks, Harvey. You've been really nice." God, I was still pissed.

"Any time."

We both frowned.

"Well," he amended, "maybe not any time. Tomorrow maybe stick to mineral water?"

I nodded. Then I stopped, partly because I was still dizzy, and partly because I had no idea what he was talking about.

"Tomorrow?"

"Dinner. Remember?"

That clinched it. I knew he was evil. Or insane. Why else would he be persisting in asking me out when I'd passed out on him and thrown up in his bathroom?

"Uh, yeah. Dinner." My brain was broken. I could think of no excuse.

"I'll call you later." He looked me over. "Maybe tomorrow. Get some sleep."

I nodded. "See you, Harvey."

He came over and kissed my cheek. I knew I was all clammy. He must be up to something.

"See you," he said quietly, and I wobbled out of his room, down past a wet patch on the stairs, ahem, and out through the lobby where I swear everyone was looking at me. God, did I have vomit in my hair or something?

It took me a while to find Luke's car. It was so generic. When I eventually got in, he was steaming with anger.

"Don't," I held up a hand. "I already know."

"You're such a bloody idiot." He started the engine and reversed out of the space at about fifty miles an hour. My stomach lurched.

"I know," I mumbled, hand to mouth.

"What the fuck were you thinking?"

"I don't know."

"Jesus, Sophie, you're still half-cut. You're going home, and you're going to bed."

Right now, that seemed like a very good idea to me.

All the way home he yelled at me, taking every corner so fast I nearly threw up again. I had to open the window and hang my head out, taking desperately deep breaths. If I was sick in the car, Luke would probably kick me out and run me over.

I got inside the flat, peeled off my clothes on the way to the bedroom and crashed out in my underwear. I didn't give a damn about whether Luke was watching me or not. I needed to sleep. I felt like seven kinds of shit.

It was dark when I woke up. There'd been a bottle of water by the bed and I'd half-woken several times to swig from it and stagger to the loo before falling back down onto my bed. My bed. My lovely, soft, warm comfy bed. Mmm. I never wanted to leave it.

Until I heard voices out in the living room. Male voices. Two. Laughing. And the TV was on, too. I staggered to my feet. I didn't feel quite so bad any more. The water seemed to have worked.

There was football on my TV and Luke and Tom were sprawled on the sofa, beers in hand. Look at that, football. Didn't know I could pick it up. Wished I couldn't. Maybe if I call Sky they'll take it off my TV package.

"So it's okay for you to drink, but not me?" I said, trying to sound indignant but ending up sounding plaintive.

They both looked up at me. Luke closed his eyes and muttered something. Tom shook his head in wonder. "Sophie. Babe."

I looked down at myself. I was sporting a g-string and a push-up bra that was slightly too small and not containing my already well-padded boobs very well.

"Shit." I beat a hasty retreat into the bedroom, wrapped my fuzzy terry dressing gown around me as securely as possible and splashed cold water on my face. I looked horrific. Even after I'd taken my smudged, panda-ish make-up off, I looked grey and clammy. The bruise on my face no longer looked cool and sexy. It looked ugly.

I trudged back out into the living room. Tom looked disappointed at my new apparel. Luke looked relieved.

"Are you done embarrassing yourself for today?" he asked.

Somehow I doubted so. I sniffed and ignored him. There was a pizza box open on the coffee table and a few slices left in it.

"You ordered pizza?"

"Well, it's a funny thing," Luke said, "I opened the door and there was this guy just standing there offering me pizza. Even when I hadn't ordered it."

So he was being sarcastic. At least he was talking to me.

"How long have you been here?" I asked Tom.

"Oh, a while." He didn't take his eyes off the TV. "You okay?"

"Never better." I threw myself at the beanbag by Luke's feet and reached for some pizza. Pizza always makes me feel better.

"I mean after last night. I called to see how you were and Luke told me to come over."

I flicked my gaze up at Luke but he was still watching the TV.

"Did he now?"

"Didn't know you two were an item."

"That makes two of us," Luke said, still not looking at me. Hmm. Maybe he wasn't talking to me after all.

Tom looked between the two of us, his eyes smiling but the rest of his face immobile. "Right," he said slowly. "So, that guy from yesterday, Soph, was he just a mate then?"

"Was," I said.

"You turn him in?"

"We took care of him," Luke said. He sounded like a hitman.

"So do I like have to make a statement or something?"

"Write it down," Luke said. "I'll take it in."

Tom frowned, but he didn't argue. The match ended, Man U won and I finished off the pizza, feeling better for it. In half an hour, I'd drunk a whole two litre bottle of water. I felt better for that, too, although my bladder was bursting.

When I came back from the loo, Tom was shrugging into his coat. "Said I'd be back an hour ago," he said. I nodded.

"Nice of you to drop by."

"Just to see you're okay." He kissed my cheek. Aw. Sweet lovely Tom.

I bet those are words that aren't said very often.

"How are you getting home?" I asked, knowing he didn't drive.

"Train."

Luke caught my eye and shook his head. I knew what he was thinking. The last person who'd helped me apprehend a criminal had been shredded.

"I'll give you a lift."

"Are you legal to drive?"

I scowled at him. "Yes."

Luke raised his eyebrows, but said nothing. I stomped back into the bedroom, pulled on a sweater and jeans and came back out for my trainers and keys. Luke was still standing there, watching me. I know I looked a wreck but really, he wasn't allowed to comment.

"*What?*"

"What are you going to drive?"

"Te—" Ted was at Luke's house. "Bollocks."

"I'll give you a lift," Luke said to Tom, who nodded.

"Wait! I'm coming too. I want my car."

Luke rolled his eyes but didn't complain. First time for everything.

We were all silent in the car. Tom was in the front and messed around with the radio, trying to get X-FM and mercifully failing. I had a feeling that Luke's musical tastes might differ from Tom's quite considerably.

"Are you coming to the Cambridge gig on Saturday?" Tom asked as he got out of the car.

"Where?"

"Dunno. Ask Chalker."

"Like he ever knows anything," I grumbled as I got into the front seat. "See you, Tom."

"See you."

He and Luke nodded at each other, then Tom was gone, sneaking into the garden for a crafty fag before his parents saw him. Luke turned the car around and drove away.

"Will you be all right on your own tonight?"

"If I throw up any more, I'll be bringing up organs," I said. "I'll be fine. I feel okay."

This was a lie. My brain felt fat and sluggish and my body matched. But I didn't feel like I was going to die any more, which was a definite improvement.

We got back to Luke's house, the yard silhouetted by a security light, and sat silently for a few seconds in the dark car. I took a deep breath, filling my lungs, feeling better for it.

"Look," we both began at the same time, and then both stopped. "You first," Luke said.

"I'm really sorry about this afternoon. I don't know what was wrong with me."

"You were really drunk?"

"Well, yes..."

"Everyone gets pissed once in a while, Sophie," Luke said, and I wondered, *Even you*? "Just don't do it on duty, okay?"

"Did you get anything from his room?"

He shrugged. "If he's involved in this, he's hiding it damn well."

"He wants to see me tomorrow."

"Even after your spectacular—"

"Yes, thank you. I figure he must be up to something if he still wants to see me."

Luke paused, smiling. "You're not that unattractive when you're drunk," he said, unfastening his seat belt. "Are you sure you don't want to stay?"

I'd probably be sick on him. "I'll be fine. Thanks."

He nodded and got out of the car. "By the way," he said as I was unlocking Ted, "I changed the security codes. Knock next time."

I rolled my eyes and drove home. But I didn't go back to sleep. I was all slept-out. I started up the computer and looked over Harvey's alumni website again. He was definitely up to something. If it wasn't a collaboration with Wright, then what was it?

I needed to get him and Wright together. Then maybe I'd be able to see.

I texted Luke, *Do you know where Wright is?*

He replied in seconds. *Checked in to B&B in village 2hrs ago. Why?*

I wasn't sure why. *Think I need to see him and Harvey together. Still don't think Harvey is partner. Wright said was a woman.*

Wright's an idiot, Luke replied, and I couldn't argue with that. *We'll check out B&B tomo. Go to sleep.*

But I could argue with that. I wasn't happy with waiting. I needed to know something.

It could be that Sven had spiked my drink for his own selfish purposes. Or, given the fingers and the sniper and the firebomb, it could be that he was involved with whoever was trying to kill me. Whoever had killed Chris. Whoever was involved with the Brownie twins and whoever was Wright's partner. I'd stake good money it was the same person.

But I wouldn't bet on it being Sven.

I grabbed my keys and double locked the door, and I drove up to the office. I had keys for the outside door, and I was hoping and praying that my pass would swipe me in. The green one failed, but the red one worked.

Note to self: do not keep PIN code on a Post-it stuck to pass.

The office was quiet and eerie when it was dark. I don't know why I didn't switch on the lights. I suppose I wanted to be unseen. I don't think many people use the business park after hours, but there could be someone around. Maybe Harvey. He seemed to have a knack for turning up in places he shouldn't be.

Oh, Jesus. Suddenly it came to me. I knew who Harvey was.

I couldn't wait for the computer to boot up. I wasn't sure where the files were kept and it seemed like forever until I got the one I wanted. The log of people who'd gone airside the night Chris was killed. Ana's name was there, but Chris's wasn't. I'd been assuming he'd been killed airside. But maybe he'd been killed somewhere else and taken through to the undercroft.

No. No, you couldn't just take a body through. The scanners were manned all night. Someone would have noticed. Just to be sure, I brought up a log of all baggage screened overnight. None.

Which meant that, either dead or alive, someone had deleted Chris Mansfield from the log.

I drummed my fingers on the desk, thinking. He'd been deleted. And whoever had killed him had been deleted, too.

I stared at Alexa's screen-saver of George Clooney pictures. There was an answer to this. Someone had deleted the information. What I needed was a BAA recycle bin so I could trawl through the deleted names.

Idly, I searched the computer for Chris's name and ID. It took forever, but one match came up.

In the computer's recycle bin.

Was her computer networked? Had someone deleted the file from here? I opened up the deleted, but not eliminated, log. There was Chris's name. And there was…

I felt the nausea rise in my throat again. Quickly, I searched the recycle bin for media files. Whoever had done this had been stupid or careless, or both, because there they were, the BAA footage files from the night Chris was killed. I knew the spliced footage had been added before 0236, because that's when the mouse ran across the floor. But what I had here were nearly two hours of footage, starting at just after two in the morning and running through until just before Ana came on screen.

It was grainy and I couldn't make out who they were. But I was pretty sure they weren't who the log said they were. I was pretty sure those passes had been stolen. Or the names had been planted. That was all I could think of to explain it.

I replayed the footage over again. There. Chris had walked into the undercroft, presumably waiting for Ana. He'd been early by about half an hour. Or she'd been late. Neither of us had thought to ask her if she'd been on time.

But what Chris hadn't known was that the undercroft wasn't empty. Someone had been using it for a meeting. In the Ace staff room. Which was supposed to be empty. Which was why Chris walked in there. And why he was killed.

And then they took his body and put it in the belt mechanism. I didn't know why. Maybe they were coming back for it later. Maybe they wanted to make a point.

They were long gone by the time Ana made her appearance. I'd even watched them clean up the blood.

I sat back in my chair. Probably I ought to tell Luke about this. But there was something else I had to do first.

I got out my phone and called Macbeth, hoping he'd be in. It was well after midnight, although I wasn't sure why that bothered me.

"Hey, babe," he answered. "You locked in again?"

"Locked out," I said. "You know the lab under the office?"

"I know it," he said.

"Can you get in?"

"I can get in anywhere."

Ten minutes later he strolled through the door. "What you wanna do down there you don't want Luke to know about?"

"It's what I want to say that I don't want him to know."

Macbeth shrugged. "Can I know?"

"You can watch."

He looked excited at the prospect and quickly pulled the files off the bookshelf to find the hidden keypad. The door swooshed open and we stepped into the lift.

"You do know how to get through this lock, right?" I asked nervously. "I mean, it's not going to fill up with poisonous gas or something if you don't put the right code in in thirty seconds?"

Macbeth was looking at me like I'd grown another head. "Girl, you watch too much TV," he said, and swiped his pass on the machine. He keyed in a code, spoke his name—sadly, not his real name—and the lift started moving.

"How come you get access and I don't?"

"I didn't get blind drunk this afternoon," he replied, grinning.

"God, does everyone know about that?"

He shrugged and grinned some more.

The lift doors opened and I could see Sven slumped in the corner of his cage, a dark lump in the shadowy corner. "Hey," I yelled, "wake up. I need to talk to you."

But then Macbeth switched on the light, and my blood suddenly froze in my veins, because it wasn't Sven lying in the corner of the cell. It was One. And he was dead.

Chapter Seventeen

"Jesus fucking Christ," Macbeth said.

"I know," I said.

"That dude is dead."

"I know," I said.

We both stood and stared. In other circumstances we might have opened up the cell and checked for a pulse or something. But that seemed rather ridiculous when we could both see, quite clearly, a tiny bullet hole on one side of One's head. And a giant bloody hole on the other side.

"He ain't the guy was down here earlier."

I concentrated on breathing. "When did you come down here?"

"This afternoon. 'Bout four."

"Was there a formerly cute Norwegian guy in here then?"

"Formerly cute?"

"I changed my mind after he tried to drug me."

"Blue shirt, vomit in his hair?"

"That's the bunny."

"You reckon he killed Albert?"

"Well, I think I just saw footage of him killing Chris Mansfield," I said, "so I wouldn't rule it out."

Macbeth walked over and ran his hands over the door of the cell. "But he couldn't've broken out," he muttered. "No one could. I made this thing everything-proof. This here is the only door I can't break through."

I believed him.

"But if Sven didn't break out, then someone must have let him out," I said.

"Maybe Albert went in there and this Sven guy killed him," Macbeth said.

It was weird to hear One called Albert. "No—" I began, and he cut me off.

"No, 'cos you need to swipe it shut. And this dude still has his pass," he peered through the glass.

"Plus, isn't it voice activated?"

"Sure is." Macbeth turned back to look at me. "Which means only five people could've done it."

"Four," I said. "I never got my voice activation activated." To prove it, I swiped my card in the slot and keyed in my code. There flashed a green light to say the code was accepted.

"Sophie Green," I said, and the light turned red. Denied.

"Which leaves Alexa, Maria, Luke and me," Macbeth said. "And I know I did not do it. Albert had my respect."

I wasn't going to argue with Macbeth. "It wasn't Luke," I said. "He's been at mine all afternoon."

"You sure 'bout that?"

"Why would Luke kill One?"

Macbeth shrugged. "Why would anybody?"

"Do you know where Maria was?"

"No. I ain't seen her since this morning."

It didn't matter. I knew who'd done it. And I was very frightened.

I took Macbeth back up to the computer and showed him the deleted log of people who'd been down to the undercroft. Christopher Mansfield. Sven Christensen. Alexa Martin.

"Our Alexa?"

"I thought maybe it'd been a plant," I said. "Or someone had stolen her pass. Because, look," I opened up the deleted footage and showed him the two people in the staff room before Chris walked in. A tall blond man and a petite blonde woman. Both standing. No wheelchair.

"She was faking that?"

"Must have been." I was shivering. I'd trusted Alexa. I'd liked her. Was I really that bad a judge of character?

Macbeth had his phone out. "I'm calling Maria. Get Luke."

I nodded and dialled him, but the number was engaged. Shit. "Luke," I said to his voice mail, "listen, this is very important. Call me *immediately*. I'm at the office. Sven has escaped and One has been killed and I'm pretty sure it was Alexa who did both. I found the deleted footage from the night Chris was killed. It was Alexa and Sven." Macbeth was signalling to me. "Macbeth's here with me... but..." I held the phone away from my ear and listened to him. "But he's going to go and see if he can find Alexa. Maria's on her way. I'm going to stay here. Get your arse up here ASAP!"

I ended the call. "You'll be all right?" Macbeth asked.

"I don't think One's going to do me any harm."

"They could come back." He took something from inside his Puffa and handed it to me. A gun. "You know how to use this?"

I hesitated. Could I bluff it out?

No. I could not.

"Nine millimetre Beretta," Macbeth said. "Semiautomatic. Just point and shoot."

"How come you're allowed a gun and I'm not?" I said, taking it and holding it gingerly.

Macbeth grinned. "Who said I was allowed? Safety catch is here. Don't use it unless you have to. It's fully loaded," he said, going to the door. "I'll see you later."

Then he was gone, and I was alone in the dark room.

I sat there for a while, my heart beating fast, trying to think of something to do. Alexa lived in town and Maria was going straight there. Macbeth was going to back her up. I was going to wait for Luke.

God, I was sick of waiting for Luke. My warrant card said I was a special agent. I had a gun, albeit unofficially. Yet here I was, waiting for someone more qualified than me to come and look after me. And look at how it turned out with the revolver. I'd been so damned scared of it I'd given it back.

I was pathetic.

I glared at the computer screen.

No, wait, there was something I could do.

I brought up the hotel reservations listing and found Wright's B&B. Shit, it wasn't far from where my parents lived. I'd been to school with the son of the owner. I dialled the number and waited for a long while as it rang out.

"Hello?" came a sleepy voice.

"I'm sorry for ringing so late. But I'm told my boss is staying with you? David Wright."

"Yes. He checked in this afternoon."

"Is he there?"

"Asleep, as far as I know."

Excellent.

"I need to give him an urgent message. It's very important that he gets this word for word and as soon as possible."

"I'll wake him up—"

"Just give him the message. They know about the deal. Meet me at the office."

"That's the message?"

"That's it."

"And your name?"

"Alexa Martin. He'll know me. I'm his business partner."

I was slightly scared Luke would turn up before Wright, but even if he did then I could say it was coincidence and get Luke to help me with the takedown. I could tell him the truth later. That I lured Wright here and handcuffed him to, erm, the desk while I got the important information out of him. Yeah.

I swiped open the door and left it ajar so he could come straight in. And he did. Completely alone. Calling out for Alexa.

I leapt out from my hiding place behind the desk and tackled him, every sore bone in my body crying out as we thudded to the floor. I had my gun ready and pointed at his head. I was doing fantastically until the door burst open and someone all in black yelled, "Freeze!" and aimed a gun at me.

I swung the pistol at him. "You freeze," I yelled, at the same instant I took in the hazel eyes, the shiny hair, the expression of disbelief.

For a second or two we were locked like that, me straddling Wright, aiming at Harvey, while Harvey stood and aimed at me, our eyes on each other, neither quite believing what we saw. Of course, Harvey probably believed it less. I'd sort of guessed who he was; I'd be pretty surprised if he could reconcile "secret agent" and "drunken floozy" with each other.

Then Wright threw me off, moving with surprising agility for someone so large, and I fumbled to get the safety off and aim after him, but he shoved past Harvey, who rang out a shot, and vanished.

Harvey ran after him, but by the time I'd got outside, Wright had already driven away. Harvey fired after him but the car swerved and the bullet missed.

I grabbed the keys from my bag, letting the SO17 door swing shut and lock itself. At least I hope it locked itself. I jumped into Ted and gunned the engine, and to my amazement Harvey banged on the window to be let in.

"Don't you have your own car?"

"Are you going after Wright?"

I nodded.

"Then we'll go together. Two guns are better than one." He'd hardly shut the door by the time I took off, rattling through the business park as fast as Ted would let me. "By the way, Sophie Green, who the hell are you?"

"I could ask the same question," I said, swinging us around a corner, making Harvey wince.

"James Harvard, CIA," he said, badging me. I only glanced at it for a second and pretty much had to take it on faith that the badge was real. But I'd pretty much figured him out earlier. He was part of exactly the same game as me.

"Damn," I said, "Luke was right." And also hysterically wrong.

"Luke?"

"He said you were James Harvard. He also said you were Wright's partner…"

"Seriously?" He shook his head. "How do you even know about this Wright stuff? Who are you?"

"Sophie Green. I'm not a stewardess."

"No shit."

"I'm a secret agent."

He laughed.

I swung a corner extra hard.

"No, really," Harvey said, smile fading.

"Yes," I glared at him, "really. There's a badge in my bag. Well, a warrant card."

He obviously didn't believe me, because he looked through my bag for my wallet. "In here?"

"No, on the chain. With my BAA pass."

"This says you're a Passenger Service Agent."

"That's my day job."

"Jesus." He read my warrant card and seemed satisfied, if a little bewildered. "So you're after this guy too?"

"We have reason to believe he's involved in the murder of a hundred and forty-five people," I said.

"A hundred forty-five?"

"Plane crash. Mostly. The other two—" we reached the exit and I craned to see which way he'd gone, before deciding on right, "—were people who got in the way. My boss was one of them."

"And who's your boss? I never heard of SO17."

"Lot of people haven't. We're very small. Just me and Luke and a couple of others." I glanced over at him. Black jeans and sweater, gun holstered openly at his side. "So why are you after Wright?"

"Fraud."

"Gee, you Americans take fraud very seriously."

"Didn't you see *Catch Me If You Can*? He's been skimming for years. Wrightbank made masses of money and Wright took most of it."

"I thought that was the FBI, not the CIA."

"He's also been involved in some heavy-duty sabotage. You know he has a partner?"

"Yes," I said through gritted teeth.

"You know who it is?"

"Luke thinks it's you."

Harvey frowned at me, then his face cleared. "That's why you turned up this afternoon!"

"Yep."

"Were the cocktails part of the plan?"

"If you mention them again, I'll have to shoot you."

He grinned. "Where are we going?"

"I'm going after Wright. You can go where you like."

"I don't see him."

"My car has many useful attributes. Amazing speed is not one of them." Zero to sixty took a long while. Top speed meant waiting for next year.

"No, I mean I don't see any sign of him. He's not on the road." Harvey twisted his head to peer far to the left. "What's that over there?"

"Um, the motorway."

"I mean on the other side."

"The high school?"

"I see headlights."

"Probably just some kids hiding out..."

"Would you go back to your high school to hide out?"

I wouldn't go back to my high school if they sold Gucci. Half price.

I turned off the main road into the school grounds and cut my lights.

"Good thinking," Harvey said, "but you still don't have the quietest car in the world."

I parked Ted up and we got out and headed over to the sports field. The ground was slick and muddy and I wished I was wearing something other than my pretty trainers. My pretty, ruined trainers.

"Damn," I whispered.

"What?"

"I got mud in my shoe."

"If that's the worst thing that happens to you—"

He stopped because a bullet whistled past his head, and we both dropped to the ground. Now all my clothes were muddy. Great.

"Stay here," Harvey whispered. "I'll go see if I can get behind them."

That was great, but I didn't even know where they were, so behind them was going to be interesting. I watched him crawl away and lay there, cold and muddy, Macbeth's gun in my hand, feeling very small and scared.

They were doing some building work on the other side of the field and there were a few huts set up on the edge of the site. I glanced over at them, and my heart stopped for a second. There were lights inside. I could see lights.

I edged away from the muddy field, staying low, my heart hammering. Hey, at least it was beating again. I thought I'd died for a second there. Wright knew we'd be following him. He knew we were both armed and now we knew he was, too. And there was a distinct possibility that he wasn't alone.

Therefore what I did next might seem extremely foolish. But I think we've established by now that pretty much the only thing I'm really good at is being foolish, so I did it anyway. I crept and crawled through the shadows to the hut with the lights on, and when I got there, I saw Sven prowling round the outside with a gun.

God. I used to fancy him. Now he looked pale and deranged, and instead of having the Johnny Depp/Christian Slater cute maniac thing going on, he just looked damaged. And kind of scary.

I say kind of, because he still had vomit in his hair. Obviously he'd not been out of the cell that long.

I saw him stare in my direction for a long time, and my skin came up in goosebumps. It occurred to me that I could be in this totally alone—I wouldn't know a real CIA badge if it came up and snogged me, for all I knew Harvey could have been hitching a ride with me back to his partner, Wright—and that what I really needed was Luke to turn up and save the day.

But Luke had no idea where I was and besides, how was I ever going to be a secret agent if I didn't get off my arse and do some day-saving by myself?

I was just about to lift my gun and take a rather ill-advised shot at Sven, when I caught a movement behind him. There was someone following him. Someone svelte and stealthy, dressed in black, taking careful steps, a pistol raised. A woman.

Maria.

I let out a long breath of relief, which Sven must have heard because he suddenly swung his gun around in my direction and then there was a shot and I hit the ground, shaking.

It took me quite a while to realise that I was not the one who'd been shot. It took one more bullet report to convince me that I'd not been hit.

But someone had, and I realised as I saw Sven start running towards me, that it wasn't him. I lifted my gun and aimed and squeezed the trigger and *nothing happened.*

I stared in shock. It was broken! Macbeth gave me a broken gun!

Sven was three feet away now, pistol aimed at me, and I saw him nudge something on the barrel with his thumb. The safety! Of course! I pulled the catch, squeezed the trigger and shot Sven just as he landed on top of me.

He lay still, and so did I, winded, horrified. I'd just shot him. I'd just shot him—I pushed him off me and stared in horror at the blood leaking from the hole in his chest—I'd shot him and he was dead. There was blood on me too, on my clothes, on my skin. He was dead.

Oh, Jesus. I am in bad trouble.

I heaved myself over his body and ran to the shadows under the hut. Maria lay there, a bleeding bruise on her head, her hand pressed to her flat stomach where the bullet had lodged. I fumbled for her pulse and found it. She was alive. Fuck knows how, but she was alive.

I was just about to run back to the car for my phone to call for help when I heard movement from inside the hut. Whoever was inside was coming outside and I heard Alexa's voice say, "...Hope the little bugger hasn't got himself shot. He's a bit too cute to—"

And then she stopped, because she saw me, and she reached for a gun and so did Wright, and I aimed mine. And for a few seconds we all aimed at each other, hardly breathing.

"How theatrical," Alexa said. "You do see the dilemma, don't you, Sophie? I always thought you were quite bright, contrary to appearances."

I looked between them. Dilemma? My whole freaking life was a dilemma. I was kneeling there with two people aiming guns at me. And I only had one gun. Which I didn't know how to use.

"I can only shoot one of you," I said.

"Leaving the other to kill you. Unless we both shoot you at the same time." She glanced at Wright, who nodded eagerly.

"Making the body count one-four-seven," I said. If they thought Maria was still alive, they might shoot her again. "A whole planeful of people. All those children. Do you have something against schools, Lex?"

She laughed. "I was a goddess at school."

"When did you get the wheelchair?"

She cocked her head. "When I was discharged from the SAS because I'd never walk again. When they never checked properly. Clearly, their diagnosis was wrong."

"But you never told anyone?"

"I never needed to. People never correct a disabled person. People never check their work. People never suggest they might be wrong, because that would be politically incorrect."

Jesus. So that was why One had never checked her files? Because he was afraid of upsetting her?

Or because he was crap with computers? Talk about a tin-pot operation.

"I checked your work," I said boldly. I was still crouched by Maria and my legs were starting to cramp. "I found the deleted files. You killed Chris Mansfield."

"Wrong place, wrong time," she shrugged. "I hear he went down there to screw his girlfriend. Speaking of which, how are you getting on with Luke?"

"He's not my girlfriend."

She laughed. "You're funny. I always liked that about you. Shame," she slid back something on her gun, and I panicked, because I didn't know if I'd have to do the same, "I'm going to have to kill you."

"Luke will know," I said quickly, my voice rising. "He'll find me and Maria. He'll match up the bullets. He'll know you killed One—"

"Sven killed One," Alexa dismissed.

"And I killed Sven," I said clearly, gladly.

Wright raised his gun. "You—" He fired a shot, and then all was chaos. Wright's bullet pinged off the hut behind me. I raised my gun to shoot him but there was another shot, someone had got there first. Wright slumped face down in the mud and Alexa, her gun still trained on me, flicked her head over to the direction the bullet had come from.

Then, so fast I hardly saw her move, she'd swung the gun around and shot the shooter. Macbeth. I saw him fall to the ground. He made a heavy thud.

Really panicking now, I pushed myself upright, tears in my eyes, and shot at Alexa. But a cramp made me stumble and I fired off-target, missing her body but hitting her hands.

Her gun fell to the floor and she clutched at her right hand.

"You fucking bitch," she cried. "What was that for?"

I stared at her.

"Oh. Right. Oh, come on, he was expendable anyway. Like you. Not a proper agent."

Bitch.

"You'd be surprised how fast I'm learning," I said.

"I tried to put you off. I thought you would quit easier."

"The fingers?"

"They were gross." Alexa managed a smile, although I could see tears on her face. "Weren't they gross?"

"Some of them were mouldy," I said.

"You see? A normal person would be put off by mouldy fingers."

"A normal person wouldn't get hired by a government special operation."

"Oh, he only hired you because he wanted to shag you."

My finger tightened on the trigger. "Were you Wright's partner?"

She dropped to her knees, still cradling her bleeding hand. "Why do you care?"

"You had all those people killed!"

"Oh, that. Had to bring down share prices somehow."

"Why? He's been skimming. He's loaded!"

"He's been skimming?" Alexa shot Wright's body a contemptuous look. "Stupid fuck. He never spent a cent, did you know that? He was such a cheapskate, all the time."

"He wanted the airline cheap?"

"Wanted to get everything cheap. First Ace, then trains, and cars. Wanted to be a transport magnate. Buy up something small and expand it. Kill the competition."

I had a feeling that wasn't a metaphor.

"That was it? He just wanted transport companies?"

"Plane, trains and automobiles. Like a little boy."

"And you were his partner?"

"I was his bloody puppet master. He couldn't even fasten his fly without my help."

Charming image.

"And now you can't fasten it either. Did you have to kill all those people?"

"I didn't kill them. It was an accident."

"The whole crash was a complete accident?"

Alexa shrugged. She was sitting on a piece of wood now, most of her body covered with blood from her hand. "I may have loosened a few screws. Sven did most of it."

"How long was he involved in this?"

"What is this, twenty questions? Since he started at Ace. We needed someone on the inside. I had my pass but he knew people. He was trusted. He was David's nephew, you know. Not Norwegian at all." Figured. From now on I was going to ask all foreigners for proof of nationality before believing they weren't faking it. "Is he dead?"

I wasn't sure. "Yes."

"Did you ever fuck him?"

"No."

"Nah," she shrugged again, "you weren't missing much. He wanted you, though. He wanted you so much he tried to drug you."

"I know."

"Yeah. Should have been you in that cell. Well, not that cell, wouldn't want Luke to find you." She dragged in a deep breath. "Are we going to be here all night? Can't you call an ambulance or something?"

She didn't deserve one. "Like you called an ambulance for One?"

She slumped. "One was an interfering old bugger. I ran SO17, not him."

I believed her. "Did you have to kill him?"

"He saw me getting Sven out. He had to die. Look, Sophie, I'm sorry. Just put the bloody gun down and call me a bloody ambulance. I could die from blood loss."

"Don't you think you deserve it?"

She stared at me. "I was paralysed," she said. "I couldn't move my legs for thirteen bloody months! They told me I would never walk again and if it hadn't been for David, I never would have."

"What do you mean?"

"Reconstructive surgery isn't cheap, you know. Neurosurgeons and the like. Funny thing was, I could have done it myself if I hadn't been paralysed."

Yeah, that was funny.

"Sophie." She looked so small and broken. "I've confessed. Lock me up. Put me in that manky car of yours and take me away. But please don't let me bleed to death."

"You deserve it." Mostly for calling Ted manky.

"No, I deserve an eternity of torment in Holloway."

She had a point. Transferring the gun to one hand, I walked forward carefully, holding out my free hand to pull her to her feet. She looked up at me, smiled gratefully, then slammed a piece of splintered wood into my leg.

I yelped and screamed and went down to the ground. The gun went off and I honestly don't know who pulled the trigger, just that there was blood on my face, blood everywhere, pain everywhere, I thought I was dead or dying, and then another shot rang out, and another, and Alexa suddenly went still, and I blinked up to see Luke and Harvey looking down at me.

Chapter Eighteen

For a second, nobody spoke. I narrowed down the pain to my head and my leg. I wasn't dying. Go figure.

"Where did you go?"

Harvey nodded at Luke. "Backup."

"You went for backup? You left me alone with all these psychos?"

"And two other special agents." Harvey dropped down by Macbeth. "Hey. Are you okay?"

To my amazement, Macbeth opened his eyes. "Okay," he said. "I was faking it." He winked at me. Good grief. "Got a lot of muscle to hide a bullet in. Maria?"

Luke ran over to her. "Alive," he said, "but only just. She needs medical help. Urgently."

I somehow pulled myself to my feet. If I thought about Maria lying there dying, my leg didn't hurt so much. "I'll go," I said. "I have my car. The Princess Alexandra isn't too far."

Harvey tilted my face up. "Is that your blood?"

"I—I don't think so. I think it's hers." We both looked down at Alexa, still and bloody. She looked small and vulnerable, innocent, maybe. But I was shaking with anger at what she'd done. Or maybe I was in shock.

"She confessed everything," Macbeth said, hauling himself to his feet. "Sophie was wicked."

I'm afraid I blushed.

"Can you drive?" Luke asked, picking up Maria and starting back towards the car park. I limped after him, Macbeth following. Harvey stayed with the bodies. Oh Christ, the bodies. This was so surreal.

"I think so."

"I need a definite."

"Yes." I opened up the back of the car, and he placed Maria on the floor between the seats. Macbeth climbed in after her, and I went round to the cab.

"Are you sure you can drive?" Luke asked me as I started the engine, and I nodded tiredly.

"I'm sure. I have a licence and all."

He nodded. "Drive safe."

I have never driven safely and I'm certainly not about to start now. "Luke, are you mad at me?"

He stared. "Why would I be mad?"

"I did a lot of things I shouldn't."

"You got the bad guy. Guys. Girl." He touched the blood on my face. "I'm proud of you."

I managed a smile. "Really?"

"Yeah." He pulled me towards him and kissed me, and everything stopped hurting.

"Mmm," I sighed. "Do that again."

"No time. You have to go. I have to get these bodies off the school premises."

I nodded reluctantly. "There's a phrase I never want to hear again." I shut the door. "I'll see you later."

"Bye."

I drove away, and he stood there watching me until I turned the corner out of sight.

The drive up to the hospital was horrible. Horrible. Every gear change was agony, and there are a lot of roundabouts on the way there. I took most of them in the wrong gear because it hurt too much to dip the clutch. Defenders have really hard clutches. Macbeth, sitting behind me, was breathing very shallowly, and when I chanced a look back at him I saw that he was pressing his hand tight against his stomach.

"I thought it just hit muscle," I said.

"Yeah," he breathed, "muscle bleeds."

"I'm going as fast as I can."

"Not me I'm worried about." He glanced at Maria, who he'd pulled onto the seat beside him, her head in his lap. She was bleeding all over.

I was really glad I had vinyl seats.

I pulled up on front of the hospital, the car slewed across double yellows. It wasn't an ambulance bay so I didn't care. I locked my door, put my warrant card between my teeth and picked Maria up in my arms. She was heavy, but I didn't see any alternative. I was too tired and too hurt to really think about it.

"Lock the door," I said to Macbeth. "If someone nicks my car, I'll be really pissed off."

He could hardly stand. He was covered in blood. He put the keys back in my bag over my shoulder and had to lean on me as we stumbled through the doors, looking horribly out of place in the bright, clean, warm A&E reception.

Everyone turned and stared at us, and for a few seconds, I was too tired to speak. Then I opened my mouth and started yelling for help.

It was still dark when I got home, driven by a nurse so kindly I nearly cried when she offered me a lift. People had rushed to help Maria and Macbeth, and by extension, me, taking out the splinters of wood from my leg and replacing them with stitches. They put stitches in my head as well, a new cut on my forehead that looked like it might have been made by a bullet whistling by. I hadn't even really realised I'd been hit. They dosed me up with new painkillers and sent me home, and I took one look at my bed and fell in, fully clothed.

I woke up several hours later, just as the sky was starting to get light, with the definite feeling that there was someone in my room. I grabbed Macbeth's gun from my night stand and aimed it groggily.

"If you shoot me," came a lovely warm, dry voice, "then I won't be able to give you your reward."

I blinked at Luke. He was standing in the doorway, looking dirty and bloody and exhausted and irresistible.

"Reward?" I croaked.

He came in and sat on the bed as I put the gun away. "I spoke to the hospital. Macbeth's okay. Maria's in a bad state, but she's going to be fine."

I slumped against the pillows. "Really fine?"

He nodded. "Really fine. How are you feeling?"

"I'm—" Luke's fingers touched the dressing on my forehead, and my voice started to squeak, "I'm okay."

"That was some takedown."

"Did you..." I didn't know how to put this. "Did you get rid of the bodies?"

Luke laughed. "We don't dump them in landfills, Sophie. We took them to the morgue. Both of them."

"There were—"

"Wright and Sven. Both dead. Alexa," he twirled a lock of my slightly bloody hair, "less so."

"But—"

"Unconscious and bleeding profusely, but not dead. Able to make a full confession. Currently under armed police guard in, ironically, the same wing as Macbeth."

"That is ironic." I took a deep breath. There was something that had been bugging me. "Luke, am I in trouble?"

He looked surprised. "You saved the day, Soph. Why would you be in trouble?"

"I killed Sven with what I'm pretty sure is an unlicensed firearm, I may have shot Alexa and I got two SO17 agents severely injured."

Luke shrugged. "I repeat, why would you be in trouble? The good guys are alive. The bad guys got caught. Everything else can be fixed. And Sven, by the way, was really a Steven. And as for licensing..."

He reached out and picked up the gun, looking at it. "This is illegal in a whole lot of ways." He bit his lip. "There's something I have to tell you."

"Oh, God, I am in trouble."

"Well, you could be. I never told you this, but your stun gun is illegal."

I couldn't tell him I already knew that. Could I?

"Then why'd you let me have it?"

"Hell, Sophie, I couldn't leave you entirely unprotected."

"Have you ever heard the one about getting hung for a sheep or a lamb?" I asked him, and he grinned.

"I have. And," he reached inside his jacket for something, "I've decided to go for the sheep."

He handed me a shiny, perfect little gun. I held it like a newborn and stared in rapture.

"You got me a gun?"

"You want to know what I was doing while you were leaving hysterical voice mails on my mobile? I was speaking to my good friend Mike at the firearms licensing department and asking why your application hadn't come through. He said it had been cancelled. By one Alexa Martin."

I gaped. Alexa had tried to stop me getting a gun?

Luke had tried to get me one?

I had one?

"So I told him that was bollocks and you would be sending in your signature very shortly. And then I got a housecall from your friend Harvey—did you know he was CIA?" I nodded. "Thanks for sharing. He said you had a gun and were in trouble. I figured, must be a Tuesday."

"Did you shoot Alexa?"

"Everybody shot Alexa. She's like a bad tempered colander. She'll be locked away for a very," he brushed the hair from my face, "very long time."

I hefted the gun in my hands. "That reward you mentioned," I said. "For saving the day?" He nodded. "Is this it?"

"No." Luke took the gun away from me and lifted my chin. "This is."

And then he kissed me. And then he pulled back the covers and took off my sweater. And then he...

Mmm. I could get used to this reward system.

About the Author

Kate was born in 1982 and still hasn't grown up yet. She lives in England with her family and two cats who are her babies in every sense. Except, obviously, the biological one. She's been writing since her teens and is damn glad it's finally taking off since this means she won't have to go back to working airport check-in any more. Kate is single but aspirational (Prince William likes Kates, right?) and asks all potential dates to send in pictures of themselves and their Aston Martins.

To learn more about Kate Johnson please visit www.katejohnson.co.uk. To learn more about Sophie, please visit www.myspace.com/sophiesuperspy. Send an email to Kate at katejohnsonauthor@googlemail.com or join her Yahoo! group to join in the fun with other readers as well as Kate's alter-ego: http://groups.yahoo.com/group/catmarsters.

Look for these titles

Now Available:

The Twelve Lies of Christmas

Coming Soon:

Ugley Business
A is for Apple

On the twelfth day of Christmas, my true love lied to me.

The Twelve Lies of Christmas

Nate Kelly is a spy. At least, he is until Christmas, when he's retiring to take up something more peaceful, like alligator wrestling or bomb disposal. Because while he's tired of being shot at, he's also not sure he really wants to live the life of a civilian. First, of course, he has to finish his current case, complete with arms dealers, mobsters, and celebrity parties.

Not to mention the glamorous Russian femme fatale who's hacking into the same computer files as Nate, lying to the same people, and incidentally has the worst Russian accent he's ever heard. But just because she's his enemy's enemy, doesn't necessarily mean she's his friend.

Available now in ebook from Samhain Publishing.

Enjoy the following excerpt from...
The Twelve Lies of Christmas

It's a truth universally acknowledged that the average British footballer has the taste and refinement of a dead gnat. Daz, who owned an entire team of such aesthetes, was no exception. The courtyard of his large, ivy-covered house held a statue of three women with enormous breasts, pouring water all over each other and leering. They were surrounded by so many supercars it looked as if they'd been breeding. Whole families of Ferraris clustered together, balefully eyeing up the contingent from Lamborghini.

Inside, the house was the usual footballer's insult to all that is tasteful and elegant. The requisite shag pile carpet squidged underfoot, and I felt absolutely sure that somewhere there would be a library full of unread leather-bound classics.

"Anatole, mate," Daz greeted him enthusiastically. His pupils looked a little uneven: so it was one of those parties, eh?

His eyes wandered over me and he said dismissively, "Servants are downstairs, mate."

Yuri gave me a superior look. I doffed an imaginary cap, and ambled towards the kitchen to find myself a bottle of beer.

I wasn't planning on drinking the beer. But it's a hell of a useful prop.

A week or two before, an SO17 operative, posing as a glossy gossip mag journalist, had obtained access to Daz's home and security systems. She'd provided me with a floor plan and computer codes for the system which ran everything from his automatic lights to the burglar alarm.

Beer in hand, I passed a couple of rooms where tattooed premier league footballers danced, shirtless, on tables, while their painfully thin, bleached'n'tanned, over-manicured, over-exposed wives and girlfriends lolled about drinking Cristal and gossiping about each others' boob jobs. Daz's office was on the upper floor, which was officially off limits to the party-goers. This rule was enforced by a door hidden by the turn of the grand staircase, which could only be opened by means of a swipe card and keypad code.

But I wasn't headed there yet. Security cameras whirred in every room, and it occurred to me that if I could sell their contents to the tabloids, I could make a fortune.

I made my way down the driveway, breath making clouds in the cold, damp air, to the guards hut at the entrance to the grounds. There were a couple of men on duty here, checking invitations and watching C-list celebs making fools of themselves on the CCTV. In the corner, a tacky soap opera was airing yet another Christmas special on a TV so small and tinny it was almost unwatchable.

I clinked together a couple of beer bottles. They were unopened, but the sleeping pills in my pocket could be added in the blink of an eye.

"Hey lads, thought you might fancy a..." I pushed the door open, and trailed off. Both men were fast asleep, lolling in their chairs, snoring loudly. One of them was covered in tea from the mug he'd dropped on the floor.

Someone had already been here.

Shit.

I sniffed at the spilt tea, but it didn't yield any special secrets to me. There was a sweet smell in the air, but it wasn't anything that had been added to the guards' drinks. Setting down my bottles, I glanced around for a security camera and saw one pointed at the computer bank.

Well, that was helpful.

Tapping into the system, I started to check the records of the guards hut camera, only to discover that it hadn't recorded anything for the last half hour...and that the preceding ten minutes had been wiped from the system's memory.

When I checked the rest of the circuit, I found that while every camera was displaying an image on the screens, none of it was being recorded.

Curiouser and curiouser. I logged into the system memory to see who had switched off the recording. And discovered that it had been done by Daz King.

Or, at least, someone with Daz's security code.

I sniffed the air again. That sweet smell was a little bit like perfume. Actually, a lot like perfume.

Well well, I thought. Looks like we have a femme fatale on our hands here, Nate. And three guesses as to who it is?

Luke thinks it's hilarious that I named my gun, but I know for a fact that he talks to his. Anyway, I like my gun. It's been very helpful to me in tight spots. It's called Belinda, after the girl who helped me pass English when I was 16.

I had Belinda—the gun, this time, not the girl—in a brace under my jacket, and my hand hovered ready to draw her as I made my way to Daz's study. But the room appeared empty, the only light coming from the computer screen which made everything look green and rather spooky.

But being a big strong scary spy, I wasn't scared. Much.

A quick sweep of the room revealed no one hiding in a darkened corner, so I set down my gun and checked out the computer. There were no programs open, so if anyone had been here before me, I didn't know what they were looking for. And I wasn't sure I had the luxury of hanging around to find out.

I stuck a USB stick into the computer, and started downloading files. I didn't check their contents, just got everything from the hard drive, as well as an internet cache and list of bookmarks. I could check them all out later. It'd be easier if I could just lift the whole hard drive out, but then Daz might get suspicious.

Drumming my fingers on my thigh—so as not to create any noise that might alert anyone else to my presence, or hide theirs from me—I watched the transfer bar creep up, little by little.

And became aware of a noise.

At first I thought it was heavy breathing, and made a face of disgust. No doubt Daz had lured some young lovely upstairs for a quickie. Hopefully, they'd be heading to one of the bedrooms, and not in here.

But I made ready to snatch the USB stick free and leap into the shadows, just in case.

Then I realized that the noise was not coming from outside the room. It was coming—I listened carefully—from a small cupboard on the far side.

A cupboard I'd dismissed when I entered as far too small for a person to hide in.

Stupid Nate. I picked up Belinda and crept as silently as possible towards the cupboard, praying that the floor wouldn't squeak. It didn't, and I made it over there without making a sound—at least, not one that could be picked up over the wheezing coming from the cupboard.

It sounded to me like someone hyperventilating. Maybe having an asthma attack. Maybe suffocating. There was a strong possibility that Daz had locked someone in there on purpose to die. It was a horrible idea, but then he was a horrible man.

I took a breath, counted to three, and yanked open the door with one hand while aiming my gun with the other.

And stared.

"Huh," I said.

Printed in the United States
95952LV00007B/3/A

9 781599 986357